# OFF THE CHARTS

The stars were doing the crawling together that marked the last moments before transition to another area of space. They suddenly blinked out and were replaced by another starry firmament.

The Captain lounged back. "Well," he said happily, "I see we made it again." He got up and headed for the hatch.

Max looked up, trying to recall what piece of this new sky they were facing. Kelly was looking up, too. "Yes, we came through," Max heard him mutter. "But *where?*"

The *Asgard* had come out in unknown space. It wasn't on any of their charts, and they were hopelessly lost!

"Robert A. Heinlein is probably more responsible than any other man for the curious development of modern science fiction . . . He made his name as a science fiction writer with vigorous stories about the impact of futuristic technology on society. He speculated fearlessly . . .

—*The New Yorker*

# Starman Jones

## Robert A. Heinlein

A Del Rey Book

BALLANTINE BOOKS • NEW YORK

For my friend Jim Smith

VL: 6 & up
IL: 7 & up

A Del Rey Book
Published by Ballantine Books

Copyright © 1953 by Robert A. Heinlein

All rights reserved. Published in the United States by Ballantine Books, a division of Random House, Inc., New York, and simultaneously in Canada by Random House of Canada, Limited, Toronto, Canada.

ISBN 0-345-30104-8

This edition published by arrangement with Charles Scribner's Sons

Manufactured in the United States of America

First Ballantine Books Edition: February 1975
Eleventh Printing: April 1983

Cover art by Rick Sternback

# CONTENTS

# STARMAN
# JONES

# 1

# THE TOMAHAWK

Max liked this time of day, this time of year. With the crops in, he could finish his evening chores early and be lazy. When he had slopped the hogs and fed the chickens, instead of getting supper he followed a path to a rise west of the barn and lay down in the grass, unmindful of chiggers. He had a book with him that he had drawn from the county library last Saturday, Bonforte's *Sky Beasts: A Guide to Exotic Zoology*, but he tucked it under his head as a pillow. A blue jay made remarks about his honesty, then shut up when he failed to move. A red squirrel sat on a stump and stared at him, then went on burying nuts.

Max kept his eyes to the northwest. He favored this spot because from it he could see the steel stilts and guide rings of the Chicago, Springfield, & Earthport Ring Road emerge from a slash in the ridge to his right. There was a guide ring at the mouth of the cut, a great steel hoop twenty feet high. A pair of stilt-like tripods supported another ring a hundred feet out from the cut. A third and last ring, its stilts more than a hundred feet high to keep it level with the others, lay west of him where the ground dropped still more sharply into the valley below. Half way up it he could see the power-link antenna pointing across the gap.

On his left the guides of the C.S.&E. picked up again on the far side of the gap. The entering ring was larger to allow for maximum windage deviation; on its stilts was the receptor antenna for the power link. That ridge was steeper; there was only one more ring before the road disappeared into a tunnel. He had read that, on the Moon, entrance rings were no larger than pass-along rings, since there was never any wind to cause variation in ballistic. When he was a child this entrance ring had been slightly smaller and, during an unprecedented windstorm, a train had struck the ring and produced an unbelievable wreck, with more than four hundred people killed. He had not seen it and his father had not allowed him to poke around afterwards because of the carnage, but the scar of it could still be seen on the lefthand ridge, a darker green than the rest.

He watched the trains go by whenever possible, not wishing the passengers any bad luck—but still, if there should happen to be a catastrophe, he didn't want to miss it.

Max kept his eyes fixed on the cut; the *Tomahawk* was due any instant. Suddenly there was a silver gleam, a shining cylinder with needle nose burst out of the cut, flashed through the last ring and for a breathless moment was in free trajectory between the ridges. Almost before he could swing his eyes the projectile entered the ring across the gap and disappeared into the hillside—just as the sound hit him.

It was a thunderclap that bounced around the hills. Max gasped for air. "Boy!" he said softly. "Boy, oh boy!" The incredible sight and the impact on his ears always affected him the same way. He had heard that for the passengers the train was silent, with the sound trailing them, but he did not know; he had never ridden a train and it seemed unlikely, with Maw and the farm to take care of, that he ever would.

He shifted to a sitting position and opened his book, holding it so that he would be aware of the southwestern sky. Seven minutes after the passing of the *Tomahawk* he should be able to see, on a clear evening, the launching orbit of the daily Moonship. Although much father away and much less dramatic than the nearby jump of the ring train it was this that he had come to see. Ring trains were all right, but spaceships were his love—even a dinky like the moon shuttle.

But he had just found his place, a description of the intelligent but phlegmatic crustaceans of Epsilon Ceti IV, when he was interrupted by a call behind him. "Oh, Maxie! Maximilian! Max . . . mil . . . *yan!*"

He held still and said nothing.

"*Max!* I can see you, Max—you come at once, hear me?"

He muttered to himself and got to his feet. He moved slowly down the path, watching the sky over his shoulder until the barn cut off his view. Maw was back and that was that—she'd make his life miserable if he didn't come in and help. When she had left that morning he had had the impression that she would be gone overnight—not that she had said so; she never did—but he had learned to read the signs. Now he would have to listen to her complaints and her petty gossip when he wanted to read, or just as bad, be disturbed by the slobbering stereovision serials she favored. He had often been tempted to sabotage the pesky SV set—by rights with an ax! He hardly ever got to see the programs he liked.

When he got in sight of the house he stopped suddenly. He had supposed that Maw had ridden the bus from the Corners and walked up the draw as usual. But there was a sporty little unicycle standing near the stoop—and there was someone with her.

He had thought at first it was a "foreigner"—but when he got closer he recognized the man. Max would rather have seen a foreigner, any foreigner. Biff Montgomery was a hillman but he didn't work a farm; Max couldn't remember having seen him do any honest work. He had heard it said that Montgomery sometimes hired out as a guard when one of the moonshine stills back in the hills was operating and it might be so —Montgomery was a big, beefy man and the part might fit him.

Max had known Montgomery as long as he could remember, seen him loafing around Clyde's Corners. But he had ordinarily given him "wagon room" and had had nothing to do with him—until lately: Maw had started being seen with him, even gone to barn dances and huskings with him. Max had tried to tell her that Dad wouldn't have liked it. But you couldn't argue with Maw—what she didn't like she just didn't hear.

But this was the first time she had ever brought him to the house. Max felt a slow burn of anger starting in him.

"Hurry up, Maxie!" Maw called out. "Don't stand there like a dummy." Max reluctantly moved along and joined them. Maw said, "Maxie, shake hands with your new father," then looked roguish, as if she had said something witty. Max stared and his mouth sagged open.

Montgomery grinned and stuck out a hand. "Yep, Max, you're Max Montgomery now—I'm your new pop. But you can call me Monty."

Max stared at the hand, took it briefly. "My name is Jones," he said flatly.

"Maxie!" protested Maw.

Montgomery laughed jovially. "Don't rush him, Nellie my love. Let Max get used to it. Live and let live; that's my motto." He turned to his wife. "Half a mo', while I get the baggage." From one saddlebag of the unicycle he extracted a wad of mussed clothing; from the other, two flat pint bottles. Seeing Max watching him he winked and said, "A toast for the bride."

His bride was standing by the door; he started to brush on past her. She protested, "But Monty darling, aren't you going to—"

Montgomery stopped. "Oh. I haven't much experience in these things. Sure." He turned to Max—"Here, take the baggage"—and shoved bottles and clothes at him. Then he swung her up in his arms, grunting a bit, and carried her over the threshold, put her down and kissed her while she squealed and blushed. Max silently followed them, put the items on the table and turned to the stove. It was cold, he had not used it since breakfast. There was an electric range but it had burned out before his father had died and there had never been money to repair it. He took out his pocket knife, made shavings, added kindling and touched the heap with an Everlite. When it flared up he went out to fetch a pail of water.

When he came back Montgomery said, "Wondered

where you'd gone. Doesn't this dump even have running water?"

"No." Max set the pail down, then added a couple of chunks of cord wood to the fire.

His Maw said, "Maxie, you should have had dinner ready."

Montgomery interceded pleasantly with, "Now, my dear, he didn't know we were coming. And it leaves time for a toast." Max kept his back to them, giving his full attention to slicing side meat. The change was so overwhelming that he had not had time to take it in.

Montgomery called to him. "Here, son! Drink your toast to the bride."

"I've got to get supper."

"Nonsense! Here's your glass. Hurry up."

Montgomery had poured a finger of amber liquid into the glass; his own glass was half full and that of his bride at least a third. Max accepted it and went to the pail, thinned it with a dipper of water.

"You'll ruin it."

"I'm not used to it."

"Oh, well. Here's to the blushing bride—and our happy family! Bottoms up!"

Max took a cautious sip and put it down. It tasted to him like the bitter tonic the district nurse had given him one spring. He turned back to his work, only to be interrupted again. "Hey, you didn't finish it."

"Look, I got to cook. You don't want me to burn supper, do you?"

Montgomery shrugged. "Oh, well—the more for the rest of us. We'll use yours for a chaser. Sonny boy, when I was your age I could empty a tumbler neat and then stand on my hands."

Max had intended to sup on side meat and warmed-over biscuits, but there was only half a pan left of the biscuits. He scrambled eggs in the grease of the side meat, brewed coffee, and let it go at that. When they sat down Montgomery looked at it and announced, "My dear, starting tomorrow I'll expect you to live up to what you told me about your cooking. Your boy isn't much of a cook." Nevertheless he ate heartily. Max decided not to tell him that he was a better cook than Maw—he'd find out soon enough.

Presently Montgomery sat back and wiped his mouth, then poured himself more coffee and lighted a cigar. Maw said, "Maxie, dear, what's the dessert?"

"Dessert? Well—there's that ice cream in the freezer, left over from Solar Union Day."

She looked vexed. "Oh, dear! I'm afraid it's not there."

"Huh?"

"Well, I'm afraid I sort of ate it one afternoon when you were out in the south field. It was an awfully hot day."

Max did not say anything, he was unsurprised. But she was not content to leave it. "You didn't fix any dessert, Max? But this is a *special* occasion."

Montgomery took his cigar out of his mouth. "Stow it, my dear," he said kindly. "I'm not much for sweets, I'm a meat-and-potatoes man—sticks to the ribs. Let's talk of pleasanter things." He turned to Max. "Max, what can you do besides farm?"

Max was startled. "Huh? I've never done anything else. Why?"

Montgomery touched the ash of the cigar to his plate. "Because you are all through farming."

For the second time in two hours Max had more change than he could grasp. "Why? What do you mean?"

"Because we've sold the farm."

Max felt as if he had had a rug jerked out from under him. But he could tell from Maw's face that it was true. She looked the way she always did when she had put one over on him—triumphant and slightly apprehensive.

"Dad wouldn't like that," he said to her harshly. "This land has been in our family for four hundred years."

"Now, Maxie! I've told you I don't know how many

times that I wasn't cut out for a farm. I was city raised."

"Clyde's Corners! Some city!"

"It wasn't a farm. And I was just a young girl when your father brought me here—you were already a big boy. I've still got my life before me. I can't live it buried on a farm."

Max raised his voice. "But you promised Dad you'd . . ."

"Stow it," Montgomery said firmly. "And keep a civil tongue in your head when you speak to your mother —and to me."

Max shut up.

"The land is sold and that's that. How much do you figure this parcel is worth?"

"Why, I've never thought about it."

"Whatever you thought, I got more." He gave Max a wink. "Yes, sir! It was a lucky day for your mother and you when she set her cap for me. I'm a man with his ear to the ground. I knew why an agent was around buying up these worn-out, worthless pieces of property. I . . ."

"I use government fertilizers."

"Worthless I said and worthless I meant. For farming, that is." He put his finger along his nose, looked sly, and explained. It seemed that some big government power project was afoot for which this area had been selected—Montgomery was mysterious about it, from which Max concluded that he didn't know very much. A syndicate was quietly buying up land in anticipation of government purchase. "So we held 'em up for five times what they expected to pay. Pretty good, huh?"

Maw put in, "You see, Maxie? If your father had known that we would ever get . . ."

"Quiet, Nellie!"

"But I was just going to tell him how much . . ."

" 'Quiet!' I said."

She shut up. Montgomery pushed his chair back, stuck his cigar in his mouth, and got up. Max put water on to heat for the dishes, scraped the plates and took the leavings out to the chickens. He stayed out quite a spell, looking at the stars and trying to think. The idea of having Biff Montgomery in the family shook him to his bones. He wondered just what rights a stepfather had, or, rather a step-stepfather, a man who had married his stepmother. He didn't know.

Presently he decided that he had to go back inside, much as he hated to. He found Montgomery standing at the bookshelf he had built over the stereo receiver; the man was pawing at the books and had piled several on the receiver. He looked around. "You back? Stick around, I want you to tell me about the live stock."

Maw appeared in the doorway. "Darling," she said to Montgomery, "can't that wait till morning?"

"Don't be in a hurry, my dear," he answered. "That auctioneer fellow will be here early. I've got to have the inventory ready." He continued to pull books down. "Say, these are pretty things." He held in his hands half a dozen volumes, printed on the finest of thin paper and bound in limp plastic. "I wonder what they're worth? Nellie, hand me my specs."

Max advanced hastily, reached for them. "Those are mine!"

"Huh?" Montgomery glanced at him, then held the books high in the air. "You're too young to own anything. No, everything goes. A clean sweep and a fresh start."

"They're mine! My uncle gave them to me." He appealed to his mother. "Tell him, Maw."

Montgomery said quietly, "Yes, Nellie, set this youngster straight—before I have to correct him."

Nellie looked worried. "Well, I don't rightly know. They did belong to Chet."

"And Chet was your brother? Then you're Chet's heir, not this young cub."

"He wasn't her brother, he was her brother-in-law!"

"So? No matter. Your father was your uncle's heir, then, and your mother is your father's heir. Not you, you're a minor. That's the law, son. Sorry." He put the books on the shelf but remained standing in front of them.

Max felt his right upper lip begin to twitch uncontrollably; he knew that he would not be able to talk coherently. His eyes filled with tears of rage so that he could hardly see. "You . . . you *thief!*"

Nellie let out a squawk. "Max!"

Montgomery's face became coldly malignant. "Now you've gone too far. I'm afraid you've earned a taste of the strap." His fingers started unbuckling his heavy belt.

Max took a step backward. Montgomery got the belt loose and took a step forward. Nellie squealed, "Monty! *Please!*"

"Keep out of this, Nellie." To Max he said, "We might as well get it settled once and for all who is boss around here. Apologize!"

Max did not answer. Montgomery repeated, "Apologize, and we'll say no more about it." He twitched the belt like a cat lashing its tail. Max took another step back; Montgomery stepped forward and grabbed at him.

Max ducked and ran out the open door into darkness. He did not stop until he was sure that Montgomery was not following. Then he caught his breath, still raging. He was almost sorry that Montgomery had not chased him; he didn't think that anyone could match him on his home grounds in the dark. He knew where the wood pile was; Montgomery didn't. He knew where the hog wallow was. Yes, he knew where the well was—even *that*.

It was a long time before he quieted down enough to think rationally. When he did, he was glad it had ended so easily, Montgomery outweighed him a lot and was reputed to be a mean one in a fight.

If it *had* ended, he corrected. He wondered if Montgomery would decide to forget it by morning. The light was still on in the living room; he took shelter in the barn and waited, sitting down on the dirt floor and leaning against the planks. After a while he felt terribly tired. He considered sleeping in the barn but there was no fit place to lie down, even though the old mule was dead. Instead he got up and looked at the house.

The light was out in the living room, but he could see a light in the bedroom; they were still awake, surely. Someone had closed the outer door after his flight; it did not lock so there was no difficulty getting in, but he was afraid that Montgomery might hear him. His own room was a shed added at the kitchen end of the main room, opposite the bedroom, but it had no outside door.

No matter—he had solved that problem when he had first grown old enough to wish to get in and out at night without consulting his elders. He crept around the house, found the saw horse, placed it under his window, got on and wiggled loose the nail that held the window. A moment later he stepped silently down into his own room. The door to the main part of the house was closed but he decided not to risk switching on the light; Montgomery might take it into his head to come out into the living room and see a crack of light under his door. He slipped quietly out of his clothes and crawled into his cot.

Sleep wouldn't come. Once he began to feel that warm drowsiness, then some tiny noise had brought him wide, stiff awake. Probably just a mouse—but for an instant he had thought that Montgomery was standing over his bed. With his heart pounding, he sat up on the edge of his cot, still in his skin.

Presently he faced up to the problem of what he was to do—not just for the next hour, not just tomorrow morning, but the following morning and all the mornings after that. Montgomery alone presented no problem; he would not voluntarily stay in the same county with the man. But how about Maw?

His father had told him, when he had known that he was dying, "Take care of your mother, son." Well, he had done so. He had made a crop every year—food in the house and a little money, even if things had been close. When the mule died, he had made do, borrowing McAllister's team and working it out in labor.

But had Dad meant that he had to take care of his stepmother even if she remarried? It had never occurred to him to consider it. Dad had told him to look out for her and he had done so, even though it had put a stop to school and did not seem to have any end to it.

But she was no longer Mrs. Jones but Mrs. Montgomery. Had Dad meant for him to support Mrs. Montgomery?

Of course not! When a woman married, her husband supported her. Everybody knew that. And Dad wouldn't expect him to put up with Montgomery. He stood up, his mind suddenly made up.

The only question was what to take with him.

There was little to take. Groping in the dark he found the rucksack he used for hunting hikes and stuffed into it his other shirt and his socks. He added Uncle Chet's circular astrogation slide rule and the piece of volcanic glass his uncle had brought back for him from the Moon. His citizen's identification card, his toothbrush, and his father's razor—not that he needed *that* very often—about completed the plunder.

There was a loose board back of his cot. He felt for it, pulled it out and groped between the studs—found nothing. He had been hiding a little money from time to time against a rainy day, as Maw couldn't or wouldn't save. But apparently she had found it on one of her snooping tours. Well, he still had to leave; it just made it a little more difficult.

He took a deep breath. There was something he *must* get . . . Uncle Chet's books . . . and they were still (presumably) on the shelf against the wall common with the bedroom. But he *had* to get them, even at the risk of meeting Montgomery.

Cautiously, most slowly, he opened the door into the living room, stood there with sweat pouring down him. There was still a crack of light under the bedroom door and he hesitated, almost unable to force himself to go on. He heard Montgomery muttering something and Maw giggle.

As his eyes adjusted he could see by the faint light leaking out under the bedroom door something piled at the outer door. It was a deadfall alarm of pots and pans, sure to make a dreadful clatter if the door were opened. Apparently Montgomery had counted on him coming back and expected to be ready to take care of him. He was very glad that he had sneaked in the window.

No use putting it off—he crept across the floor, mindful of the squeaky board near the table. He could not see but he could feel and the volumes were known to his fingers. Carefully he slid them out, being sure not to knock over the others.

He was all the way back to his own door when he remembered the library book. He stopped in sudden panic.

He couldn't go back. They might hear him this time —or Montgomery might get up for a drink of water or something.

But in his limited horizon, the theft of a public library book—or failure to return it, which was the same thing—was, if not a mortal sin, at least high on the list of shameful crimes. He stood there, sweating and thinking about it.

Then he went back, the whole long trek, around the squeaky board and tragically onto one he had not remembered. He froze after he hit it, but apparently it had not alarmed the couple in the room beyond. At last he was leaning over the SV receiver and groping at the shelf.

Montgomery, in pawing the books, had changed their arrangement. One after another he had to take them down and try to identify it by touch, opening each and feeling for the perforations on the title page.

It was the fourth one he handled. He got back to his room hurrying slowly, unbearably anxious but afraid to move fast. There at last, he began to shake and had to wait until it wore off. He didn't chance closing his door but got into his clothes in the dark. Moments later he crept through his window, found the saw horse with his toe, and stepped quietly to the ground.

His shoes were stuffed on top of the books in his rucksack; he decided to leave them there until he was well clear of the house, rather than chance the noise he might make with his feet shod. He swung wide around the house and looked back. The bedroom light was still on; he started to angle down toward the road when he noticed Montgomery's unicycle. He stopped.

If he continued he would come to the road the bus passed along. Whether he turned right or left there, Montgomery would have a fifty-fifty chance of catching him on the unicycle. Having no money he was dependent on Shank's ponies to put distance under him; he could not take the bus.

Shucks! Montgomery wouldn't try to fetch him back. He would say good riddance and forget him!

But the thought fretted him. Suppose Maw urged him? Suppose Montgomery wouldn't forget an insult and would go to any trouble to "get even"?

He headed back, still swinging wide of the house, and cut across the slopes toward the right of way of the C.S.&E.

# 2

# GOOD SAMARITAN

He wished for a light, but its lack did not bother him much. He knew this country, every slope, almost every tree. He stayed high, working along the hillside, until he reached the exit ring where the trains jumped the gap, and there he came out on the road used by the ring road's maintenance crews. He sat down and put on his shoes.

The maintenance road was no more than a track cut through trees; it was suited to tractor treads but not to wheels. But it led down across the gap and up to where the ring road disappeared in the tunnel through the far ridge. He followed it, making good time in the born mountaineer's easy, loose-jointed walk.

Seventy minutes later he was across the gap and passing under the entrance ring. He went on until he was near the ring that marked the black entrance to the tunnel. He stopped at what he judged to be a safe distance and considered his chances.

The ridge was high, else the rings would have been built in a cut rather than a tunnel. He had often hunted on it and knew that it would take two hours to climb it—in daylight. But the maintenance road ran right through the hill, under the rings. If he followed it, he could go through in ten or fifteen minutes.

Max had never been through the ridge. Legally it was trespass—not that that bothered him, he was trespassing now. Occasionally a hog or a wild animal would wander into the tunnel and be trapped there when a train hurtled through. They died, instantly and without a scratch. Once Max had spotted the carcass of a fox just inside the tunnel and had ducked in and salvaged it. There were no marks on it, but when he skinned it he found that it was a mass of tiny hemorrhages. Several years earlier a man had been caught inside; the maintenance crew brought out the body.

The tunnel was larger than the rings but no larger than necessary to permit the projectile to ride ahead of its own reflected shock wave. Anything alive in the tunnel could not avoid the wave; that unbearable thunderclap, painful at a distance, was so loaded with energy as to be quick death close up.

But Max did not want to climb the ridge; he went over the evening schedule of trains in his mind. The *Tomahawk* was the one he had watched at sundown; the *Javelin* he had heard while he was hiding in the barn. The *Assegai* must have gone by quite a while ago though he didn't remember hearing it; that left only the midnight *Cleaver*. He then looked at the sky.

Venus had set, of course, but he was surprised to see Mars still in the west. The Moon had not risen. Let's see—full moon was last Wednesday. Surely . . .

The answer he got seemed wrong, so he checked himself by taking a careful eyesight of Vega and compared it with what the Big Dipper told him. Then he whistled softly—despite everything that had happened it was only ten o'clock, give or take five minutes; the stars could not be wrong. In which case the *Assegai* was not due for another three-quarters of an hour. Except for the faint chance of a special train he had plenty of time.

He headed into the tunnel. He had not gone fifty yards before he began to be sorry and a bit panicky; it was as dark as a sealed coffin. But the going was much easier as the bore was lined to permit smooth shock-wave reflections. He had been on his way several minutes, feeling each step but hurrying, when his eyes, adjusting to complete darkness, made out a faint grey circle far ahead. He broke into a trot and then into a dead run as his fear of the place piled up.

He reached the far end with throat burned dry and heart laboring; there he plunged downhill regardless of the sudden roughening of his path as he left the tunnel and hit the maintenance track. He did not slow up until he stood under stilt supports so high that the ring above looked small. There he stood still and fought to catch his breath.

He was slammed forward and knocked off his feet.

He picked himself up groggily, eventually remembered where he was and realized that he had been knocked cold. There was blood on one cheek and his hands and elbows were raw. It was not until he noticed these that he realized what had happened; a train had passed right over him.

It had not been close enough to kill, but it had been close enough to blast him off his feet. It could not have been the *Assegai;* he looked again at the stars and confirmed it. No, it must have been a special—and he had beaten it out of the tunnel by about a minute.

He began to shake and it was minutes before he pulled himself together, after which he started down the maintenance road as fast as his bruised body could manage. Presently he became aware of an odd fact; the night was silent.

But night is never silent. His ears, tuned from babyhood to the sounds and signs of his hills, should have heard an endless pattern of little night noises—wind in the leaves, the scurrying of his small cousins, tree frogs, calls of insects, owls.

By brutal logic he concluded correctly that he could not hear—"deef as a post"—the shock wave had left him deaf. But there was no way to help it, so he went on; it did not occur to him to return home. At the bottom of this draw, where the stilts were nearly three hundred feet high, the maintenance road crossed a farm road. He turned down hill onto it, having accomplished his first purpose of getting into territory where Montgomery would be less likely to look for him. He was in another watershed now; although still only a few miles from home, nevertheless by going through the ridge he had put himself into a different neighborhood.

He continued downhill for a couple of hours. The road was hardly more than a cart track but it was easier than the maintenance road. Somewhere below, when the hills gave way to the valley where the "foreigners" lived, he would find the freight highway that paralleled the ring road on the route to Earthport—Earthport being his destination although he had only foggy plans as to what he would do when he got there.

The Moon was behind him now and he made good time. A rabbit hopped onto the road ahead, sat up and stared, then skittered away. Seeing it, he regretted not having brought along his squirrel gun. Sure, it was worn out and not worth much and lately it had gotten harder and harder to buy the slugs thrown by the obsolete little weapon—but rabbit in the pot right now would go mighty nice, mighty nice! He realized that he was not only weary but terribly hungry. He had just picked at his supper and it looked like he'd breakfast on his upper lip.

Shortly his attention was distracted from hunger to a ringing in his ears, a ringing that got distressingly worse. He shook his head and pounded his ears but it did not help; he had to make up his mind to ignore it. After another half mile or so he suddenly noticed that he could hear himself walking. He stopped dead, then clapped his hands together. He could hear them smack, cutting through the phantom ringing. With a lighter heart he went on.

At last he came out on a shoulder that overlooked the broad valley. In the moonlight he could make out the sweep of the freight highway leading southwest and could detect, he thought, its fluorescent traffic guide lines. He hurried on down.

He was nearing the highway and could hear the rush of passing freighters when he spotted a light ahead. He approached it cautiously, determined that it was neither vehicle nor farm house. Closer approach showed it to be a small open fire, visible from uphill but shielded from the highway by a shoulder of limestone. A man was squatting over it, stirring the contents of a can resting on rocks over the fire.

Max crept nearer until he was looking down into the hobo jungle. He got a whiff of the stew and his mouth watered. Caught between hunger and a hillman's ingrown distrust of "foreigners" he lay still and stared. Presently the man set the can off the fire and called out, "Well, don't hide there! Come on down."

Max was too startled to answer. The man added, "Come on down into the light. I won't fetch it up to you."

Max got to his feet and shuffled down into the circle of firelight. The man looked up. "Howdy. Draw up a chair."

"Howdy." Max sat down across the fire from the tramp. He was not even as well dressed as Max and he needed a shave. Nevertheless he wore his rags with a jaunty air and handled himself with a sparrow's cockiness.

The man continued to stir the mess in the can then spooned out a sample, blew on it, and tasted it. "About right," he announced. "Four-day mulligan, just getting ripe. Find yourself a dish." He got up and picked over a pile of smaller cans behind him, selected one. Max hesitated, then did the same, settling on one that had once contained coffee and appeared not to have been used since. His host served him a liberal portion of stew, then handed him a spoon. Max looked at it.

"If you don't trust the last man who used it," the man said reasonably, "hold it in the fire, then wipe it. Me, I don't worry. If a bug bites me, he dies horribly." Max took the advice, holding the spoon in the flames until the handle became too hot, then wiped it on his shirt.

The stew was good and his hunger made it superlative. The gravy was thick, there were vegetables and unidentified meat. Max didn't bother his head about the pedigrees of the materials; he simply enjoyed it. After a while his host said, "Seconds?"

"Huh? Sure. Thanks!"

The second can of stew filled him up and spread through his tissues a warm glow of well-being. He stretched lazily, enjoying his fatigue. "Feel better?" the man asked.

"Gee, yes. Thanks."

"By the way, you can call me Sam."

"Oh, my name is Max."

"Glad to know you, Max."

Max waited before raising a point that had been bothering him. "Uh, Sam? How did you know I was there? Did you hear me?"

Sam grinned. "No. But you were silhouetted against the sky. Don't ever do that, kid, or it may be the last thing you do."

Max twisted around and looked up at where he had lurked. Sure enough, Sam was right. He'd be dogged!

Sam added, "Traveled far?"

"Huh? Yeah, quite a piece."

"Going far?"

"Uh, pretty far, I guess."

Sam waited, then said, "Think your folks'll miss you?"

"Huh? How did you know?"

"That you had run away from home? Well, you have, haven't you?"

"Yeah. Yeah, I guess I have."

"You looked beat when you dragged in here. Maybe it's not too late to kill the goose before your bridges are burned. Think about it, kid. It's rough on the road. I know."

"Go back? I won't ever go back!"

"As bad as that?"

Max stared into the fire. He needed badly to get his thoughts straight, even if it meant telling a foreigner his private affairs—and this soft-spoken stranger was easy to talk to. "See here, Sam, did you ever have a stepmother?"

"Eh? Can't remember that I ever had any. The Central Jersey Development Center for State Children used to kiss me good night."

"Oh." Max blurted out his story with an occasional sympathetic question from Sam to straighten out its confusion. "So I lit out," he concluded. "There wasn't anything else to do. Was there?"

Sam pursed his lips. "I reckon not. This double step-father of yours—he sounds like a mouse studying to be a rat. You're well shut of him."

"You don't think they'll try to find me and haul me back, do you?"

Sam stopped to put a piece of wood on the fire. "I am not sure about that."

"Huh? Why not? I'm no use to him. He doesn't like me. And Maw won't care, not really. She may whine a bit, but she won't turn her hand."

"Well, there's the farm."

"The farm? I don't care about that, not with Dad gone. Truthfully, it ain't much. You break your back trying to make a crop. If the Food Conservation Act hadn't forbidden owners to let farm land fall out of use, Dad would have quit farming long ago. It would take something like this government condemnation to make it possible to find anybody to take it off your hands."

"That's what I mean. This joker got your mother to sell it. Now my brand of law may not be much good, but it looks as if that money ought to come to you."

"What? Oh, I don't care about the money. I just want to get away from them."

"Don't talk that way about money; the powers-that-be will have you shut up for blasphemy. But it probably doesn't matter how you feel, as I think Citizen Montgomery is going to want to see you awful bad."

"Why?"

"Did your father leave a will?"

"No. Why? He didn't have anything to leave but the farm."

"I don't know the ins and outs of your state laws, but it's a sure thing that at least half of that farm belongs to you. Possibly your stepmother has only life-time tenure in her half, with reversion to you when she dies. But it's a certainty that she can't grant a good deed without your signature. Along about time your county courthouse opens up tomorrow morning the buyers are going to find that out. Then they'll come high-tailing up, looking for her—and you. And ten minutes later this Montgomery hombre will start looking for you, if he hasn't already."

"Oh, me! If they find me, can they make me go back?"

"Don't let them find you. You've made a good start."

Max picked up his rucksack. "I guess I had better get moving. Thanks a lot, Sam. Maybe I can help you someday."

"Sit down."

"Look, I had better get as far away as I can."

"Kid, you're tired out and your judgment has slipped. How far can you walk tonight, the shape you're in? Tomorrow morning, bright and early, we'll go down to the highway, follow it about a mile to the freighters' restaurant south of here and catch the haulers as they come out from breakfast, feeling good. We'll promote a ride and you'll go farther in ten minutes than you could make all night."

Max had to admit that he was tired, exhausted really, and Sam certainly knew more about these wrinkles than he did. Sam added, "Got a blanket in your bindle?"

"No. Just a shirt . . . and some books."

"Books, eh? Read quite a bit myself, when I get a chance. May I see them?"

Somewhat reluctantly Max got them out. Sam held them close to the fire and examined them. "Well, I'll be a three-eyed Martian! Kid, do you know what you've got here?"

"Sure."

"But you ought not to have these. You're not a member of the Astrogators' Guild."

"No, but my uncle was. He was on the first trip to Beta Hydrae," he added proudly.

"No foolin'!"

"Sure as taxes."

"But you've never been in space yourself? No, of course not."

"But I'm going to be!" Max admitted something that he had never told anyone, his ambition to emulate his uncle and go out to the stars. Sam listened thoughtfully. When Max stopped, he said slowly, "So you want to be an astrogator?"

"I certainly do."

Sam scratched his nose. "Look, kid, I don't want to throw cold water, but you know how the world wags. Getting to be an astrogator is almost as difficult as getting into the Plumbers' Guild. The soup is thin these days and there isn't enough to go around. The guild won't welcome you just because you are anxious to be apprenticed. Membership is hereditary, just like all the other high-pay guilds."

"But my uncle was a member."

"Your uncle isn't your father."

"No, but a member who hasn't any sons gets to nominate someone else. Uncle Chet explained it to me. He always told me he was going to register my nomination."

"And did he?"

Max was silent. At the time his uncle had died he had been too young to know how to go about finding out. When his father had followed his uncle events had closed in on him—he had never checked up, subconsciously preferring to nurse the dream rather than test it. "I don't know," he said at last. "I'm going to the Mother Chapter at Earthport and find out."

"Hmmm—I wish you luck, kid." He stared into the fire, sadly it seemed to Max. "Well, I'm going to grab some shut-eye, and you had better do the same. If you're chilly, you'll find some truck back under that rock shelf—burlap and packing materials and such. It'll keep you warm, if you don't mind risking a flea or two."

Max crawled into the dark hole indicated, found a half-way cave in the limestone. Groping, he located the primitive bedding. He had expected to be wakeful, but he was asleep before Sam finished covering the fire.

He was awakened by sunlight blazing outside. He crawled out, stood up and stretched the stiffness out of his limbs. By the sun he judged it to be about seven o'clock in the morning. Sam was not in sight. He looked around and shouted, not too loudly, and guessed that Sam had gone down to the creek for a drink and a cold wash. Max went back into the shelter and hauled out his rucksack, intending to change his socks.

His uncle's books were missing.

There was a note on top of his spare shirt: "Dear Max," it said, "There is more stew in the can. You can warm it up for breakfast. So long—Sam P.S. Sorry."

Further search disclosed that his identification card was missing, but Sam had not bothered with his other pitiful possessions. Max did not touch the stew but set out down the road, his mind filled with bitter thoughts.

# 3

# EARTHPORT

The farm road crossed under the freight highway; Max came up on the far side and headed south beside the highway. The route was marked by "NO TRESPASS" signs but the path was well worn. The highway widened to make room for a deceleration strip. At the end of its smooth reach, a mile away, Max could see the restaurant Sam had mentioned.

He shinnied over the fence enclosing the restaurant and parking grounds and went to the parking stalls where a dozen of the big land ships were lined up. One was quivering for departure, its flat bottom a few inches clear of the metallic pavement. Max went to its front end and looked up at the driver's compartment. The door was open and he could see the driver at his instrument board. Max called out, "Hey, Mister!"

The driver stuck his head out. "What's itching you?"

"How are the chances of a lift south?"

"Beat it, kid." The door slammed.

None of the other freighters was raised off the pavement; their control compartments were empty. Max was about to turn away when another giant scooted down the braking strip, reached the parking space, crawled slowly into a stall, and settled to the ground. He considered approaching its driver, but decided to wait until the man had eaten. He went back toward the restaurant building and was looking through the door, watching hungry men demolish food while his mouth watered, when he heard a pleasant voice at his shoulder.

"Excuse me, but you're blocking the door."

Max jumped aside. "Oh! Sorry."

"Go ahead. You were first." The speaker was a man about ten years older than Max. He was profusely freckled and had a one-sided grin. Max saw on his cap the pin of the Teamsters' Guild. "Go on in," the man repeated, "before you get trampled in the rush."

Max had been telling himself that he might catch Sam inside—and, after all, they couldn't charge him just for coming in, if he didn't actually *eat* anything. Underlying was the thought of asking to work for a meal, if the manager looked friendly. The freckled-faced man's urging tipped the scales; he followed his nose toward the source of the heavenly odors pouring out the door.

The restaurant was crowded; there was one vacant table, for two. The man slid into a chair and said, "Sit down." When Max hesitated, he added, "Go ahead, put it down. Never like to eat alone." Max could feel the manager's eyes on him, he sat down. A waitress handed them each a menu and the hauler looked her over appreciatively. When she left he said, "This dump used to have automatic service—and it went broke. The trade went to the *Tivoli*, eighty miles down the stretch. Then the new owner threw away the machinery and hired girls and business picked up. Nothing makes food taste better than having a pretty girl put it in front of you. Right?"

"Uh, I guess so. Sure." Max had not heard what was said. He had seldom been in a restaurant and then only in the lunch counter at Clyde's Corners. The prices he read frightened him; he wanted to crawl under the table.

His companion looked at him. "What's the trouble, chum?"

"Trouble? Uh, nothing."

"You broke?" Max's miserable expression answered him. "Shucks, I've been there myself. Relax." The man waggled his fingers at the waitress. "Come here, honey chile. My partner and I will each have a breakfast steak with a fried egg sitting on top and this and that on the side. I want that egg to be just barely dead. If it is cooked solid, I'll nail it to the wall as a warning to others. Understand me?"

"I doubt if you'll be able to get a nail through it," she retorted and walked away, swaying gently. The hauler kept his eyes on her until she disappeared into the kitchen. "See what I mean? How can machinery compete?"

The steak was good and the egg was not congealed. The hauler told Max to call him "Red" and Max gave his name in exchange. Max was pursuing the last of the yolk with a bit of toast and was considering whether it was time to broach the subject of a ride when Red leaned forward and spoke softly. "Max—you got anything pushing you? Free to take a job?"

"What? Why, maybe. What is it?"

"Mind taking a little run southwest?"

"Southwest? Matter of fact, I was headin' that way."

"Good. Here's the deal. The Man says we have to have two teamsters to each rig—or else break for eight hours after driving eight. I can't; I've got a penalty time to meet—and my partner washed out. The flathead got taken drunk and I had to put him down to cool. Now I've got a check point to pass a hundred thirty miles down the stretch. They'll make me lay over if I can't show another driver."

"Gee! But I don't know how to drive, Red. I'm awful sorry."

Red gestured with his cup. "You won't have to. You'll always be the off-watch driver. I wouldn't trust little *Molly Malone* to somebody who didn't know her ways. I'll keep myself awake with Pep pills and catch up on sleep at Earthport."

"You're going all the way to *Earthport?*"

"Right."

"It's a deal!"

"Okay, here's the lash up. Every time we hit a check point you're in the bunk, asleep. You help me load and unload—I've got a partial and a pick-up at Oke City—and I'll feed you. Right?"

"Right!"

"Then let's go. I want to scoot before these other dust jumpers get underway. Never can tell, there might be a spotter." Red flipped a bill down and did not wait for change.

The *Molly Malone* was two hundred feet long and stream lined such that she had negative lift when cruising. This came to Max's attention from watching the instruments; when she first quivered and raised, the dial marked ROAD CLEARANCE showed nine inches, but as they gathered speed down the acceleration strip it decreased to six.

"The repulsion works by an inverse-cube law," Red explained. "The more the wind pushes us down the harder the road pushes us up. Keeps us from jumping over the skyline. The faster we go the steadier we are."

"Suppose you went so fast that the wind pressure forced the bottom down to the road? Could you stop soon enough to keep from wrecking it?"

"Use your head. The more we squat the harder we are pushed up—inverse-cube, I said."

"Oh." Max got out his uncle's slide rule. "If she just supports her own weight at nine inches clearance, then at three inches the repulsion would be twenty-seven times her weight and at an inch it would be seven hundred and twenty-nine, and at a quarter of an inch—"

"Don't even think about it. At top speed I can't get her down to five inches."

"But what makes her *go?*"

"It's a phase relationship. The field crawls forward and Molly tries to catch up—only she can't. Don't ask me the theory, I just push the buttons." Red struck a cigarette and lounged back, one hand on the tiller. "Better get in the bunk, kid. Check point in forty miles."

The bunk was thwartships abaft the control compartment, a shelf above the seat. Max climbed in and wrapped a blanket around himself. Red handed him a cap. "Pull this down over your eyes. Let the button show." The button was a teamster's shield, Max did as he was told.

Presently he heard the sound of wind change from a soft roar to a sigh and then stop. The freighter settled to the pavement and the door opened. He lay still, unable to see what was going on. A strange voice said, "How long you been herding it?"

"Since breakfast at Tony's."

"So? How did your eyes get so bloodshot?"

"It's the evil life I lead. Want to see my tongue?"

The inspector ignored this, saying instead, "Your partner didn't sign his trick."

"Whatever you say. Want me to wake the dumb geek?"

"Umm . . . don't bother. You sign for him. Tell him to be more careful."

"Right."

The *Molly Malone* pulled out and picked up speed. Max crawled down. "I thought we were sunk when he asked for my signature."

"That was on purpose," Red said scornfully. "You have to give them something to yap about, or they'll dig for it."

Max liked the freighter. The tremendous speed so close to the ground exhilarated him; he decided that if he could not be a spaceman, this life would not be bad —he'd find out how high the application fee was and start saving. He liked the easy way Red picked out on the pavement ahead the speed line that matched the *Molly's* speed and then laid the big craft into a curve. It was usually the outermost line, with the *Molly* on her side and the horizon tilted up at a crazy angle.

Near Oklahoma City they swooped under the ring guides of the C.S.&E. just as a train went over—the *Razor*, by Max's calculations. "I used to herd those things," Red remarked, glancing up.

"You *did?*"

"Yep. But they got to worrying me. I hated it every time I made a jump and felt the weight sag out from under me. Then I got a notion that the train had a mind of its own and was just waiting to turn aside instead of entering the next guide ring. That sort of thing is no good. So I found a teamster who wanted to better himself and paid the fine to both guilds to let us swap. Never regretted it. Two hundred miles an hour when you're close to the ground is enough."

"Uh, how about space ships?"

"That's another matter. Elbow room out there. Say, kid, while you're at Earthport you should take a look at the big babies. They're quite something."

The library book had been burning a hole in his rucksack; at Oklahoma City he noticed a postal box at the freight depot and, on impulse, dropped the book into it. After he had mailed it he had a twinge of worry that he might have given a clue to his whereabouts which would get back to Montgomery, but he suppressed the worry—the book *had* to be returned. Vagrancy in the eyes of the law had not worried him, nor trespass, nor impersonating a licensed teamster—but filching a book was a sin.

Max was asleep in the bunk when they arrived. Red shook him. "End of the line, kid."

Max sat up, yawning. "Where are we?"

"Earthport. Let's shake a leg and get this baby unloaded."

It was two hours past sunrise and growing desert hot by the time they got the *Molly* disgorged. Red stood him to a last meal. Red finished first, paid, then laid a bill down by Max's plate. "Thanks, kid. That's for luck. So long." He was gone while Max still had his mouth hanging open. He had never learned his friend's name, did not even know his shield number.

Earthport was much the biggest settlement Max had ever seen and everything about it confused him—the hurrying self-centered crowds, the enormous buildings, the slidewalks in place of streets, the noise, the desert sun beating down, the flatness—why, there wasn't anything you could call a hill closer than the skyline!

He saw his first extra-terrestrial, an eight-foot native of Epsilon Gemini V, striding out of a shop with a package under his left arms—as casually, Max thought, as a farmer doing his week's shopping at the Corners. Max stared. He knew what the creature was from pictures and SV shows, but seeing one was another matter. Its multiple eyes, like a wreath of yellow grapes around the head, gave it a grotesque faceless appearance. Max let his own head swivel to follow it.

The creature approached a policeman, tapped the top of his cap, and said, "Excuse me, sahr, but can you tirect me to the Tesert Palms Athletic Club?" Max could not tell where the noise came out.

' Max finally noticed that he seemed to be the only one staring, so he walked slowly on, while sneaking looks over his shoulder—which resulted in his bumping into a stranger. "Oh, excuse me!" Max blurted. The stranger looked at him. "Take it easy, cousin. You're in the big city now." After that he tried to be careful.

He had intended to seek out the Guild Hall of the Mother Chapter of Astrogators at once in the forlorn hope that even without his books and identification card he might still identify himself and find that Uncle Chet had provided for his future. But there was so much to see that he loitered. He found himself presently in front of Imperial House, the hotel that guaranteed to supply any combination of pressure, temperature, lighting, atmosphere, pseudogravitation, and diet favored by any known race of intelligent creatures. He hung around hoping to see some of the guests, but the only one who came out while he was there was wheeled out in a pressurized travel tank and he could not see into it.

He noticed the police guard at the door eyeing him and started to move on—then decided to ask directions, reasoning that if it was all right for a Geminian to question a policeman it certainly must be all right for a human being. He found himself quoting the extra-terrestrial. "Excuse me, sir, but could you direct me to the Astrogators' Guild Hall?"

The officer looked him over. "At the foot of the Avenue of Planets, just before you reach the port."

"Uh, which way do . . ."

"New in town?"

"Yeah. Yes, sir."

"Where are you staying?"

"Staying? Why, nowhere yet. I just got here. I . . ."

"What's your business at the Astrogators' Hall?"

"It's on account of my uncle," Max answered miserably.

"Your uncle?"

"He . . . he's an astrogator." He mentally crossed his fingers over the tense.

The policeman inspected again. "Take this slide to the next intersection, change and slide west. Big building with the guild sunburst over the door—can't miss it. Stay out of restricted areas." Max left without waiting to find out how he was to know a restricted area. The Guild Hall did prove easy to find; the slide-walk to the west ducked underground and when it emerged at its swing-around Max was deposited in front of it.

But he had not eyes for it. To the west where avenue and buildings ended was the field and on it space ships, stretching away for miles—fast little military darts, stubby Moon shuttles, winged ships that served the satellite stations, robot freighters, graceless and powerful. But directly in front of the gate hardly half a mile away was a great ship that he knew at once, the starship *Asgard*. He knew her history, Uncle Chet had served in her. A hundred years earlier she had been built out in space as a space-to-space rocket ship; she was then the *Prince of Wales*. Years passed, her tubes were ripped out and a mass-conversion torch was kindled in her; she became the *Einstein*. More years passed, for nearly twenty she swung empty around Luna, a lifeless, outmoded hulk. Now in place of the torch she had Horst-Conrad impellers that clutched at the fabric of space itself; thanks to them she was now able to touch Mother Terra. To commemorate her rebirth she had been dubbed *Asgard*, heavenly home of the gods.

Her massive, pear-shaped body was poised on its smaller end, steadied by an invisible scaffolding of thrust beams. Max knew where they must be, for there was a ring of barricades spotted around her to keep the careless from wandering into the deadly loci.

He pressed his nose against the gate to the field and tried to see more of her, until a voice called out, "Away from there, Jack! Don't you see that sign?"

Max looked up. Above his head was a sign: RESTRICTED AREA. Reluctantly he moved away and walked back to the Guild Hall.

# 4

## THE ASTROGATORS' GUILD

Everything about the hall of the Mother Chapter was to Max's eyes lavish, churchlike, and frightening. The great doors opened silently as he approached, dilating away into the walls. His feet made no sound on the tesselated floor. He started down the long, high foyer, wondering where he should go, when a firm voice stopped him. "May I help you, please?"

He turned. A beautiful young lady with a severe manner held him with her eye. She was seated behind a desk. Max went up to her. "Uh, maybe you could tell me, Ma'am, who I ought to see. I don't rightly know just . . ."

"One moment. Your name, please?" Several minutes later she had wormed out of him the basic facts of his quest. "So far as I can see, you haven't any status here and no excuse for appealing to the Guild."

"But I told you . . ."

"Never mind. I'm going to put it up to the legal office." She touched a button and a screen raised up on her desk; she spoke to it. "Mr. Hanson, can you spare a moment?"

"Yes, Grace?"

"There is a young man here who claims to be a legacy of the Guild. Will you talk with him?"

The voice answered, "Look, Grace, you know the procedures. Get his address, send him on his way, and send his papers up for consideration."

She frowned and touched another control. Although Max could see that she continued to talk, no sound reached him. Then she nodded and the screen slid back into the desk. She touched another button and said, "Skeeter!"

A page boy popped out of a door behind her and looked Max over with cold eyes. "Skeeter," she went on, "take this visitor to Mr. Hanson."

The page sniffed. "Him?"

"Him. And fasten your collar and spit out that gum."

Mr. Hanson listened to Max's story and passed him on to his boss, the chief legal counsel, who listened to a third telling. That official then drummed his desk and made a call, using the silencing device the girl had used.

He then said to Max, "You're in luck, son. The Most Worthy High Secretary will grant you a few minutes of his time. Now when you go in, don't sit down, remember to speak only when spoken to, and get out quickly when he indicates that the audience is ended."

The High Secretary's office made the lavishness that had thus far filled Max's eyes seem like austerity. The rug alone could have been swapped for the farm on which Max grew up. There was no communication equipment in evidence, no files, not even a desk. The High Secretary lounged back in a mammoth easy chair while a servant massaged his scalp. He raised his head as Max appeared and said, "Come in, son. Sit down there. What is your name?"

"Maximilian Jones, sir."

They looked at each other. The Secretary saw a lanky youth who needed a haircut, a bath, and a change of clothes; Max saw a short, fat little man in a wrinkled uniform. His head seemed too big for him and Max could not make up his mind whether the eyes were kindly or cold.

"And you are a nephew of Chester Arthur Jones?"

"Yes, sir."

"I knew Brother Jones well. A fine mathematician." The High Secretary went on, "I understand that you have had the misfortune to lose your government Citizen's Identification. Carl."

He had not raised his voice but a young man appeared with the speed of a genie. "Yes, sir?"

"Take this young man's thumb print, call the Bureau of Identification—not here, but the main office at

New Washington. My compliments to the Chief of Bureau and tell him that I would be pleased to have immediate identification while you hold the circuit."

The print was taken speedily; the man called Carl left. The High Secretary went on, "What was your purpose in coming here?" Diffidently Max explained that his uncle had told him that he intended to nominate him for apprenticeship in the guild.

The man nodded. "So I understand. I am sorry to tell you, young fellow, that Brother Jones made no nomination."

Max had difficulty in taking in the simple statement. So much was his inner pride tied to his pride in his uncle's profession, so much had he depended on his hope that his uncle had named him his professional heir, that he could not accept at once the verdict that he was nobody and nothing. He blurted out, "You're *sure*? Did you look?"

The masseur looked shocked but the High Secretary answered calmly, "The archives have been searched, not once, but twice. There is no possible doubt." The High Secretary sat up, gestured slightly, and the servant disappeared. "I'm sorry."

"But he *told* me," Max said stubbornly. "He said he was going to."

"Nevertheless he did not." The man who had taken the thumb print came in and offered a memorandum to the High Secretary, who glanced at it and waved it away. "I've no doubt that he considered you. Nomination to our brotherhood involves a grave responsibility; it is not unusual for a childless brother to have his eye on a likely lad for a long time before deciding whether or not he measures up. For some reason your uncle did not name you."

Max was appalled by the humiliating theory that his beloved uncle might have found him unworthy. It could not be true—why, just the day before he died, he had said—he interrupted his thoughts to say, "Sir—I think I know what happened."

"Eh?"

"Uncle Chester died suddenly. He meant to name me, but he didn't get a chance. I'm sure of it."

"Possibly. Men have been known to fail to get their affairs in order before the last orbit. But I must assume that he knew what he was doing."

"But—"

"That's all, young man. No, don't go away. I've been thinking about you today." Max looked startled, the High Secretary smiled and continued, "You see, you are the second 'Maximilian Jones' who has come to us with this story."

"Huh?"

"Huh indeed." The guild executive reached into a pocket of his chair, pulled out some books and a card, handed them to Max, who stared unbelievingly.

"Uncle Chet's books!"

"Yes. Another man, older than yourself, came here yesterday with your identification card and these books. He was less ambitious than you are," he added dryly. "He was willing to settle for a rating less lofty than astrogator."

"What happened?"

"He left suddenly when we attempted to take his finger prints. I did not see him. But when you showed up today I began to wonder how long a procession of 'Maximilian Jones's' would favor us. Better guard that card in the future—I fancy we have saved you a fine."

Max placed it in an inner pocket. "Thanks a lot, sir." He started to put the books in his rucksack. The High Secretary gestured in denial.

"No, no! Return the books, please."

"But Uncle Chet gave them to me."

"Sorry. At most he loaned them to you—and he should not have done even that. The tools of our profession are never owned individually; they are loaned to each brother. Your uncle should have turned them in when he retired, but some of the brothers have a sentimental fondness for having them in their possession. Give them to me, please."

Max still hesitated. "Come now," the guildsman said

reasonably. "It would not do for our professional secrets to be floating around loose, available to anyone.
Even the hairdressers do not permit that. We have a
high responsibility to the public. Only a member of
this guild, trained, tested, sworn, and accepted, may
lawfully be custodian of those manuals."

Max's answer was barely audible. "I don't see the
harm. I'm not going to get to use them, it looks like."

"You don't believe in anarchy, surely? Our whole society is founded on entrusting grave secrets only to
those who are worthy. But don't feel sad. Each brother, when he is issued his tools, deposits an earnest with
the bursar. In my opinion, since you are the nearest
relative of Brother Jones, we may properly repay the
earnest to you for their return. Carl."

The young man appeared again. "The deposit mon-
ies, please." Carl had the money with him—he seemed
to earn his living by knowing what the High Secretary
was about to want. Max found himself accepting an
impressive sheaf of money, more than he had ever
touched before, and the books were taken from him
before he could think of another objection.

It seemed time to leave, but he was motioned back
to his chair. "Personally, I am sorry to disappoint you,
but I am merely the servant of my brothers; I have no
choice. However . . ." The High Secretary fitted his
finger tips together. "Our brotherhood takes care of its
own. There are funds at my disposal for such cases.
How would you like to go into training?"

"For the *Guild?*"

"No, no! We don't grant brotherhood as charity. But
for some respectable trade, metalsmith, or chef, or tailor—what you wish. Any occupation not hereditary.
The brotherhood will sponsor you, pay your 'prentice
fee and, if you make good, lend you your contribution
when you are sworn in."

Max knew he should accept gratefully. He was
being offered an opportunity free that most of the
swarming masses never got on any terms. But the
cross-grained quirk in him that had caused him to

spurn the stew that Sam had left behind made this generous offer stick in his craw. "Thanks just the same," he answered in tones almost surly, "but I don't rightly think I can take it."

The High Secretary looked bleak. "So? It's your life." He snapped his fingers, a page appeared, and Max was led quickly out of the Hall.

He stood on the steps of the Guild Hall and wondered dejectedly what he should do next. Even the space ships on the field at the foot of the street did not attract; he could not have looked at one without feeling like crying. He looked to the east instead.

A short distance away a jaunty figure leaned against a trash receptacle. As Max's eyes rested on the man he straightened up, flipped a cigarette to the pavement, and started toward him.

Max looked at him again. "Sam!" It was undoubtedly the wayfarer who had robbed him—well dressed, clean shaved—but Sam nonetheless. Max hurried toward him.

"Howdy, Max," Sam greeted him with an unembarrassed grin, "how did you make out?"

"I ought to have you arrested!"

"Now, now—keep your voice down. You're making yourself conspicuous."

Max took a breath and lowered his voice. "You stole my books."

"*Your* books? They weren't yours—and I returned them to their owners. You want to arrest me for that?"

"But you . . . Well, anyhow you . . ."

A voice, civil, firm, and official, spoke at Max's elbow. "Is this person annoying you, sir?" Max turned and found a policeman standing behind him. He started to speak, then bit off the words as he realized the question had been addressed to Sam.

Sam took hold of Max's upper arm in a gesture that was protective and paternal, but quite firm. "Not at all, officer, thank you."

"Are you sure? I received word that this chico was headed this way and I've had my eye on him."

"He's a friend of mine. I was waiting for him here."

"As you say. We have a lot of trouble with vagrants. They all seem to head for Earthport."

"He's not a vagrant. He's a young friend of mine from the country and I'm afraid he's gotten a bit confused. I'll be responsible."

"Very well, sir."

"Not at all." Max let himself be led away. When they were out of earshot Sam said, "That was close. That nosy clown would have had us both in the bull pen. You did all right, kid—kept your lip zipped at the right time."

They were around the corner into a less important street before Sam let go his grip. He stopped and faced Max, grinning. "Well, kid?"

"I should 'a' told that cop about you!"

"Why didn't you? He was right there."

Max found himself caught by contradictory feelings. He was angry with Sam, no doubt about it, but his first unstudied reaction at seeing him had been the warm pleasure one gets from recognizing a familiar face among strangers—the anger had come a split second later. Now Sam looked at him with easy cynicism, a quizzical smile on his face. "Well, kid?" he repeated. "If you want to turn me in, let's go back and get it over with. I won't run."

Max looked back at him peevishly. "Oh, forget it!"

"Thanks. I'm sorry about it, kid. I really am."

"Then why did you do it?"

Sam's face changed suddenly to a sad, far-away look, then resumed its cheerful cynicism. "I was tempted by an idea, old son—every man has his limits. Some day I'll tell you. Now, how about a bit to eat and a gab? There's a joint near here where we can talk without having the nosies leaning over our shoulders."

"I don't know as I want to."

"Oh, come now! The food isn't much but it's better than mulligan."

Max had been ready with a stiff speech about how he would not turn Sam in, but he certainly did not want to eat with him; the mention of mulligan brought him up short. He remembered uneasily that Sam had not inquired as to *his* morals, but had shared his food.

"Well . . . okay."

"That's my boy!" They went on down the street. The neighborhood was a sort to be found near the port in any port city; once off the pompous Avenue of the Planets it became more crowded, noisier, more alive, and somehow warmer and more friendly despite a strong air of "keep your hand on your purse." Hole-in-the-wall tailor shops, little restaurants none too clean, cheap hotels, honky-tonks, fun arcades, exhibits both "educational" and "scientific," street vendors, small theaters with gaudy posters and sounds of music leaking out, shops fronting for betting parlors, tattoo parlors fronting for astrologers, and the inevitable Salvation Army mission gave the street flavor its stylish cousins lacked. Martians in trefoil sunglasses and respirators, humanoids from Beta Corvi IH, things with exoskeletons from Allah knew where, all jostled with humans of all shades and all blended in easy camaraderie.

Sam stopped at a shop with the age-old symbol of three golden spheres. "Wait here. Be right out."

Max waited and watched the throng. Sam came out shortly without his coat. "Now we eat."

"Sam! Did you pawn your coat?"

"Give the man a cigar! How did you guess?"

"But . . . Look, I didn't know you were broke; you looked prosperous. Get it back, I'll . . . I'll pay for our lunch."

"Say, that's sweet of you, kid. But forget it. I don't need a coat this weather. Truth is, I was dressed up just to make a good impression at—well, a little matter of business."

Max blurted out, "But how did you . . .", then shut up. Sam grinned. "Did I steal the fancy rags? No. I encountered a citizen who believed in percentages and engaged him in a friendly game. Never bet on percentages, kid; skill is more fundamental. Here we are."

The room facing the street was a bar, beyond was a restaurant. Sam led him on through the restaurant, through the kitchen, down a passage off which there were card rooms, and ended in a smaller, less pretentious dining room; Sam picked a table in a corner. An enormous Samoan shuffled up, dragging one leg. Sam nodded, "Howdy, Percy." He turned to Max. "A drink first?"

"Uh, I guess not."

"Smart lad. Lay off the stuff. Irish for me, Percy, and we'll both have whatever you had for lunch." The Samoan waited silently. Sam shrugged and laid money on the table, Percy scooped it up.

Max objected, "But I was going to pay."

"You can pay for the lunch. Percy owns the place," he added. "He's offensively rich, but he didn't get that way by trusting the likes of me. Now tell me about yourself, old son. How you got here? How you made out with the astrogators . . . everything. Did they kill the fatted calf?"

"Well, no." There seemed to be no reason not to tell Sam and he found that he wanted to talk. Sam nodded at the end.

"About what I had guessed. Any plans now?"

"No. I don't know what to do now, Sam."

"Hmm . . . it's an ill wind that has no turning. Eat your lunch and let me think."

Later he added, "Max, what do you *want* to do?"

"Well . . . I wanted to be an astrogator . . ."

"That's out."

"I know."

"Tell me, did you want to be an astrogator and nothing else, or did you simply want to go into space?"

"Why, I guess I never thought about it any other way."

"Well, think about it."

Max did so. "I want to space. If I can't go as an astrogator, I want to go anyhow. But I don't see how. The Astrogators' Guild is the only one I stood a chance for."

"There are ways."

"Huh? Do you mean put in for emigration?"

Sam shook his head. "It costs more than you could save to go to one of the desirable colonies—and the ones they give you free rides to I wouldn't wish on my worst enemies."

"Then what do you mean?"

Sam hesitated. "There are ways to wangle it, old son —if you do what I say. This uncle of yours—you were around him a lot?"

"Why, sure."

"Talked about space with you?"

"Certainly. That's all we talked about."

"Hmm . . . how well do you know the patter?"

# 5

# ". . . YOUR MONEY AND MY KNOW-HOW . . ."

"The patter?" Max looked puzzled. "I suppose I know what everybody knows."

"Where's the worry hole?"

"Huh? That's the control room."

"If the cheater wants a corpse, where does he find it?"

Max looked amused. "That's just stuff from SV serials, nobody talks like that aboard ship. The cook is the cook, and if he wanted a side of beef, he'd go to the reefer for it."

"How do you tell a 'beast' from an animal?"

"Why, a 'beast' is a passenger, but an animal is just an animal, I guess."

"Suppose you were on a ship for Mars and they announced that the power plant had gone blooie and the ship was going to spiral into the Sun? What would you think?"

"I'd think somebody was trying to scare me. In the first place, you wouldn't be 'on' a ship—'in' is the right word. Second, a spiral isn't one of the possible orbits. And third, if a ship was headed for Mars from Earth, it couldn't fall into the Sun; the orbit would be incompatible."

"Suppose you were part of a ship's crew in a strange port and you wanted to go out and look the place over. How would you go about asking the captain for permission?"

"Why, I wouldn't."

"You'd just jump ship?"

"Let me finish. If I wanted to hit dirt, I'd ask the first officer; the captain doesn't bother with such things. If the ship was big enough, I'd have to ask my department head first." Max sat up and held Sam's eye. "Sam—you've been spaceside. Haven't you?"

"What gave you that notion, kid?"

"What's your guild?"

"Stow it, Max. Ask me no questions and I'll sell you no pigs in a poke. Maybe I've studied up on the jive just as you have."

"I don't believe it," Max said bluntly.

Sam looked pained. Max went on, "What's this all about? You usk me a bunch of silly questions—sure, I know quite a bit about spaceside; I've been reading about it all my life and Uncle Chet would talk by the hour. But what of it?"

Sam looked at him and said softly, "Max—the *Asgard* is raising next Thursday—for starside. Would you like to be in her?"

Max thought about it. To be in the fabulous *Asgard*, to be heading out to the stars, to be—he brushed the vision aside. "Don't talk that way, Sam! You know I'd give my right arm. Why needle me?"

"How much money have you?"

"Huh? Why?"

"How much?"

"I haven't even had time to count it." Max started to haul out the wad of bills he had been given; Sam hastily and unobtrusively stopped him.

"Psst!" he protested. "Don't flash a roll in here. Do you want to eat through a slit in your throat? Keep it down!"

Startled, Max took the advice. He was still more startled when he finished the tally; he had known that he had been given quite a lot of money but this was more than he had dreamed. "How much?" Sam persisted. Max told him, Sam swore softly. "Well, it will just have to do."

"Do for what?"

"You'll see. Put it away."

As Max did so he said wonderingly, "Sam, I had no idea those books were so valuable."

"They aren't."

"Huh?"

"It's malarkey. Lots of guilds do it. They want to

make it appear that their professional secrets are precious, so they make the candidate put up a wad of dough for his reference books. If those things were published in the ordinary way, they'd sell at a reasonable price."

"But that's right, isn't it? As the Worthy High Secretary explained, it wouldn't do for just anybody to have that knowledge."

Sam made a rude noise and pretended to spit. "What difference would it make? Suppose you still had them—you don't have a ship to conn."

"But . . ." Max stopped and grinned. "I can't see that it did any good to take them away from me anyhow. I've read them, so I know what's in them."

"Sure you know. Maybe you even remember some of the methods. But you don't have all those columns of figures so you can look up the one you need when you need it. That's what they care about."

"But I do! I read them, I tell you." Max wrinkled his forehead, then began to recite: " 'Page 272, Calculated Solutions of the Differential Equation of Motion by the Ricardo Assumption—' " He began to reel off a series of seven-place figures. Sam listened in growing surprise, then stopped him.

"Kid, you really remember that? You weren't making it up?"

"Of course not, I *read* it."

"Well, I'll be a beat up. . . . Look, you're a page-at-a-glance reader? Is that it?"

"No, not exactly. I'm a pretty fast reader, but I do have to read it. But I don't forget. I never have been able to see how people forget. I can't forget anything."

Sam shook his head wonderingly. "I've been able to forget a lot of things, thank Heaven." He thought for a moment. "Maybe we should forget the other caper and exploit this talent of yours. I can think of angles."

"What do you mean? And what other caper?"

"Hmm . . . no, I was right the first time. The idea is to get away from here. And with your funny memory the chances are a whole lot better. Even though you sling the slang pretty well I was worried. Now I'm not."

"Sam, stop talking riddles. What are you figuring on?"

"Okay, kid, I'll lay it on the table." He glanced around, leaned forward, and spoke even more quietly. "We take the money and I spread it around carefully. When the *Asgard* raises, we're signed on as crewmen."

"As apprentices? We wouldn't even have time for ground school. And besides you're too old to 'prentice."

"Use your head! We don't have enough to pay one apprentice fee, let alone two, in any space guild—and the *Asgard* isn't signing 'prentices anyhow. We'll be experienced journeymen in one of the guilds, with records to prove it."

When the idea soaked in, Max was shocked. "But they put you in jail for that!"

"Where do you think you are now?"

"Well, I'm not in jail. And I don't want to be."

"This whole planet is one big jail, and a crowded one at that. What chance have you got? If you aren't born rich, or born into one of the hereditary guilds, what can you do? Sign up with one of the labor companies."

"But there are non-hereditary guilds."

"Can you pay the fee? You've got a year, maybe two until you're too old to 'prentice. If you were sharp with cards you might manage it—but can you earn it? You should live so long! Your old man should have saved it; he left you a farm instead." Sam stopped suddenly, bit his thumb. "Max, I'll play fair. Your old man did leave you a fair start in life. With the money you've got you can go home, hire a shyster, and maybe squeeze that Montgomery item out of the money he swindled for your farm. Then you can buy your apprenticeship in some guild. Do it, kid. I won't stand in your way." He watched Max narrowly.

Max reflected that he had just refused a chance to

pick a trade and be given a free start. Maybe he should reconsider. Maybe . . . "No! That's not what I want. This . . . this, uh, scheme of yours; how do we do it?"

Sam relaxed and grinned. "My boy!"

Sam got them a room over Percy's restaurant. There he coached him. Sam went out several times and Max's money went with him. When Max protested Sam said wearily, "What do you want? To hold my heart as security? Do you want to come along and scare 'em out of the dicker? The people I have to reason with will be taking chances. Or do you think you can arrange matters yourself? It's your money and my know-how . . . that's the partnership."

Max watched him leave the first time with gnawing doubts, but Sam came back. Once he brought with him an elderly, gross woman who looked Max over as if he were an animal up for auction. Sam did not introduce her but said, "How about it? I thought a mustache would help."

She looked at Max from one side, then the other. "No," she decided, "that would just make him look made up for amateur theatricals." She touched Max's head with moist, cold fingers; when he drew back, she admonished, "Don't flinch, honey duck. Aunt Becky has to work on you. No, we'll move back his hair line above his temples, thin it out on top, and kill its gloss. Some faint wrinkles tattooed around his eyes. Mmm . . . that's all. Mustn't overdo it."

When this fat artist was through Max looked ten years older. Becky asked if he wanted his hair roots killed, or would he prefer to have his scalp return to normal in time? Sam started to insist on permanence, but she brushed him aside. "I'll give him a bottle of 'Miracle Gro'—no extra charge, it's just rubbing alcohol—and he can make a big thing of using it. How about it, lover? You're too pretty to age you permanently."

Max accepted the "Miracle Gro"—hair restored or your money back.

Sam took away his citizen's identification card, returned with another one. It had his right name, a
wrong age, his right serial number, a wrong occupation, his own thumb print, and a wrong address. Max
looked at it curiously. "It looks real."

"It should. The man who made it makes thousands
of real ones—but he charges extra for this." That night
Sam brought him a book titled *Ship Economy* and embossed with the seal of the Guild of Space Stewards,
Cooks, and Purser's Clerks. "Better stay up all night
and see how much you can soak up. The man it belongs to won't sleep more than ten hours even with the
jolt Percy slipped into his nightcap. Want a pill to
keep you awake?"

"I don't think so." Max examined it. It was in fine
print and quite thick. But by five in the morning he
had finished it. He woke Sam and gave it back, then
went to sleep, his head buzzing with stowage and
dunnage, moment arms and mass calculations, hydroponics techniques, cargo records, tax forms, diets, food
preservation and preparation, daily, weekly, and
quarterly accounts, and how to get rats out of a compartment which must not be evacuated. Simple stuff, he
decided—he wondered why such things were considered too esoteric for laymen.

On the fourth day of his incarceration Sam fitted
him out with spaceside clothes, none of them new, and
gave him a worn plastileather personal record book.
The first page stated that he was an accepted brother
of the Stewards, Cooks, and Purser's Clerks, having
honorably completed his apprenticeship. It listed his
skills and it appeared that his dues had been paid
each quarter for seven years. What appeared to be his
own signature appeared above that of the High Steward, with the seal of the guild embossed through both.
The other pages recorded his trips, his efficiency ratings, and other permanent data, each properly signed
by the first officers and pursers concerned. He noted
with interest that he had been fined three days pay in
the *Cygnus* for smoking in an unauthorized place and

that he had·once for six weeks been allowed to strike
for chartsman, having paid the penalty to the Chartsmen & Computers Guild for the chance.

"See anything odd?" asked Sam.

"It all looks funny to me."

"It says you've been to Luna. Everybody's been to
Luna. But the ships you served in are mostly out of
commission and none of the pursers happens to be in
Earthport now. The only starship you ever jumped in
was lost on the trip immediately after the one you
took. Get me?"

"I think so."

"When you talk to another spaceman, no matter
what ship he served in, it's not one you served in—you
won't be showing this record to anybody but the purser and your boss anyhow."

"But suppose *they* served in one of these?"

"Not in the *Asgard*. We made darn sure. Now I'm
going to take you out on an evening of gaiety. You'll
drink warm milk on account of your ulcer and you'll
complain when you can't get it. And that's just about
all you'll talk about—your symptoms. You'll start a reputation right now for being untalkative; you can't
make many mistakes with your mouth shut. Watch
yourself, kid, there will be spacemen around you all
evening. If you mess it up, I'll leave you dirtside and
raise without you. Let me see you walk again."

Max walked for him. Sam cursed gently. "Cripes,
you still walk like a farmer. Get your feet out of those
furrows, boy."

"No good?"

"It'll have to do. Grab your bonnet. We'll strike
while the iron's in the fire and let the bridges fall
where they may."

# 6

## "SPACEMAN" JONES

The *Asgard* was to raise the next day. Max woke early and tried to wake Sam, but this proved difficult. At last the older man sat up. "Oh, what a head! What time is it?"

"About six."

"And you woke me? Only my feeble condition keeps me from causing you to join your ancestors. Go back to sleep."

"But today's the day!"

"Who cares? She raises at noon. We'll sign on at the last minute; that way you won't have time to make a slip."

"Sam? *How do you know they'll take us?*"

"Oh, for Pete's sake! It's all arranged. Now shut up. Or go downstairs and get breakfast—but don't talk to anybody. If you're a pal, you'll bring me a pot of coffee at ten o'clock."

"And breakfast?"

"Don't mention food in my presence. Show some respect." Sam pulled the covers up over his head.

It was nearly eleven thirty when they presented themselves at the gate of the port; ten minutes later before the bus deposited them at the base of the ship. Max looked up at its great, bulging sides but was cut short by a crewman standing at the lift and holding a list. "Names."

"Anderson."

"Jones."

He checked them off. "Get in the ship. You should have been here an hour ago." The three climbed into the cage; it swung clear of the ground and was reeled in, swaying, like a bucket on a well rope.

Sam looked down and shuddered. "Never start a trip feeling good," he advised Max. "It might make you sorry to be leaving." The cage was drawn up inside the ship; the lock closed after them and they stepped out into the *Asgard*. Max was trembling with stage fright.

He had expected to be sworn into the ship's company by the first officer, as called for by law. But his reception was depressingly unceremonious. The crewman who had checked them into the ship told them to follow him; he led them to the Purser's office. There the Chief Clerk had them sign and thumbprint the book, yawning the while and tapping his buck teeth. Max surrendered his forged personal record book, while feeling as if the deception were stamped on it in bold letters. But Mr. Kuiper merely chucked it into a file basket. He then turned to them. "This is a taut ship. You've started by very nearly missing it. That's a poor start."

Sam said nothing. Max said, "Yessir."

The Chief Clerk went on, "Stow your gear, get your chow, and report back." He glanced at a wall chart. "One of you in D-112, the other in E-009."

Max started to ask how to get there, but Sam took his elbow and eased him out of the office. Outside he said, "Don't ask any questions you can avoid. We're on Baker deck, that's all we need to know." Presently they came to a companionway and started back down. Max felt a sudden change in pressure, Sam grinned. "She's sealed. Won't be long now."

They were in D-112, an eight-man bunkroom, and Sam was showing him how to set the lock on the one empty locker when there was a distant call on a loudspeaker. Max felt momentarily dizzy and his weight seemed to pulse. Then it stopped. Sam remarked, "They were a little slow synchronizing the field—or else this bucket of bolts has an unbalanced phaser." He clapped Max on the back. "We made it, kid."

They were in space.

E-009 was down one more deck and on the far side; they left Sam's gear there and started to look for lunch. Sam stopped a passing engineer's mate. "Hey, shipmate—we're fresh caught. Where's the crew's mess?"

"Clockwise about eighty and inboard, this deck." He looked them over. "Fresh caught, eh? Well, you'll find out."

"Like that, huh?"

"Worse. A madhouse squared. If I wasn't married, I'd 'a' stayed dirtside." He went on his way.

Sam said, "Ignore it, kid. All the oldtimers in a ship claim its the worst madhouse in space. A matter of pride." But their next experience seemed to confirm it; the serving window in the mess room had closed at noon, when the ship lifted; Max mournfully resigned himself to living with a tight belt until supper. But Sam pushed on into the galley and came out presently with two loaded trays. They found empty places and sat down.

"How did you do it?"

"Any cook will feed you if you let him explain first what a louse you are and how by rights he doesn't have to."

The food was good—real beef patties, vegetables from the ship's gardens, wheat bread, a pudding, and coffee. Max polished his platter and wondered if he dared ask for seconds. He decided against it. The talk flowed around him and only once was there danger that his tyro status might show up, that being when a computerman asked him a direct question as to his last trip.

Sam stalled it off. "Imperial survey," he answered briefly. "We're both still covered."

The computerman grinned knowingly. "Which jail were you in? The Imperial Council hasn't ordered a secret survey in years."

"This one was so secret they forgot to tell you about it. Write 'em a letter and burn them out about it," Sam stood up. "Finished, Max?"

On the way back to the Purser's Office Max worried as to his probable assignment, checking over in his mind the skills and experience he was alleged to have. He need not have worried; Mr. Kuiper, with a fine disregard for such factors, assigned him as stableman.

The *Asgard* was a combined passenger liner and freighter. She carried this trip Hereford breeding stock, two bulls and two dozen cows, and an assortment of other animals consigned for ecologic and economic reasons to colonies—pigs, chickens, sheep, a pair of Angora goats, a family of llamas. It was contrary to Imperial policy to plant most terrestrial fauna on other planets; the colonials were expected to establish economy with indigenous flora and fauna—but some animals have been bred for so many generations for the use of man that they are not easily replaced by exotic creatures. On Gamma Leonis VI(b), New Mars, the saurians known locally as "chuckleheads" or "chucks" could and did replace Percherons as draft animals with greater efficiency and economy—but men disliked them. There was never the familial trust that exists between horses and men; unless a strain of chucks should develop a degree of rapport with men (which seemed unlikely) they would eventually die out and be replaced by the horse, for the unforgivable sin of failing to establish a firm treaty with the most ravenous, intolerant, deadly, and successful of the animals in the explored universe, Man.

There was also a cage of English sparrows. Max never did find out where these noisy little scavengers were believed to be necessary, nor was he acquainted with the complex mathematical analysis by which such conclusions were reached. He simply fed them and tried to keep their quarters clean.

There were cats in the *Asgard*, too, but most of these were free citizens and crewmen, charged with holding down the rats and mice that had gone into space along with mankind. One of Max's duties was to change the sand boxes on each deck and take the soiled ones to the oxydizer for processing. The other cats were pets, property of passengers, unhappy prisoners in the kennel off the stables. The passengers' dogs lived there, too; no dogs were allowed to run free.

Max wanted to look back at Earth and see it as a shrinking globe in the sky, but that was a privilege reserved for passengers. He spent the short period when it would have been possible in hauling (by hand) green timothy hay from the hydroponics air-conditioning plant to the stables and in cleaning said stables. It was a task he neither liked nor disliked; by accident he had been assigned to work that he understood.

His immediate boss was the Chief Ship's Steward, Mr. Giordano. Mr. "Gee" split the ship's housekeeping with Mr. Dumont, Chief Passengers' Steward; their domains divided at Charlie deck. Thus Mr. Dumont had passengers' quarters, officers' country, offices, and the control and communication stations, while Giordano was responsible for everything down (or aft) to but not including the engineering space—crew's quarters, mess, and galley, stores, stables and kennel, hydroponics deck, and cargo spaces. Both worked for the Purser, who in turn was responsible to the First Officer.

The organization of starships derived in part from that of military vessels, in part from ocean liners of earlier days, and in part from the circumstances of interstellar travel. The first officer was boss of the ship and a wise captain did not interfere with him. The captain, although by law monarch of his miniature world, turned his eyes outward; the first officer turned his inward. As long as all went well the captain concerned himself only with the control room and with astrogation; the first officer bossed everything else. Even astrogators, communicators, computermen, and chartsmen were under the first officer, although in practice he had nothing to do with them when they were on duty since they worked in the "worry hole" under the captain.

The chief engineer was under the first officer, too,

but he was nearly an autonomous satrap. In a taut, well-run ship he kept his bailiwick in such shape that the first officer did not need to worry about it. The chief engineer was responsible not only for the power plant and the Horst-Conrad impellers but for all auxiliary engineering equipment wherever located—for example the pumps and fans of the hydroponics installations, even though the purser, through his chief ship's steward, took care of the farming thereof.

Such was the usual organization of starship liner-freighters and such was the *Asgard*. It was not identical with the organization of a man-of-war and very different from that of the cheerless transports used to ship convicts and paupers out to colonies that were being forced—in *those* ships, the purser's department was stripped to a clerk or two and the transportees did all the work, cooking, cleaning, handling cargo, everything. But the *Asgard* carried paid passengers, some of whom measured their wealth in megabucks; they expected luxury hotel service even light-years out in space. Of the three main departments of the *Asgard*, astrogation, engineering, and housekeeping, the Purser's was by far the largest.

A first officer could reach that high status from chief astrogator, from chief engineer, or from purser, but only if he were originally an astrogator could he go on to captain. The three officer types were essentially mathematicians, business managers, or physicists; a captain necessarily had to be able to practice the mathematical skill of astrogation. First Officer Walther, as was usually the case with a liner, had formerly been a purser.

The *Asgard* was a little world, a tiny mobile planet. It had its monarch the captain, its useless nobility the passengers, its technical and governing class, and its hewers of wood and drawers of water. It contained flora and fauna in ecological balance; it carried its miniature sun in its power plant. Although its schedule contemplated only months in space, it was capable of staying in space indefinitely. The chef might run out of caviar, but there would be no lack of food, nor of air, nor of heat and light.

Max decided that he was lucky to be assigned to Mr. Giordano rather than to Chief Clerk Kuiper. Mr. Kuiper supervised his clerks minutely, but Mr. Gee did not often stir his fat frame out of his office-stateroom. He was a jovial boss—provided everything ran to suit him. Mr. Gee found it an effort to go all the way down to the stables; once he became convinced that Max was giving the animals proper care and keeping the place clean he gave up inspecting, merely requiring Max to report daily. This gave Giordano more time for his principal avocation, which was distilling a sort of vodka in a cubby in his stateroom, using materials grown in the hydroponds—also in his charge. He carried on a clandestine trade in his product with the crew. By keeping his mouth shut and his ears open Max learned that this was a usual prerogative of a chief ship's steward, ignored as long as the steward had the judgment to limit his operations. The ship, of course, had a wine mess and bar, but that was for the "beasts"—crewmen could not patronize it.

"I was once in a ship," Sam told Max, "where the First clamped down—busted up the still, busted the steward to cleaning decks, and generally threw the book." He stopped to puff on his cigar, a gift from the passenger steward; they were hiding out in Max's stables, enjoying a rest and a gab. "Didn't work out."

"Why not?"

"Use your head. Forces must balance, old son. For every market there is a supplier. That's the key to the nutshell. In a month there was a still in durn near every out-of-the-way compartment in the ship and the crew was so demoralized it wasn't fit to stuff vacuum. So the Captain had a talk with the First and things went back to normal."

Max thought it over. "Sam? Were you that ship's steward?"

"Huh? What gave you that idea?"

"Well . . . you've been in space before; you no longer make any bones about it. I just thought—well, you've never told me what your guild was, nor why you were on dirt, or why you had to fake it to get back to space again. I suppose it's none of my business."

Sam's habitual cynical smile gave way to an expression of sadness. "Max, a lot of things can happen to a man when he thinks he has the world by the tail. Take the case of a friend of mine, name of Roberts. A sergeant in the Imperial Marines, good record, half a dozen star jumps, a combat decoration or two. A smart lad, boning to make warrant officer. But he missed his ship once—hadn't been on Terra for some time and celebrated too much. Should have turned himself in right away, of course, taken his reduction in rank and lived it down. Trouble was he still had money in his pocket. By the time he was broke and sober it was too late. He never quite had the guts to go back and take his court martial and serve his sentence. Every man has his limits."

Max said presently, "You trying to say you used to be a marine?"

"Me? Of course not, I was speaking of this guy Richards, just to illustrate what can happen to a man when he's not looking. Let's talk of more pleasant things. Kid, what do you plan to do next?"

"What do you mean?"

"Well, what do you figure on doing after this jump?"

"Oh. More of the same, I guess. I like spacing. I suppose I'll try to keep my nose clean and work up to chief steward or chief clerk."

Sam shook his head. "Think it through, kid. What happens when your record in this ship is mailed to the guild? And another copy is mailed to the Department of Guilds and Labor?"

"What?"

"I'll tell you. Maybe nothing happens at first, maybe you can space for another cruise. But eventually the red tape unwinds, they compare notes and see that

while your ship lists you as an experienced steward's
mate, there isn't any Max Jones in their files. Comes
the day you ground at Terra and a couple of clowns
with sidearms are waiting at the foot of the lift to drag
you off to the calabozo."

"But Sam! I thought it was all fixed?"

"Don't blow a gasket. Look at me, I'm relaxed—and
it applies to me, too. More so, for I have other reasons
we needn't go into to want to let sleeping dogs bury
their own dead. As for it being 'all fixed,' it is—everything I promised. You're here, aren't you? But as for
the files: old son, it would have taken ten times the
money to tamper with guild files, and as for locating a
particular microfilm in New Washington and substituting a fake that would show the record you are
supposed to have—well, I wouldn't know how to start,
though no doubt it could be done, with enough time,
money, and finesse."

Max felt sensations almost identical with those he
had experienced when Montgomery had announced
that the farm was sold. Despite his menial position he
liked it aboard ship, he had had no intention of ever
doing anything else. He got along with his boss, he
was making friends, he was as cozy as a bird in its
nest. Now the nest was suddenly torn down. Worse,
he was in a trap.

He turned white. Sam put a hand on his shoulder.
"Stop spinning, kid! You're not in a jam."

"Jail—"

"Jail my aunt's Sunday hat! You're safe as dirt until
we get back. You can walk away from the *Asgard* at
Earthport with your wages in your pocket and have
days at least, maybe weeks or months, before anyone
will notice, either at the guild mother hall or at New
Washington. You can lose yourself among four billion
people. You won't be any worse off than you were
when you first ran into me—you were trying to get
lost then, remember?—and you'll have one star trip
under your belt to tell your kids about. Or they may
never look for you; some clerk may chuck your trip rec-

ord into the file basket and leave it there until it gets
lost rather than bother. Or you might be able to per-
suade a clerk in Mr. Kuiper's office to lose the dupli-
cates, not mail them in. Nelson, for example; he's got a
hungry look." Sam eyed him carefully, then added,
"Or you might do what I'm going to do."

Only part of what Sam had said had sunk in. Max
let the record play back and gradually calmed down
as he began to understand that his situation was not
entirely desperate. He was inclined to agree about
Nelson, as Nelson had already suggested indirectly
that sometimes the efficiency marks on the ship's
books were not necessarily the ones that found their
way into the permanent records—under certain circumstances. He put the idea aside, not liking it and
having no notion anyhow of how to go about offering
a bribe.

When he came, in his mental play back, to Sam's
last remark, it brought him to attention. "What are
you going to do?"

Sam eyed the end of his cigar stub. "I'm not going
back."

This required no diagram to be understood. But,
under Imperial decrees, the suggested offense carried
even heavier punishment than faking membership in a
guild. Deserting was almost treason. "Keep talking,"
Max said gruffly.

"Let's run over where we touch this cruise. Garson's
Planet—domed colonies, like Luna and Mars. In a
domed colony you do exactly what the powers-that-be
say, or you stop breathing. You might hide out and
have a new identity grafted on, but you would still be
in the domes. No good, there's more freedom even
back on Terra. Nu Pegasi VI, Halcyon—not bad
though pretty cold at aphelion. But it is still importing
more than it exports which means that the Imperials
run the show and the locals will help dig out a wanted
man. Now we come to Nova Terra, Beta Aquarii X—
and that, old son, is what the doctor ordered and why
the preacher danced."

"You've been there?"

"Once. I should have stayed. Max, imagine a place like Earth, but sweeter than Terra ever was. Better weather, broader richer lands . . . forests aching to be cut, game that practically jumps into the stew pot. If you don't like settlements, you move on until you've got no neighbors, poke a seed in the ground, then jump back before it sprouts. No obnoxious insects. Practically no terrestrial diseases and no native diseases that like the flavor of our breed. Gushing rivers. Placid oceans. Man, I'm telling you!"

"But wouldn't they haul us back from there?"

"Too big. The colonists *want* more people and they won't help the Imperials. The Imperial Council has a deuce of a time just collecting taxes. They don't even try to arrest a deserter outside the bigger towns." Sam grinned. "You know why?"

"Why?"

"Because it didn't pay. An Imperial would be sent to Back-and-Beyond to pick up someone; while he was looking he would find some golden-haired daughter of a rancher eyeing him—they run to eight or nine kids, per family and there are always lots of eligible fillies, husband-high and eager. So pretty quick he is a rancher with a beard and a new name and a wife. He was a bachelor and he hasn't been home lately—or maybe he's married back on Terra and doesn't want to go home. Either way, even the Imperial Council can't fight human nature."

"I don't want to get married."

"That's your problem. But best of all, the place still has a comfortable looseness about it. No property taxes, outside the towns. Nobody would pay one; they'd just move on, if they didn't shoot the tax collector instead. No guilds—you can plow a furrow, saw a board, drive a truck, or thread a pipe, all the same day and never ask permission. A man can do anything and there's no one to stop him, no one to tell him he wasn't born into the trade, or didn't start young enough, or hasn't paid his contribution. There's more work than there are men to do it and the colonists just don't care."

Max tried to imagine such anarchy and could not, he had never experienced it. "But don't the guilds object?"

"What guilds? Oh, the mother lodges back earthside squawked when they heard, but not even the Imperial Council backed them up. They're not fools—and you don't shovel back the ocean with a fork."

"And that's where you mean to go. It sounds lovely," Max said wistfully.

"I do. It is. There was a girl—oh, she'll be married now; they marry young—but she had sisters. Now here is what I figure on—and you, too, if you want to tag along. First time I hit dirt I'll make contacts. The last time I rate liberty, which will be the night before the ship raises if possible, I'll go dirtside, then in a front door and out the back and over the horizon so fast I won't even be a speck. By the time I'm marked 'late returning' I'll be hundreds of miles away, lying beside a chuckling stream in a virgin wilderness, letting my beard grow and memorizing my new name. Say the word and you'll be on the bank, fishing."

Max stirred uneasily. The picture aroused in him a hillbilly homesickness he had hardly been aware of. But he could not shuffle off his proud *persona* as a spaceman so quickly. "I'll think about it."

"Do that. It's a good many weeks yet, anyhow." Sam got to his feet. "I'd better hurry back before Ole Massa Dumont wonders what's keeping me. Be seeing you, kid—and remember: it's an ill wind that has no turning."

## ELDRETH

Max's duties did not take him above "C" deck except to service the cats' sand boxes and he usually did that before the passengers were up. He wanted to visit the control room but he had no opportunity, it being still higher than passengers' quarters. Often an owner of one of the seven dogs and three cats in Max's custody would come down to visit his pet. This sometimes resulted in a tip. At first his cross-grained hillbilly pride caused him to refuse, but when Sam heard about it, he swore at him dispassionately. "Don't be a fool! They can afford it. What's the sense?"

"But I would exercise their mutts anyhow. It's my job." He might have remained unconvinced had it not been that Mr. Gee asked him about it at the end of his first week, seemed to have a shrewd idea of the usual take, and expected a percentage—"for the welfare fund."

Max asked Sam about the fund, was laughed at. "That's a very interesting question. Are there any more questions?"

"I suppose not."

"Max, I like you. But you haven't learned yet that when in Rome, you shoot Roman candles. Every tribe has its customs and what is moral one place is immoral somewhere else. There are races where a son's first duty is to kill off his old man and serve him up as a feast as soon as he is old enough to swing it—civilized races, too. Races the Council recognizes diplomatically. What's your moral judgment on that?"

Max had read of such cultures—the gentle and unwarlike Bnathors, or the wealthy elephantine amphibians of Paldron who were anything but gentle, probably others. He did not feel disposed to pass judgment on nonhumans. Sam went on, "I've known stewards who would make Jelly Belly look like a philanthropist.

Look at it from his point of view. He regards these things as prerogatives of his position, as rightful a part of his income as his wages. Custom says so. It's taken him years to get to where he is; he expects his reward."

Sam, Max reflected, could always out-talk him.

But he could not concede that Sam's thesis was valid; there were things that were right and others that were wrong and it was not just a matter of where you were. He felt this with an inner conviction too deep to be influenced by Sam's cheerful cynicism. It worried Max that he was where he was as the result of chicanery, he sometimes lay awake and fretted about it.

But it worried him still more that his deception might come to light. What to do about Sam's proposal was a problem always on his mind.

The only extra-terrestrial among Max's charges was a spider puppy from the terrestrian planet Hespera. On beginning his duties in the *Asgard* Max found the creature in one of the cages intended for cats; Max looked into it and a sad, little, rather simian face looked back at him. "Hello, Man."

Max knew that some spider puppies had been taught human speech, after a fashion, but it startled him; he jumped back. He then recovered and looked more closely. "Hello yourself," he answered. "My, but you are a fancy little fellow." The creature's fur was a deep, rich green on its back, giving way to orange on the sides and blending to warm cream color on its little round belly.

"Want out," stated the spider puppy.

"I can't let you out. I've got work to do." He read the card affixed to the cage: "Mr. Chips" it stated, *Pseudocanis hexapoda hesperae,* Owner: Miss E. Coburn, A-092; there followed a detailed instruction as to diet and care. Mr. Chips ate grubs, a supply of which was to be found in freezer compartment H-118, fresh fruits and vegetables, cooked or uncooked, and should receive iodine if neither seaweed nor artichokes was available. Max thumbed through his mind, went over what he had read about the creatures, decided the instructions were reasonable.

"*Please* out!" Mr. Chips insisted.

It was an appeal hard to resist. No maiden fayre crying from a dungeon tower had ever put it more movingly. The compartment in which the cats were located was small and the door could be fastened; possibly Mr. Chips could be allowed a little run—but later; just now he had to take care of other animals.

When Max left, Mr. Chips was holding onto the bars and sobbing gently. Max looked back and saw that it was crying real tears; a drop trembled on the tip of its ridiculous little nose; it was hard to walk out on it. He had finished with the stables before tackling the kennel; once the dogs and cats were fed and their cages policed he was free to give attention to his new friend. He had fed it first off, which had stopped the crying. When he returned, however, the demand to be let out resumed.

"If I let you out, will you get back in later?"

The spider puppy considered this. A conditional proposition seemed beyond its semantic attainments, for it repeated, "Want out." Max took a chance.

Mr. Chips landed on his shoulder and started going through his pockets. "Candy," it demanded. "Candy?"

Max stroked it. "Sorry, chum. I didn't know."

"Candy?"

"No candy." Mr. Chips investigated personally, then settled in the crook of Max's arm, prepared to spend a week or more. It wasn't, Max decided, much like a puppy and certainly not like a spider, except that six legs seemed excessive. The two front ones had little hands; the middle legs served double duty. It was more like a monkey, but felt like a cat. It had a slightly spicy fragrance and seemed quite clean.

Max tried talking to it, but found its intellectual attainments quite limited. Certainly it used human words meaningfully but its vocabulary was not richer than that which might be expected of a not-too-bright toddler.

When Max tried to return it to its cage there ensued twenty minutes of brisk exercise, broken by stalemates. Mr. Chips swarmed over the cages, causing hysterics among the cats. When at last the spider puppy allowed itself to be caught it still resisted imprisonment, clinging to Max and sobbing. He ended by walking it like a baby until it fell asleep.

This was a mistake. A precedent had been set and thereafter Max was not permitted to leave the kennel without walking the baby.

He wondered about the "Miss Coburn" described on the tag as Mr. Chips' owner. All of the owners of cats and dogs had shown up to visit their pets, but Mr. Chips remained unvisited. He visualized her as a sour and hatchet-faced spinster who had received the pet as a going-away present and did not appreciate it. As his friendship with the spider puppy grew his mental picture of Miss E. Coburn became even less attractive.

The *Asgard* was over a week out and only days from its first spatial transition before Max had a chance to compare conception with fact. He was cleaning the stables, with Mr. Chips riding his shoulder and offering advice, when Max heard a shrill voice from the kennel compartment. "Mr. *Chips!* Chipsie! Where are you?"

The spider puppy sat up suddenly and turned its head. Almost immediately a young female appeared in the door; Mr. Chips squealed, "Ellie!" and jumped to her arms. While they were nuzzling each other Max looked her over. Sixteen, he judged, or seventeen. Or maybe even eighteen—shucks, how was a fellow to tell when womenfolk did such funny things to their faces? Anyhow she was no beauty and the expression on her face didn't help it any.

She looked up at him and scowled. "What were you doing with Chipsie? Answer me that!"

It got his back fur up. "Nothing," he said stiffly. "If

you will excuse me, ma'am, I'll get on with my work."
He turned his back and bent over his broom.

She grabbed his arm and swung him around. "Answer me! Or . . . or—I'll tell the Captain, that's what
I'll do!"

Max counted ten, then just to be sure, recalled the
first dozen 7-place natural logarithms. "That's your
privilege, ma'am," he said with studied calmness, "but
first, what's your name and what is your business
here? I'm in charge of these compartments and responsible for these animals—as the Captain's representative." This he knew to be good space law, although the concatenation was long.

She looked startled. "Why, I'm Eldreth Coburn," she
blurted as if anyone should know.

"And your business?"

"I came to see Mr. Chips—of course!"

"Very well, ma'am. You may visit your pet for a reasonable period," he added, quoting verbatim from his
station instruction sheet. "Then he goes back in his
cage. Don't disturb the other animals and don't feed
them. That's orders."

She started to speak, decided not to and bit her lip.
The spider puppy had been looking from face to face
and listening to a conversation far beyond its powers,
although it may have sensed the emotions involved.
Now it reached out and plucked Max's sleeve. "Max,"
Mr. Chips announced brightly. "Max!"

Miss Coburn again looked startled. "Is that your
name?"

"Yes, ma'am. Max Jones. I guess he was trying to introduce me. Is that it, old fellow?"

"Max," Mr. Chips repeated firmly. "Ellie."

Eldreth Coburn looked down, then looked up at
Max with a sheepish smile. "You two seem to be
friends. I guess I spoke out of turn. Me and my
mouth."

"No offense meant I'm sure, ma'am."

Max had continued to speak stiffly; she answered
quickly, "Oh, but I was rude! I'm sorry—I'm always

sorry afterwards. But I got panicky when I saw the cage open and empty and I thought I had lost Chipsie."

Max grinned grudgingly. "Sure. Don't blame you a bit. You were scared."

"That's it—I was scared." She glanced at him. "Chipsie calls you Max. May I call you Max?"

"Why not? Everybody does—and it's my name."

"And you call me Eldreth, Max. Or Ellie."

She stayed on, playing with the spider puppy, until Max had finished with the cattle. She then said reluctantly, "I guess I had better go, or they'll be missing me."

"Are you coming back?"

"Oh, of course!"

"Ummm . . . Miss Eldreth . . ."

"Ellie."

"—May I ask a question?" He hurried on, "Maybe it's none of my business, but what took you so long? That little fellow has been awful lonesome. He thought you had deserted him."

"Not 'he'—'she'."

"Huh?"

"Mr. Chips is a girl," she said apologetically. "It was a mistake anyone could make. Then it was too late, because it would confuse her to change her name."

The spider puppy looked up brightly and repeated, "'Mr. Chips is a girl.' Candy, Ellie?"

"Next time, honey bun."

Max doubted if the name was important, with the nearest other spider puppy light-years away. "You didn't answer my question?"

"Oh. I was so mad about that I wanted to bite. They wouldn't let me."

"Who's 'they'? Your folks?"

"Oh, no! The Captain and Mrs. Dumont." Max decided that it was almost as hard to extract information from her as it was from Mr. Chips. "You see, I came aboard in a stretcher—some silly fever, food poisoning probably. It couldn't be much because I'm tough. But they kept me in bed and when the Surgeon did let me get up, Mrs. Dumont said I mustn't go below 'C' deck. She had some insipid notion that it wasn't proper."

Max understood the stewardess's objection; he had already discovered that some of his shipmates were a rough lot—though he doubted that any of them would risk annoying a girl passenger. Why, Captain Blaine would probably space a man for that.

"So I had to sneak out. They're probably searching for me right now. I'd better scoot."

This did not fit in with Mr. Chips' plans; the spider puppy clung to her and sobbed, stopping occasionally to wipe tears away with little fists. "Oh, dear!"

Max looked perturbed. "I guess I've spoiled him—her. Mr. Chips, I mean." He explained how the ceremony of walking the baby had arisen.

Eldreth protested, "But I must go. What'll I do?"

"Here, let's see if he—she—will come to me." Mr. Chips would and did. Eldreth gave her a pat and ran out, whereupon Mr. Chips took even longer than usual to doze off. Max wondered if spider puppies could be hypnotized; the ritual was getting monotonous.

Eldreth showed up next day under the stern eye of Mrs. Dumont. Max was respectful to the stewardess and careful to call Eldreth "Miss Coburn." She returned alone the next day. He looked past her and raised his eyebrows. "Where's your chaperone?"

Eldreth giggled. "La Dumont consulted her husband and he called in your boss—the fat one. They agreed that you were a perfect little gentleman, utterly harmless. How do you like that?"

Max considered it. "Well, I'm an ax murderer by profession, but I'm on vacation."

"That's nice. What have you got there?"

It was a three-dimensional chess set. Max had played the game with his uncle, it being one that all astrogators played. Finding that some of the chartsmen and computermen played it, he had invested his tips in a set from the ship's slop chest. It was a cheap set, having no attention lights and no arrangements for remote-control moving, being merely stacked transparent trays and pieces molded instead of carved, but it sufficed.

"It's solid chess. Ever seen it?"

"Yes. But I didn't know you played it."

"Why not? Ever play flat chess?"

"Some."

"The principles are the same, but there are more pieces and one more direction to move. Here, I'll show you."

She sat tailor-fashion opposite him and he ran over the moves. "These are robot freighters . . . pawns. They can be commissioned anything else if they reach the far rim. These four are starships; they are the only ones with funny moves, they correspond with knights. They have to make interspace transitions, always off the level they're on to some other level and the transition has to be related a certain way, like this—or this. And this is the Imperial flagship; it's the one that has to be checkmated. Then there is . . ." They ran through a practice game, with the help of Mr. Chips, who liked to move the pieces and did not care whose move it was.

Presently he said, "You catch on pretty fast."

"Thanks."

"Of course, the *real* players play four-dimensional chess."

"Do you?"

"Well, no. But I hope to learn some day. It's just a matter of holding in your mind one more spatial relationship. My uncle used to play it. He was going to teach me, but he died." He found himself explaining about his uncle. He trailed off without mentioning his own disappointment.

Eldreth picked up one of the starship pieces from a tray. "Say, Max, we're pretty near our first transition, aren't we?"

"What time is it?"

"Uh, sixteen twenty-one—say, I'd better get upstairs."

"Then it's, uh, about thirty-seven hours and seven minutes, according to the computer crew."

"Mmm . . . you seem to know about such things. Could you tell me just what it is we do? I heard the Astrogator talking about it at the table but I couldn't make head nor tail. We sort of duck into a space warp; isn't that right?"

"Oh no, not a space warp. That's a silly term—space doesn't 'warp' except in places where *pi* isn't exactly three point one four one five nine two six five three five eight nine seven nine three two three eight four six two six four three three eight three two seven, and so forth—like inside a nucleus. But we're heading out to a place where space is *really* flat, not just mildly curved the way it is near a star. Anomalies are always flat, otherwise they couldn't fit together—be congruent."

She looked puzzled. "Come again?"

"Look, Eldreth, how far did you go in mathematics?"

"Me? I flunked improper fractions. Miss Mimsey was very vexed with me."

"Miss Mimsey?"

"Miss Mimsey's School for Young Ladies, so you see I can listen with an open mind." She made a face. "But you told me that all you went to was a country high school and didn't get to finish at that. Huh?"

"Yes, but I learned from my uncle. He was a great mathematician. Well, he didn't have any theorems named after him—but a great one just the same, *I* think." He paused. "I don't know exactly how to tell you; it takes equations. Say! Could you lend me that scarf you're wearing for a minute?"

"Huh? Why, sure." She removed it from her neck.

It was a photoprint showing a stylized picture of the solar system, a souvenir of Solar Union Day. In the middle of the square of cloth was the conventional sunburst surrounded by circles representing orbits of solar planets, with a few comets thrown in. The scale was badly distorted and it was useless as a structural picture of the home system, but it sufficed. Max took it and said, "Here's Mars."

Eldreth said, "You read it. That's cheating."

"Hush a moment. Here's Jupiter. To go from Mars to Jupiter you have to go from here to here, don't you?"

"Obviously."

"But suppose I fold it so that Mars is on top of Jupiter? What's to prevent just stepping across?"

"Nothing, I guess. Except that what works for that scarf wouldn't work very well in practice. Would it?"

"No, not that near to a star. But it works fine after you back away from a star quite a distance. You see, that's just what an anomaly is, a place where space is folded back on itself, turning a long distance into no distance at all."

"Then space *is* warped."

"No, no, no! Look, I just folded your scarf. I didn't stretch it out of shape! I didn't even wrinkle it. Space is the same way; it's crumpled like a piece of waste paper—but it's not warped, just crumpled. Through some extra dimensions, of course."

"I don't see any 'of course' about it."

"The math of it is simple, but it's hard to talk about because you can't see it. Space—*our* space—may be crumpled up small enough to stuff into a coffee cup, all hundreds of thousands of light-years of it. A four-dimensional coffee cup, of course."

She sighed. "I don't see how a four-dimensional coffee cup could even hold coffee, much less a whole galaxy."

"No trouble at all. You could stuff this sheer scarf into a thimble. Same principle. But let me finish. They used to think that nothing could go faster than light. Well, that was both right and wrong. It . . ."

"How can it be both?"

"That's one of the Horst anomalies. You can't go faster than light, not in our space. If you do, you burst out of it. But if you do it where space is folded back and congruent, you pop right back into our own space again—but a long way off. How far off depends on how it's folded. And that depends on the mass in the space, in a complicated fashion that can't be described in words but can be calculated."

"But suppose you do it just anywhere?"

"That's what happened to the first ones who tried it. They didn't come back. And that's why surveys are dangerous; survey ships go poking through anomalies that have been calculated but never tried. That's also why astrogators get paid so much. They have to head the ship for a place you can't see and they have to put the ship there just under the speed of light and they have to give it the gun at just the right world point. Drop a decimal point or use a short cut that covers up an indeterminancy and it's just too bad. Now we've been gunning at twenty-four gee ever since we left the atmosphere. We don't feel it of course because we are carried inside a discontinuity field at an artificial one gravity—that's another of the anomalies. But we're getting up close to the speed of light, up against the Einstein Wall; pretty soon we'll be squeezed through like a watermelon seed between your finger and thumb and we'll come out near Theta Centauri fifty-eight light-years away. Simple, if you look at it right."

She shivered. "*If* we come out, you mean."

"Well . . . I suppose so. But it's not as dangerous as helicopters. And look at it this way: if it weren't for the anomalies, there never would have been any way for us to reach the stars; the distances are too great. But looking back, it is obvious that all that emptiness couldn't be real—there *had* to be the anomalies. That's what my uncle used to say."

"I suppose he must have been right, even if I don't understand it." She scrambled to her feet. "But I do know that I had better hoof it back upstairs, or Mrs. Dumont may change her mind." She hugged Mr. Chips and shoved the little creature into Max's arms. "Walk the baby—that's a pal."

# 8

## THREE WAYS TO GET AHEAD

Max intended to stay awake during the first transition, but he slept through it. It took place shortly after five in the morning, ship's time. When he was awakened by idlers' reveille at six it was all over. He jerked on his clothes, fuming at not having awakened earlier, and hurried to the upper decks. The passageways above Charlie deck were silent and empty; even the early risers among the passengers would not be up for another hour. He went at once to the Bifrost Lounge and crossed it to the view port, placed there for the pleasure of passengers.

The stars looked normal but the familiar, age-old constellations were gone. Only the Milky Way, our own galaxy, seemed as usual—to that enormous spiral of stars, some hundred thousand light-years across, a tiny displacement of less than sixty light-years was inconsequential.

One extremely bright yellow-white star was visible; Max decided that it must be Theta Centauri, sun of Garson's Planet, their first stop. He left shortly, not wanting to chance being found loafing in passengers' country. The sand boxes which constituted his excuse were then replaced with greater speed than usual and he was back in crew's quarters in time for breakfast.

The passage to Garson's Planet took most of a month even at the high boost possible to Horst-Conrad ship. Eldreth continued to make daily trips to see Mr. Chips—and to talk with and play 3-dee chess with Max. He learned that while she had not been born on Hespera, but in Auckland on Terra, nevertheless Hespera was her home. "Daddy sent me back to have them turn me into a lady, but it didn't take."

"What do you mean?"

She grinned. "I'm a problem. That's why I've been sent for. You're in check, Max. Chipsie! Put that back. I think the little demon is playing on your side."

He gradually pieced together what she meant. Miss Mimsey's school had been the third from which she had been expelled. She did not like Earth, she was determined to go home, and she had created a reign of terror at each institution to which she had been entrusted. Her widower father had been determined that she must have a "proper" education, but she had been in a better strategic position to impose her will—her father's Earthside attorneys had washed their hands of her and shipped her home.

Sam made the mistake of joshing Max about Eldreth. "Have you gotten her to set the day yet, old son?"

"Who set what day?"

"Now, now! Everybody in the ship knows about it, except possibly the Captain. Why play dumb with your old pal?"

"I don't know what you are talking about!"

"I wasn't criticizing, I was admiring. I'd never have the nerve to plot so high a trajectory myself. But as grandpop always said, there are just three ways to get ahead; sweat and genius, getting born into the right family, or marrying into it. Of the three, marrying the boss's daughter is the best, because— Hey! Take it easy!" Sam skipped back out of range.

"Take that back!"

"I do, I do. I was wrong. But my remarks were inspired by sheer admiration. Mistaken, I admit. So I apologize and withdraw the admiration."

"But . . ." Max grinned in spite of himself. It was impossible to stay angry at Sam. Sure, the man was a scamp, probably a deserter, certainly a belittler who always looked at things in the meanest of terms, but—well, there it was. Sam was his friend.

"I knew you were joking. How could I be figuring on getting married when you and I are going to . . ."

"Keep your voice down." Sam went on quietly, "You've made up your mind?"

"Yes. It's the only way out, I guess. I don't want to go back to Earth."

"Good boy! You'll never regret it." Sam looked thoughtful. "We'll need money."

"Well, I'll have some on the books."

"Don't be silly. You try to draw more than spending money and they'll never let you set foot on dirt. But don't worry—save your tips, all that Fats will let you keep, and I'll get us a stake. It's my turn."

"How?"

"Lots of ways. You can forget it."

"Well . . . all right. Say, Sam, just what did you mean when you—I mean, well, suppose I did want to marry Ellie—I don't of course; she's just a kid and anyhow I'm not the type to marry—but just supposing? Why should anybody care?"

Sam looked surprised. "You don't know?"

"Why would I be asking?"

"You don't know who she is?"

"Huh? Her name's Eldreth Coburn and she's on her way home to Hespera, she's a colonial. What of it?"

"You poor boy! She didn't mention that she is the only daughter of His Supreme Excellency, General Sir John FitzGerald Coburn, O.B.E., K.B., O.S.U., and probably X.Y.Z., Imperial Ambassador to Hespera and Resident Commissioner Plenipotentiary?"

"Huh? Oh my gosh!"

"Catch on, kid? With the merest trifle of finesse you can be a remittance man, at least. Name your own planet, just as long as it isn't Hespera."

"Oh, go boil your head! She's a nice kid anyhow."

Sam snickered. "She sure is. As grandpop used to say, 'It's an ill wind that gathers no moss.'"

The knowledge disturbed Max. He had realized that Eldreth must be well to do—she was a passenger, wasn't she? But he had no awe of wealth. Achievement as exemplified by his uncle held much more respect in his eyes. But the notion that Eldreth came from such an impossibly high stratum—and that he, Maximilian Jones, was considered a fortune-hunter and social climber on that account—was quite upsetting.

He decided to put an end to it. He started by letting his work pile up so that he could say truthfully that he did not have time to play three-dee chess. So Ellie pitched in and helped him. While he was playing the unavoidable game that followed he attempted a direct approach. "See here, Ellie, I don't think you ought to stay down here and play three-dee chess with me. The other passengers come down to see their pets and they notice. They'll gossip."

"Pooh!"

"I mean it. Oh, you and I know it's all right, but it doesn't look right."

She stuck out her lower lip. "Am I going to have trouble with you? You talk just like Miss Mimsey."

"You can come down to see Chipsie, but you'd better come down with one of the other pet owners."

She started to make a sharp answer, then shrugged, "Okay, this isn't the most comfortable place anyhow. From now on we play in Bifrost Lounge, afternoons when your work is done and evenings."

Max protested that Mr. Giordano would not let him; she answered quickly, "Don't worry about your boss. I can twist him around my little finger." She illustrated by gesture.

The picture of the gross Mr. Gee in such a position slowed up Max's answer, but he finally managed to get out, "Ellie, crew members can't use the passenger lounge. It's . . ."

"They can so. More than once, I've seen Mr. Dumont having a cup of coffee there with Captain Blaine."

"You don't understand. Mr. Dumont is almost an officer, and if the Captain wants him as his guest, well, that's the Captain's privilege."

"You'd be my guest."

"No, I wouldn't be." He tried to explain to her the strict regulation that crew members were not to associate with passengers. "The Captain would be angry if he could see us right now—not at you, at me. If he caught me in the passengers' lounge he'd kick me all the way down to 'H' deck."

"I don't believe it."

"But . . ." He shrugged. "All right. I'll come up this evening. He won't kick me, actually; that would be beneath him. He'll just send Mr. Dumont over to tell me to leave, then he'll send for me in the morning. I don't mind being fined a month's pay if that is what it takes to show you the way things are."

He could see that he had finally reached her. "Why, I think that's perfectly rotten! Everybody is equal. Everybody! That's the law."

"They are? Only from on top."

She got up suddenly and left. Max again had to soothe Mr. Chips, but there was no one to soothe him. He decided that the day that he and Sam disappeared over a horizon and lost themselves could not come too soon.

Eldreth returned next day but in company with a Mrs. Mendoza, the devoted owner of a chow who looked much like her. Eldreth treated Max with the impersonal politeness of a lady "being nice" to servants, except for a brief moment when Mrs. Mendoza was out of earshot.

"Max?"

"Yes, Miss?"

"I'll 'Yes, Miss' you! Look, Max, what was your uncle's name? Was it *Chester* Jones?"

"Why, yes, it was. But why . . ."

"Never mind." Mrs. Mendoza rejoined them. Max was forced to drop it.

The following morning the dry-stores keeper sought him out. "Hey, Max! The Belly wants you. Better hurry—I think you're in some sort of a jam."

Max worried as he hurried. He couldn't think of anything he had done lately; he tried to suppress the horrid fear that Ellie was involved.

It was clear that Mr. Giordano was not pleased but all that he said was, "Report to the Purser's Office. Jump." Max jumped.

The Purser was not there; Mr. Kuiper received him and looked him over with a cold eye. "Put on a clean uniform and make it quick. Then report to the Captain's cabin."

Max stood still and gulped. Mr. Kuiper barked, "Well? Move!"

"Sir," Max blurted, "I don't know where the Captain's cabin is."

"What? I'll be switched! Able deck, radius nine oh and outboard." Max moved.

The Captain was in his cabin. With him was Mr. Samuels the Purser, Mr. Walther the First Officer, and Dr. Hendrix the Astrogator. Max concluded that whatever it was he was about to be tried for, it could be nothing trivial. But he remembered to say, "Steward's Mate Third Class Jones reporting, sir."

Captain Blaine looked up. "Oh, yes. Find a chair." Max found one, sat down on the edge of it. The Captain said to the First Officer, "Under the circumstances, Dutch, I suppose it's the best thing to do—though it seems a little drastic. You agree, Hal?"

The Purser agreed. Max wondered just how drastic it was and whether he would live through it.

"We'll log it as an exception, then, Doc, and I'll write up an explanation for the board. After all, regulations were made to be broken. That's the end of it." Max decided that they were simply going to space him and explain it later.

The Captain turned back to his desk in a manner that signified that the meeting was over. The First Officer cleared his throat. "Captain . . ." He indicated Max with his eyes.

Captain Blaine looked up again. "Oh, yes! Young man, your name is Jones?"

"Yessir."

"I've been looking over your record. I see that you once tried out for chartsman for a short time in the *Thule?*"

"Uh, yes, Captain."

"Didn't you like it?"

"Well, sir." Max asked himself what Sam would say when confronted by such a ghost. "It was like this . . . to tell you the truth I didn't do much except empty ash trays in the Worry—in the control room." He held his breath.

The Captain smiled briefly. "It can sometimes work out that way. Would you be interested in trying it again?"

"What? Yes, *sir!*"

"Dutch?"

"Captain, ordinarily I see no point in a man striking twice for the same job. But there is this personal matter."

"Yes, indeed. You can spare him, Hal?"

"Oh, certainly, Captain. He's hardly a key man where he is." The Purser smiled. "Bottom deck valet."

The Captain smiled and turned to the Astrogator. "I see no objection, Doc. It's a guild matter, of course."

"Kelly is willing to try him. He's short a man, you know."

"Very well, then . . ."

"Just a moment, Captain." The Astrogator turned to Max. "Jones . . . you had a relative in my guild?"

"My uncle, sir. Chester Jones."

"I served under him. I hope you have some of his skill with figures."

"Uh, I hope so, sir."

"We shall see. Report to Chief Computerman Kelly."

Max managed to find the control room without asking directions, although he could hardly see where he was going.

# 9

# CHARTSMAN JONES

The change in Max's status changed the whole perspective of his life. His social relations with the other crew members changed not entirely for the better. The control room gang considered themselves the gentry of the crew, a status disputed by the power technicians and resented by the stewards. Max found that the guild he was leaving no longer treated him quite as warmly while the guild for which he was trying out did not as yet accept him.

Mr. Gee simply ignored him—would walk right over him if Max failed to jump aside. He seemed to regard Max's trial promotion as a personal affront.

It was necessary for him to hit the slop chest for dress uniforms. Now that his duty station was in the control room, now that he must pass through passengers' country to go to and from work, it was no longer permissible to slouch around in dungarees. Mr. Kuiper let him sign for them; his cash would not cover it. He had to sign as well for the cost of permission to work out of his guild, with the prospect of going further in debt to both guilds should he be finally accepted. He signed cheerfully.

The control department of the *Asgard* consisted of two officers and five men—Dr. Hendrix the Astrogator, his assistant astrogator Mr. Simes, Chief Computerman Kelly, Chartsman First Class Kovak, Chtsmn 2/c Smythe, and computermen Noguchi and Lundy, both second class. There was also "Sack" Bennett, communicator first class, but he was not really a part of the control gang, even though his station was in the Worry Hole; a starship was rarely within radio range of anything except at the very first and last parts of a trip. Bennett doubled as Captain Blaine's secretary and factotum and owed his nickname to the often-stated belief of the others that he spent most of his life in his bunk.

Since the *Asgard* was always under boost a continuous watch was kept; not for them were the old, easy days of rocket ships, with ten minutes of piloting followed by weeks of free fall before more piloting was required. Since the *Asgard* carried no apprentice astrogator, there were only two officers to stand watches (Captain Blaine was necessarily an astrogator himself, but skippers do not stand watches); this lack was made up by Chief Computerman Kelly, who stood a regular watch as control officer-of-the-watch. The other ratings stood a watch in four; the distinction between a computerman and a chartsman was nominal in a control room dominated by "Decimal Point" Kelly —what a man didn't know he soon learned, or found another ship.

Easy watches for everyone but Max—he was placed on watch-and-watch for instruction, four hours on followed by four hours off in which he must eat, keep himself clean, relax, and—if he found time—sleep.

But he thrived on it, arriving early and sometimes having to be ordered out of the Worry Hole. Not until much later did he find out that this stiff regime was Kelly's way of trying to break him, discover his weakness and get rid of him promptly if he failed to measure up.

Not all watches were pleasant. Max's very first watch was under Mr. Simes. He crawled up the hatch into the control room and looked around him in wonderment. On four sides were the wonderfully delicate parallax cameras. Between two of them Lundy sat at the saddle of the main computer; he looked up and nodded but did not speak. Mr. Simes sat at the control console, facing the hatch; he must have seen Max but gave no sign of it.

There were other instruments crowded around the walls, some of which Max recognized from reading and from seeing pictures, some of which were strange—

tell-tales and gauges from each of the ship's compartments, a screen to reproduce the view aft or "below," microphone and controls for the ship's announcing system, the "tank" or vernier stereograph in which plates from the parallax cameras could be compared with charts, spectrostellograph, dopplerscope, multipoint skin temperature recorder, radar repeater for landing, too many things to take in at once.

Overhead through the astrogation dome was the starry universe. He stared at it, mouth agape. Living as he had been, inside a steel cave, he had hardly seen the stars; the firmament had been more with him back home on the farm.

"Hey! You!"

Max shook his head and found Mr. Simes looking at him. "Come here." Max did so, the assistant astrogator went on, "Don't you know enough to report to the watch officer when you come on duty?"

"Uh—sorry, sir."

"Besides that, you're late." Max slid his eyes to the chronometer in the console; it still lacked five minutes of the hour. Simes continued, "A sorry state of affairs when crewmen relieve the watch later than the watch officer. What's your name?"

"Jones, sir."

Mr. Simes sniffed. He was a red-faced young man with thin, carroty hair and a sniff was his usual conversational embellishment, at least with juniors. "Make a fresh pot of coffee."

"Aye aye, sir." Max started to ask where and how, but Mr. Simes had gone back to his reading. Max looked helplessly at Lundy, who indicated a direction with his eyes. Behind the chart safe Max found a coffee maker and under it cups, saucers, sugar, and tins of cream.

He burned himself before getting the hang of gear's idiosyncrasies. Mr. Simes accepted the brew without looking at him. Max wondered what to do next, decided to offer a cup to Lundy. The computerman thanked him quietly and Max decided to risk having one himself, since it seemed to be accepted. He took it over beside the computer to drink it.

He was still doing so when the watch officer spoke up. "What is this? A tea party? Jones!"

"Yes, sir?"

"Get the place policed up. Looks as if a herd of chucks had been wallowing in it."

The room seemed clean, but Max found a few scraps of paper to pick up and stuff down the chute, after which he wiped already-gleaming brightwork. He had started to go over things a second time when Lundy motioned him over. Max then helped Lundy change plates in the parallax cameras and watched him while he adjusted the electronic timer. Mr. Simes pushed the ready button himself, which seemed to be his sole work during the watch.

Lundy removed the plates and set them up in the tank for chart comparison, took the readings and logged them. Max gave him nominal help and gathered some notion of how it was done, after which he again wiped brightwork.

It was a long watch. He went to his bunk drained of the elation he had felt.

But watches with Dr. Hendrix and with Chief Kelly were quite different. The Worry Hole was a jolly place under Kelly; he ruled as a benevolent tyrant, shouting, cursing, slandering the coffee, slurring his juniors and being sassed back. Max never touched a polish rag when Kelly was at control; he was kept too busy not merely helping but systematically studying everything in the room. "We haven't a condemned thing to do," Kelly shouted at him, "until we hit Garson's Folly. Nothing to do but to ride this groove down until we hit dirt. So you, my laddy buck, are going to do plenty. When we get there you are going to know this condemned hole better than your mother knew your father—or you can spend your time there learning what you've missed while your mates are dirtside getting blind. Get out the instruction manual for the main computer, take off the back plate and get lost in them wires. I don't want to see anything but your ugly behind the rest of this watch."

Within ten minutes Kelly was down on his knees with him, helping him trace the intricate circuits.

Max learned, greatly assisted by his photographic memory and still more by the sound grounding in theory he had gotten from his uncle. Kelly was pleased. "I reckon you exaggerated a mite when you said you hadn't learned anything in the *Thule.*"

"Well, not much."

"Johansen have the Worry Hole when you were striking?"

"Uh, yes." Max hoped frantically that Kelly would not ask other names.

"I thought so. That squarehead wouldn't tell his own mother how old he was."

There came a watch when Kelly trusted him to do a dry run for a transition approach on the computer, with Noguchi handling the tables and Kelly substituting for the astrogator by following records of the actual transition the ship had last made. The programming was done orally, as is the case when the astrogator is working under extreme pressure from latest data, just before giving the crucial signal to boost past the speed of light.

Kelly took it much more slowly than would happen in practice, while Noguchi consulted tables and called out figures to Max. He was nervous at first, his fingers trembling so that it was hard to punch the right keys —then he settled down and enjoyed it, feeling as if he and the machine had been born for each other.

Kelly was saying, "—times the binary natural logarithm of zero point eight seven oh nine two." Max heard Noguchi's voice call back the datum while he thumbed for the page—but in his mind Max saw the page in front of his eyes long before Noguchi located it; without conscious thought he depressed the right keys.

"Correction!" sang out Kelly. "Look, meathead, you don't put in them figures; you wait for translation by

Noggy here. How many times I have to tell you?"

"But I did—" Max started, then stopped. Thus far he had managed to keep anyone aboard the *Asgard* from learning of his embarrassingly odd memory.

"You did what?" Kelly started to clear the last datum from the board, then hesitated. "Come to think of it, you can't possibly feed decimal figures into that spaghetti mill. Just what *did* you do?"

Max knew he was right and hated to appear not to know how to set up a problem. "Why, I put in the figures Noguchi was about to give me."

"How's that again?" Kelly stared at him. "You a mind reader?"

"No. But I put in the right figures."

"Hmm . . ." Kelly bent over the keyboard. "Call 'em off, Noggy." The computerman reeled off a string of ones and zeroes, the binary equivalent of the decimal expression Kelly had given him; Kelly checked the depressed keys, his lips moving in concentration. He straightened up. "I once saw a man roll thirteen sevens with honest dice. Was it fool luck, Max?"

"No."

"Well! Noggy, gimme that book." Kelly went through the rest of the problem, giving Max raw data and the operations to be performed, but not translating the figures into the binary notation the computer required. He kept thumbing the book and glancing over Max's shoulder. Max fought off stage fright and punched the keys, while sweat poured into his eyes.

At last Kelly said, "Okay. Twist its tail." Max flipped the switch which allowed the computer to swallow the program and worry it for an instant; the answer popped out in lights, off or on—the machine's equivalent of binary figures.

Kelly translated the lights back into decimal notation, using the manual. He then glanced at the recorded problem. He closed the record book and handed it to Noguchi. "I think I'll have a cup of coffee," he said quietly and walked away.

Noguchi reopened it, looked at the lights shining on

the board and consulted the manual, after which he looked at Max very oddly. Max saw Kelly staring at him over a cup with the same expression. Max reached up and cleared the board entirely; the lights went out. He got down out of the computerman's saddle. Nobody said anything.

Max's next watch was with Dr. Hendrix. He enjoyed watches with the Astrogator almost as much as those with Kelly; Dr. Hendrix was a friendly and soft-spoken gentleman and gave as much attention to training Max as Kelly did. But this time Kelly lingered on after being relieved—in itself nothing, as the Chief Computerman frequently consulted with, or simply visited with, the Astrogator at such times. But today, after relieving the watch, Dr. Hendrix said pleasantly, "Kelly tells me that you are learning to use the computer, Jones?"

"Uh, yes, sir."

"Very well, let's have a drill." Dr. Hendrix dug out an old astrogation log and selected a transition-approach problem similar to the one Max had set up earlier. Kelly took the manual, ready to act as his "numbers boy"—but did not call the translations. Max waited for the first one; when it did not come, he read the figures from the page shining in his mind and punched them in.

It continued that way. Kelly said nothing, but wet his lips and checked what Max did each time the doctor offered a bit of the problem. Kovak watched from nearby, his eyes moving from actor to actor.

At last Dr. Hendrix closed the book. "I see," he agreed, as if it were an everyday occurrence. "Jones, that is an extremely interesting talent. I've read of such cases, but you are the first I have met. You've heard of Blind Tom?"

"No, sir."

"Perhaps the ship's library has an account of him." The Astrogator was silent for a moment. "I don't mean to belittle your talent, but you are not to use it during an actual maneuver. You understand why?"

"Yes, sir. I guess I do."

"Better say that you are not to use it unless you think an error has been made—in which case you will speak up at once. But the printed tables remain the final authority."

"Aye aye, sir."

"Good. See me, please, in my room when you come off watch."

It was "day time" by the ship's clocks when he went off watch. He went to the passageway outside Dr. Hendrix's room and waited; there Ellie came across him. "Max!"

"Oh. Hello, Ellie." He realized uncomfortably that he had not seen her since his tentative promotion.

"Hello he says!" She planted herself in front of him. "You're a pretty sight—with your bloodshot eyes matching the piping on your shirt. Where have you been? Too good for your old friends? You haven't even been to see Chipsie."

He had been, once, although he had not run into Ellie. He had not repeated the visit because the shipmate who had replaced him had not liked being assigned as chambermaid to cows, sheep, llamas, *et al.;* he had seemed to feel that it was Max's fault. "I'm sorry," Max said humbly, "but I haven't had time."

"A feeble excuse. Know what you are going to do now? You're going straight to the lounge and I am going to trim your ears—I've figured out a way to box your favorite gambit that will leave you gasping."

Max opened his mouth, closed it, opened it again. "No."

"Speak louder. You used a word I don't understand."

"Look, Ellie, be reasonable. I'm waiting for Dr. Hendrix and as soon as he lets me go I've got to get some sleep. I'm about ten hours minus."

"You can sleep any time."

"Not when you're standing four hours on and four off. You nap anytime you get a chance."

She looked perplexed. "You don't mean you work

every other watch? Why, that's criminal."

"Maybe so but that's how it is."

"But—I'll fix that! I'll speak to the Captain."

"Ellie! Don't you dare!"

"Why not? Captain Blaine is old sugar pie. Never you mind, I'll fix it."

Max took a deep breath, then spoke carefully. "Ellie, don't say anything to the Captain, not anything. It's a big opportunity for me and I don't mind. If you go tampering with things you don't understand, you'll ruin my chances. I'll be sent back to the stables."

"Oh, he wouldn't do that."

"You don't understand. He may be an 'old sugar pie' to you; to me he is the Captain. So don't."

She pouted. "I was just trying to help."

"I appreciate it. But don't. And anyhow, I can't come to the lounge, ever. It's off limits for me."

"But I thought—I think you're just trying to avoid me. You run around up here now and you dress in pretty clothes. Why not?"

They were interrupted by Dr. Hendrix returning to his room. "Morning, Jones. Good morning, Miss Coburn." He went on in.

Max said desperately, "Look, Ellie, I've got to go." He turned and knocked on the Astrogator's door.

Dr. Hendrix ignored having seen him with Ellie. "Sit down, Jones. That was a very interesting exhibition you put on." The Astrogator went on, "I'm curious to know how far your talent extends. Is it just to figures?"

"Why, I guess not, sir."

"Do you have to study hard to do it?"

"No, sir."

"Hmm . . . We'll try something. Have you read—let me see—any of the plays of Shakespeare?"

"Uh, we had *Hamlet* and *As You Like It* in school, and I read *A Winter's Tale*. But I didn't like it," he answered honestly.

"In that case I don't suppose you reread it. Remember any of it?"

"Oh, certainly, sir."

"Hmm—" Dr. Hendrix got down a limp volume. "Let me see. Act two, scene three; Leontes says, 'Nor night nor day nor rest: it is but weakness . . .'"

Max picked it up. ". . . it is but weakness to bear the matter thus; mere weakness. If the cause were not in being . . ." He continued until stopped.

"That's enough. I don't care much for that play myself. Even the immortal Will had his off days. But how did you happen to have read that book of tables? Shakespeare at his dullest isn't that dull. I've never read them, not what one would call 'reading.'"

"Well, sir, Uncle Chet had his astrogation manuals at home after he retired and he used to talk with me a lot. So I read them."

"Do I understand that you have memorized the entire professional library of an astrogator?"

Max took a deep breath. "Well, sir, I've read them."

Dr. Hendrix took from his shelves his own tools of his profession. He did not bother with the binary tables, that being the one Max had shown that he knew. He leafed through them, asked Max questions, finally identifying what he wanted only by page number. He closed the last of them. "Whew!" he commented, and blinked. "While I am aware that there are numerous cases of your talent in the history of psychology, I must admit it is disconcerting to encounter one." He smiled. "I wonder what Brother Witherspoon would think of this."

"Sir?"

"Our High Secretary. I'm afraid he would be shocked; he has conservative notions about protecting the 'secrets' of our profession."

Max said uncomfortably, "Am I likely to get into trouble, sir? I didn't know it was wrong to read Uncle's books."

"What? Nonsense. There are no 'secrets' to astrogation. You use these books on watch, so does every member of the 'Worry' gang. The passengers can read them, for all I care. Astrogation isn't secret; it is merely difficult. Few people are so endowed as to be able to follow accurately the mathematical reasoning necessary to plan a—oh, a transition, let us say. But it suits those who bother with guild politics to make it appear an arcane art—prestige, you know." Dr. Hendrix paused and tapped on his chair arm. "Jones, I want you to understand me. Kelly thinks you may shape up."

"Uh, that's good, sir."

"But don't assume that you know more than he does just because you have memorized the books."

"Oh, no, sir!"

"Actually, your talent isn't necessary in the control room. The virtues needed are those Kelly has—unflagging attention to duty, thorough knowledge of his tools, meticulous care for details, deep loyalty to his job and his crew and his ship and to those placed over him professionally. Kelly doesn't need eidetic memory, ordinary good memory combined with intelligence and integrity are what the job takes—and that's what I want in my control room."

"Yes, sir."

The Astrogator hesitated. "I don't wish to be offensive but I want to add this. Strange talents are sometimes associated with ordinary, or even inferior, mentality—often enough so that the psychologists use the term 'idiot savant.' Sorry. You obviously aren't an idiot, but you are not necessarily a genius, even if you can memorize the Imperial Encyclopedia. My point is: I am more interested in your horse sense and your attention to duty than I am in your phenomenal memory."

"Uh, I'll try, sir."

"I think you'll make a good chartsman, in time." Dr. Hendrix indicated that the interview was over; Max got up. "One more thing."

"Yes, sir?"

"There are excellent reasons of discipline and efficiency why crew members do not associate with passengers."

Max gulped. "I know, sir."

"Mind your P's and Q's. The members of my department are careful about this point—even then it is difficult."

Max left feeling deflated. He had gone there feeling that he was about to be awarded something—even a chance to become an astrogator. He now felt sweated down to size.

# 10

# GARSON'S PLANET

Max did not see much of Sam during the weeks following; the stiff schedule left him little time for visiting. But Sam had prospered.

Like all large ships the *Asgard* had a miniature police force, experienced ratings who acted as the First Officer's deputies in enforcing ship's regulations. Sam, with his talent for politics and a faked certification as steward's mate first class, managed during the reshuffle following Max's transfer to be assigned as master-at-arms for the Purser's department. He did well, treading on no toes, shutting his eyes to such violations as were ancient prerogatives and enforcing those rules of sanitation, economy, and behavior which were actually needed for a taut, happy ship . . . all without finding it necessary to haul offenders up before the First Officer for punishment—which suited both Mr. Walther and the crew. When Stores Clerk Maginnis partook too freely of Mr. Gee's product and insisted on serenading his bunk mates, Sam merely took him to the galley and forced black coffee down him—then the following day took him down to 'H' deck, laid his own shield of office aside, and gave Maginnis a scientific going over that left no scars but deeply marked his soul. In his obscure past Sam had learned to fight, not rough house, not in the stylized mock combat of boxing, but in the skilled art in which an unarmed man becomes a lethal machine.

Sam had selected his victim carefully. Had he reported him Maginnis would have regarded Sam as a snoop, a mere busybody to be outwitted or defied, and had the punishment been severe he might have been turned into a permanent discipline problem—not forgetting that reporting Maginnis might also have endangered a sacred cow, Chief Steward Giordano. As it was, it turned Maginnis into Sam's strongest supporter and best publicist; as Maginnis's peculiar but not unique pride required him to regard the man who defeated him as "the hottest thing on two feet, sudden death in each hand, a *real* man! No nonsense about old Sam—try him yourself and see how *you* make out. Go on, I want to lay a bet."

It was not necessary for Sam to set up a second lesson.

A senior engineer's mate was chief master-at-arms and Sam's nominal superior; these two constituted the police force of their small town. When the technician asked to go back to power room watch-standing and was replaced by an engineer's mate third, it was natural that Walther should designate Sam as Chief Master-at-Arms.

He had had his eye on the job from the moment he signed on. Any police chief anywhere has powers far beyond those set forth by law. As long as Sam stayed well buttered up with Mr. Kuiper, Mr. Giordano, and (to a lesser extent) with Mr. Dumont, as long as he was careful to avoid exerting his authority in either the engineering spaces or the Worry Hole, he was the most powerful man in the ship—more powerful in all practical matters than the First Officer himself since he was the First Officer's visible presence.

Such was the situation when the ship grounded at Garson's Planet.

Garson's Planet appears to us to be a piece of junk left over when the universe was finished. It has a surface gravity of one-and-a-quarter, too much for comfort, it is cold as a moneylender's heart, and it has a methane atmosphere unbreathable by humans. With the sky swarming with better planets it would be avoided were it not an indispensable way station. There is only one survey Horst congruency near Earth's Sun and transition of it places one near Theta Centauri—and of the thirteen planets of that sun, Garson's Planet possesses the meager virtue of being least unpleasant.

But there are half a dozen plotted congruencies accessible to Theta Centauri, which makes Garson's Planet the inevitable cross-roads for trade of the Solar Union.

Max hit dirt there just once, once was plenty. The colony at the space port, partly domed, partly dug in under the domes, was much like the Lunar cities and not unlike the burrows under any major Earth city, but to Max it was novel since he had never been on Luna and had never seen a big city on Terra other than Earthport. He went dirtside with Sam, dressed in his best and filled with curiosity. It was not necessary to put on a pressure suit; the port supplied each passenger liner with a pressure tube from ship's lock to dome lock.

Once inside Sam headed down into the lower levels. Max protested, "Sam, let's go up and look around."

"Huh? Nothing there. A hotel and some expensive shops and clip joints for the pay passengers. Do you want to pay a month's wages for a steak?"

"No. I want to see *out*. Here I am on a strange planet and I haven't *seen* it at all. I couldn't see it from the control room when we landed and now I haven't seen anything but the inside of a trans tube and this." He gestured at the corridor walls.

"Nothing to see but a dirty, thick, yellow fog that never lifts. Worse than Venus. But suit yourself. I've got things to do, but if you don't want to stick with me you certainly don't have to."

Max decided to stick. They went on down and came out in a wide, lighted corridor not unlike that street in Earthport where Percy's restaurant was located, save that it was roofed over. There were the same bars, the same tawdry inducements for the stranger to part with cash, even to the tailor shop with the permanent "CLOSING OUT" sale. Several other ships were in and the sector was crowded. Sam looked around. "Now for a place for a quiet drink and a chat."

"How about there?" Max answered, pointing to a sign reading THE BETTER 'OLE. "Looks clean and cheerful."

Sam steered him quickly past it. "It is," he agreed, "but not for us."

"Why not?"

"Didn't you notice the customers? Imperial Marines."

"What of that? I've got nothing against the Imperials."

"Mmm . . . no," Sam agreed, still hurrying, "but those boys stick together and they have a nasty habit of resenting a civilian who has the bad taste to sit down in a joint they have staked out. Want to get your ribs kicked in?"

"Huh? That wouldn't happen if I minded my own business, would it?"

"Maybe. Maybe not. Suppose a hostess decides that you're 'cute'—and the spit-and-polish boy she was with wants to make something of it? Max, you're a good boy—but there just ain't no demand for good boys. To stay out of trouble you have to stay away from it."

They threaded their way through the crowd for another hundred yards before Sam said, "Here we are—provided Lippy is still running the place." The sign read *THE SAFE LANDING;* it was larger but not as pleasant as *THE BETTER 'OLE.*

"Who's Lippy?"

"You probably won't meet him." Sam led the way in and picked out a table.

Max looked around. It looked like any other fifth-rate bar grille. "Could I get a strawberry soda here? I've had a hankering for one for ages—I used always to get one Saturdays when I went to the Corners."

"They can't rule you out for trying."

"Okay. Sam, something you said—you remember the story you told me about your friend in the Imperials? Sergeant Roberts?"

"Who?"

"Or Richards. I didn't quite catch it."

"Never heard of the guy."

"But . . ."

"Never heard of him. Here's the waiter."

Nor had the humanoid Sirian waiter heard of strawberry soda. He had no facial muscles but his back skin crawled and rippled with embarrassed lack of comprehension. Max settled for something called "Old Heidelberg" although it had never been within fifty light-years of Germany. It tasted to Max like cold soap suds, but since Sam had paid for it he nursed it along and pretended to drink it.

Sam bounced up almost at once. "Sit tight, kid. I won't be long." He spoke to the barman, then disappeared toward the back. A young woman came over to Max's table.

"Lonely, spaceman?"

"Uh, not especially."

"But *I* am. Mind if I sit down?" She sank into the chair that Sam had vacated.

"Suit yourself. But my friend is coming right back."

She didn't answer but turned to the waiter at her elbow. "A brown special, Giggles."

Max made an emphatic gesture of denial. "No!"

"What's that, dear?"

"Look," Max answered, blushing, "I may look green as paint—I am, probably. But I don't buy colored water at house prices. I don't have much money."

She looked hurt. "But you have to order or I can't sit here."

"Well . . ." He glanced at the menu. "I could manage a sandwich, I guess."

She turned again to the waiter. "Never mind the special, Giggles. A cheese on rye and plenty of mustard." She turned back to Max. "What's your name, honey?"

"Max."

"Mine's Dolores. Where are you from?"

"The Ozarks. That's Earthside."

"Now isn't that a coincidence! I'm from Winnipeg—we're neighbors!"

Max decided that it might appear so, from that distance. But as Dolores babbled on it became evident that she knew neither the location of the Ozarks nor that of Winnipeg, had probably never been on Terra in her life. She was finishing the sandwich while telling Max that she just adored spacemen, they were so romantic, when Sam returned.

He looked down at her. "How much did you take him for?"

Dolores said indignantly, "That's no way to talk! Mr. Lipski doesn't permit . . ."

"Stow it, kid," Sam went on, not unkindly. "You didn't know that my partner is a guest of Lippy. Get me? No 'specials,' no 'pay-me's'—you're wasting your time. Now how much?"

Max said hastily, "It's okay, Sam. All I bought her was a sandwich."

"Well . . . all right. But you're excused, sister. Later, maybe."

She shrugged and stood up. "Thanks, Max."

"Not at all, Dolores. I'll say hello to the folks in Winnipeg."

"Do that."

Sam did not sit down. "Kid, I have to go out for a while."

"Okay."

Max started to rise, Sam motioned him back. "No, no. This I'd better do by myself. Wait here, will you? They won't bother you again—or if they do, ask for Lippy."

"I won't have any trouble."

"I hope not." Sam looked worried. "I don't know why I should fret, but there is something about you that arouses the maternal in me. Your big blue eyes I guess."

"Huh? Oh, go sniff space! Anyway, my eyes are brown."

"I was speaking," Sam said gently, "of the eyes of your dewy pink soul. Don't speak to strangers while I'm gone."

Max used an expression he had picked up from Mr. Gee; Sam grinned and left.

But Sam's injunction did not apply to Mr. Simes. Max saw the assistant astrogator appear in the doorway. His face was redder than usual and his eyes looked vague. He let his body revolve slowly as he surveyed the room. Presently his eyes lit on Max and he grinned unpleasantly.

"Well, well, well!" he said as he advanced toward Max. "If it isn't the Smart Boy."

"Good evening, Mr. Simes." Max stood up.

"So it's 'good evening, Mr. Simes'! But what did you say under your breath?"

"Nothing, sir."

"Humph! I know! But I think the same thing about you, only worse." Max did not answer, Simes went on, "Well, aren't you going to ask me to sit down?"

"Have a seat, sir," Max said without expression.

"Well, what do you know? The Smart Boy wants me to sit with him." He sat, called the waiter, ordered, and turned back to Max. "Smart Boy, do you know why I'm sitting with you?"

"No, sir."

"To put a flea in your ear, that's why. Since you pulled that hanky-panky with the computer, you've been Kelly's hair-faired—fair-haired—boy. Fair-haired boy," he repeated carefully. "That gets you nowhere with me. Get this straight: you go sucking around the Astrogator the way Kelly does and I'll run you out of the control room. Understand me?"

Max felt himself losing his temper. "What do you mean by 'hanky-panky,' Mr. Simes?"

"You know. Probably memorized the last half dozen transitions—now you've got Kelly and the Professor thinking you've memorized the book. A genius in our midst! You know what that is? That's a lot of . . ."

Fortunately for Max they were interrupted; he felt a firm hand on his shoulder and Sam's quiet voice said, "Good evening, Mr. Simes."

Simes looked confused, then recognized Sam and brightened. "Well, if it isn't the copper. Sit down, Constable. Have a drink."

"Don't mind if I do." Sam pulled up another chair.

"Do you know Smart Boy here?"

"I've seen him around."

"Keep your eye on him. That's an order. He's very, very clever. Too clever. Ask him a number. Pick a number between one and ten."

"Seven."

Mr. Simes pounded the table. "What did I tell you? He memorized it before you got here. Someday he's going to memorize one and they'll stencil it across his chest. You know what, Constable? I don't trust smart boys. They get ideas."

Reinforced by Sam's calming presence Max kept quiet. Giggles had come to the table as soon as Sam joined them; Max saw Sam write something on the back of a menu and pass it with money to the humanoid. But Mr. Simes was too busy with his monologue to notice. Sam let him ramble on, then suddenly interrupted. "You seem to have a friend here, sir."

"Huh? Where?"

Sam pointed. At the bar Dolores was smiling and gesturing at the assistant navigator to join her. Simes focused his eyes, grinned and said, "Why, so I do! It's my Great Aunt Sadie." He got up abruptly.

Sam brushed his hands together. "That disposes of that. Give you a bad time, kid?"

"Sort of. Thanks, Sam. But I hate to see him dumped on Dolores. She's a nice kid."

"Don't worry about her. She'll roll him for every thin he has on him—and a good job, too." His eyes became hard. "I like an officer who acts like an officer. If he wants to pin one on, he should do it in his own part of town. Oh, well." Sam relaxed. "Been some changes, eh, kid? Things are different from the way they were when we raised ship at Terra."

"I'll say they are!"

"Like it in the Worry gang?"

"It's more fun than I ever had in my life. And I'm learning fast—so Mr. Kelly says. They're a swell bunch—except for *him*." He nodded toward Simes.

"Don't let him worry you. The best soup usually has a fly in it. Just don't let him get anything on you."

"I sure don't intend to."

Sam looked at him, then said softly, "Ready to take the dive?"

"Huh?"

"I'm getting our stake together. We'll be all set."

Max found it hard to answer. He had known that his transfer had not changed anything basic; he was still in as much danger as ever. But he had been so busy with the joy of hard, interesting work, so dead for sleep when he was not working, that the subject had been pushed back in his mind. Now he drew patterns on the table in the sweat from the glasses and thought about it. "I wish," he said slowly, "that there was some way to beat it."

"There is a way, I told you. Your record gets lost."

Max raised his eyes. "What good would that do? Sure, it would get me another trip. But I don't want just another trip; I want to stay with it." He looked down at the table top and carefully sketched an hyperboloid. "I'd better go with you. If I go back to Terra, it's the labor companies for me—even if I stay out of jail."

"Nonsense."

"What?"

"Understand me, kid. I'd like to have you with me. A time like that, having a partner at your elbow is the difference between—well, being down in the dumps and being on top. But you can stay in space, with a record as clean as a baby's."

"Huh? How?"

"Because you are changing guilds. Now only *one* paper has to get lost—your strike-out record with the stewards, cooks, and clerks. And they will never miss it because you aren't on their books, anyhow. You start fresh with the chartsmen and computers, all neat and legal."

Max sat still and was tempted. "How about the report to the Department of Guilds and Labor?"

"Same thing. Different forms to different offices. I checked. One form gets lost, the other goes in—and Steward's Mate Jones vanishes into limbo while Apprentice Chartsman Jones starts a clean record."

"Sam, why don't *you* do it? With the drag you've got now you could switch to . . . uh, well, to . . ."

"To what?" Sam shook his head sadly. "No, old son, there is nothing I can switch to. Besides, there are reasons why I had better be buried deep." He brightened. "Tell you what—I'll pick my new name before I take the jump and tell you. Then some day, two years, ten, twenty, you'll lay over at Nova Terra and look me up. We'll split a bottle and talk about when we were young and gay. Eh?"

Max smiled though he did not feel happy. "We will, Sam. We surely will." Then he frowned. "But, Sam, I don't know how to wangle the deal—and you'll be gone."

"I'll fix it before I leave. I've got Nelson eating out of my hand now. Like this: half cash down and half on delivery—and I'll fix it so that you have something on him—never mind what; you don't need to know yet. When you ground at Earthport, he asks you to mail the reports because you are going dirtside and he has work to finish. You check to see that the two reports you want are there, then you give him his pay off. Done."

Max said slowly, "I suppose that's best."

"Quit fretting. Everybody has a skeleton in the closet; the thing is to keep 'em there and not at the feast." He pushed an empty glass aside. "Kid, would you mind if we went back to the ship? Or had you planned to make a night of it?"

"No, I don't mind." Max's elation at setting foot on his first strange planet was gone—Garson's Hole was, he had to admit, a sorry sample of the Galaxy.

"Then let's get saddled up. I've got stuff to carry and I could use help."

It turned out to be four fairly large bundles which Sam had cached in public lockers. "What are they?" Max asked curiously.

"Tea cozies, old son. Thousands of them. I'm going to sell 'em to Procyon pinheads as skull caps." Somewhat affronted, Max shut up.

Everything coming into the ship was supposed to be inspected, but the acting master-at-arms on watch at the lock did not insist on examining the items belonging to the Chief Master-at-Arms any more than he would have searched a ship's officer. Max helped Sam carry the bundles to the stateroom which was the prerogative of the ship's chief of police.

# 11

## "THROUGH THE CARGO HATCH"

From Garson's Planet to Halcyon around Nu Pegasi is a double dogleg of three transitions, of 105, 487, and 19 light-years respectively to achieve a "straight line" distance of less than 250 light-years. But neither straight-line distance nor pseudo-distance of transition is important; the *Asgard* covered less than a light-year between gates. A distance "as the crow flies" is significant only to crows.

The first transition was barely a month out from Garson's Planet. On raising from there Kelly placed Max on a watch in three, assigning him to Kelly's own watch, which gave Max much more sleep, afforded him as much instruction (since the watch with Simes was worthless, instruction-wise), and kept Max out of Simes' way, to his enormous relief. Whether Kelly had planned that feature of it Max never knew—and did not dare ask.

Max's watch was still an instruction watch, he had no one to relieve nor to be relieved by. It became his habit not to leave the control room until Kelly did, unless told to do so. This resulted in him still being thrown into the company of Dr. Hendrix frequently, since the Astrogator relieved the Chief Computerman and Kelly would usually hang around and chat . . . during which time the Astrogator would sometimes inquire into Max's progress.

Occasionally the Captain would show up on Dr. Hendrix's watch. Shortly after leaving Garson's Planet Dr. Hendrix took advantage of one such occasion to have Max demonstrate for Captain Blaine and First Officer Walther his odd talent. Max performed without a mistake although the Captain's presence made him most selfconscious. The Captain watched closely with an expression of gentle surprise. Afterwards he

said, "Thank you, lad. That was amazing. Let me see
—what is your name?"

"Jones, sir."

"Jones, yes." The old man blinked thoughtfully. "It
must be terrifying not to be able to forget—especially
in the middle of the night. Keep a clear conscience,
son."

Twelve hours later Dr. Hendrix said to him, "Jones,
don't go away. I want to see you."

"Yes, sir."

The Astrogator spoke with Kelly for a few moments,
then again spoke to Max. "The Captain was impressed
by your vaudeville act, Jones. He is wondering whether you have any parallel mathematical ability."

"Well—no, sir. I'm not a lightning calculator, that
is. I saw one in a sideshow once. He could do things I
couldn't."

Hendrix brushed it aside. "Not important. I believe
you told me that your uncle taught you some mathematical theory?"

"Just for astrogation, sir."

"What do you think I am talking about? Do you
know how to compute a transition approach?"

"Uh, I think so, sir."

"Frankly, I doubt it, no matter how much theoretical drill Brother Jones gave you. But go ahead."

"*Now*, sir?"

"Try it. Pretend you're the officer of the watch. Kelly will be your assistant. I'll just be audience. Work
the approach we are on. I realize that we aren't close
enough for it to matter—but you are to assume that
the safety of the ship depends on it."

Max took a deep breath. "Aye aye, sir." He started
to get out fresh plates for the cameras.

Hendrix said, "No!"

"Sir?"

"If you have the watch, where's your crew? Noguchi, help him."

"Aye aye, sir." Noguchi grinned and came over.
While they were bending over the first camera, Nogu-

chi whispered, "Don't let him rattle you, pal. We'll give him a good show. Kelly will help you over the humps."

But Kelly did not help; he acted as "numbers boy" and nothing else, with no hint to show whether Max was right, or wildly wrong. After Max had his sights and had taken his comparison data between plates and charts he did not put the problem through the computer himself, but let Noguchi man the machine, with Kelly translating. After a long time and much sweat the lights blinked what he hoped was the answer.

Dr. Hendrix said nothing but took the same plates to the tank and started to work the problem again, with the same crew. Very quickly the lights blinked on again; the Astrogator took the tables from Kelly and looked up the translation himself. "We differ only in the ninth decimal place. Not bad."

"I was wrong only in the ninth place, sir?"

"I didn't say that. Perhaps I was more in error."

Max started to grin, but Dr. Hendrix frowned. "Why didn't you take doppler spectra to check?"

Max felt a cold chill. "I guess I forgot, sir."

"I thought you were the man who never forgot?"

Max thought intuitively—and correctly—that two kinds of memory were involved, but he did not have a psychologist's jargon with which to explain. One sort was like forgetting one's hat in a restaurant, that could happen to anyone; the other was being unable to re-call what the mind had once known.

Hendrix went on, "A control room man must not forget things necessary to the safety of the ship. How-ever as an exercise you solved it very well—except that you have no speed. Had we been pushing close to the speed of light, ready to cross, your ship would have been in Hades and crashed in the River Styx be-fore you got the answer. But it was a good first try."

He turned away. Kelly jerked his head toward the hatch and Max went below.

As he was falling asleep Max turned over in his

mind the notion that Dr. Hendrix might even be
thinking of him for— Oh no! He put the thought aside.
After all, Kelly could have done it; he had seen him do
early approaches many times, and faster, too. Probably Noguchi could have done it.

Certainly Noguchi could have done it, he corrected.
After all, there weren't any "secrets."

As they approached the first anomaly the easy
watch in three for officers and watch in four for the
men changed to watch-and-watch, with an astrogator,
an assistant, a chartsman, and a computerman on each
watch. Max was at last assigned to a regular watch;
the first watch was Dr. Hendrix assisted by Chartsman
1/c Kovak, Max as chartsman of the watch and Noguchi on the computer; the other watch was Mr. Simes
assisted by Chief Kelly, Smythe as chartsman and
Lundy as computerman. Max noticed that Dr. Hendrix had assigned his "first team" to Simes and had
taken the less experienced technicians himself. He
wondered why, but was pleased not to be working for
Simes.

He learned at last why they called it the "Worry
Hole." Dr. Hendrix became a frozen-masked automaton, performing approach correction after correction
and demanding quick, accurate, and silent service.
During the last twenty hours of the approach the Astrogator never left the control room, nor did anyone
else other than for short periods when nominally off
watch. Simes continued to take his regular watch but
Dr. Hendrix hung over him, checking everything that
he did. Twice he required the junior astrogator to re-
perform portions of his work and once elbowed him
aside and did it himself. The first time it happened
Max stared—then he noticed that the others were careful to be busy doing something else whenever Dr. Hendrix spoke privately to Simes.

The tension grew as the critical instant approached.
The approach to an anomalous intraspatial transition
can hardly be compared to any other form of piloting

ever performed by human beings, though it might be
compared to the impossible trick of taking off in an atmosphere plane, flying a thousand miles blind—while
performing dead reckoning so perfectly as to fly
through a narrow tunnel at the far end, without ever
seeing the tunnel. A Horst congruency cannot be seen,
it can only be calculated by abstruse mathematics of
effects of mass on space; a "gateway" is merely unmarked empty space in vaster emptiness. In approaching a planet an astrogator can see his destination, directly or by radar, and his speed is just a few
miles per second. But in making a Horstian approach
the ship's speed approaches that of light—and reaches
it, at the last instant. The nearest landmarks are many
billions of miles away, the landmarks themselves are
moving with stellar velocities and appear to be crowding together in the exaggerated parallax effects possible only when the observer is moving almost as fast as
is his single clue to location and speed—the wave fronts
of the electromagnetic spectrum.

Like searching at midnight in a dark cellar for a
black cat that isn't there.

Toward the last Kelly himself was on the computer
with Lundy at his ear. Smythe and Kovak were chart-
ing, passing new data to Dr. Hendrix, who was programming orally to the computer crew, setting up the
problems in his head and feeding them to the electronic brain almost without delay. The power room
was under his direct control now; he had a switch led
out from the control console in each hand, one to
nurse the ship along just below speed of light, the other to give the *Asgard* the final kick that would cause
her to burst through.

Max was pushed aside, no task remained in which
there was not someone more experienced. On a
different level, Simes too had been pushed aside; there
was place for only one astrogator at the moment of
truth.

Of all those in the Worry Hole only Captain Blaine
seemed to be relaxed. He sat in the chair sacred to

him, smoking quietly and watching Hendrix. The Astrogator's face was gray with fatigue, greasy with unwashed sweat. His uniform was open at the collar and looked slept in, though he certainly had not slept. Max looked at him and wondered why he had ever longed to be an astrogator, ever been foolish enough to wish to bear this undivided and unendurable burden.

But the doctor's crisp voice showed no fatigue; the endless procession of numbers marched out, sharp as print, each spoken so that there could be no mistake, no need to repeat, "nine" always sounded as one syllable, "five" always stretched into two. Max listened and learned and wondered.

He glanced up through the dome, out into space itself, space shown distorted by their unthinkable speed. The stars ahead, or above, had been moving closer together for the past several watches, the huge parallax effect displacing them to the eye so that they seemed to be retreating in the very sector of the sky they were approaching. They were seeing by infra-red waves now, ploughing into oncoming wave trains so fast that doppler effect reduced heat wave lengths to visible light.

The flood of figures stopped. Max looked down, then looked up hastily as he heard Dr. Hendrix say, "Stand by!"

The stars seemed to crawl together, then instantly they were gone to be replaced without any lapse of time whatever by another, new and totally different starry universe.

Hendrix straightened up and sighed, then looked up. "There's the Albert Memorial," he said quietly. "And there is the Hexagon. Well, Captain, it seems we made it again." He turned to Simes. "Take it, Mister." He let the Captain go first, then followed him down the hatch.

The control gang went back to easy watches; the next transition was many days away. Max continued as chartsman-of-the-watch in place of Kovak, who temporarily replaced Dr. Hendrix while the Astrogator got a week of rest. There was truly not much to do during the early part of a leg and the doctor's superb skill was not needed. But Max greatly enjoyed the new arrangements; it made him proud to sign the rough log "M. Jones, Chtsmn o/W." He felt that he had arrived—even though Simes found fault with him and Kelly continued to drill him unmercifully in control room arts.

He was surprised but not apprehensive when he was told, during an off-watch period, to report to the Astrogator. He put on a fresh uniform, slicked his hair down, and went above "C" deck. "Apprentice Chartsman Jones reporting, sir."

Kelly was there, having coffee with the Astrogator. Hendrix acknowledged Max's salutation but left him standing. "Yes, Jones." He turned to Kelly. "Suppose you break the news."

"If you say so, sir." Kelly looked uncomfortable. "Well, Jones, it's like this—you don't really belong in my guild."

Max was so shocked that he could not answer. He was about to say that he had thought—he had understood—he hadn't known— But he got nothing out; Kelly continued, "The fact is, you ought to buck for astrogator. The Doctor and I have been talking it over."

The buzzing in his head got worse. He became aware that Dr. Hendrix was repeating, "Well, Jones? Do you want to try it? Or don't you?"

Max managed to say, "Yes. Yes, sir."

"Good. Kelly and I have been watching you. He is of the opinion and so am I that you may, just possibly, have the latent ability to develop the skill and speed necessary. The question is: do *you* think so?"

"Uh . . . that is— I hope so, sir!"

"So do I," Hendrix answered dryly. "We shall see. If you haven't, you can revert to your own guild and no harm is done. The experience will make you a better chartsman." The Astrogator turned to Kelly. "I'll quiz Jones a bit, Kelly. Then we can make up our minds."

"Very good, sir." Kelly stood up.

When the Chief Computerman had gone Hendrix turned to his desk, hauled out a crewman's personal record. To Max he said harshly, "Is this yours?"

Max looked at it and gulped. "Yes, sir."

Dr. Hendrix held his eye. "Well? How good a picture is it of your career thus far? Any comment you want to make?"

The pause might have been a dozen heart beats, though to Max it was an endless ordeal. Then a catharsis came bursting up out of him and he heard himself answering, "It's not a good picture at all, sir. It's phony from one end to the other."

Even as he said it, he wondered why. He felt that he had kicked to pieces his one chance to achieve his ambition. Yet, instead of feeling tragic, he felt oddly relaxed.

Hendrix put the personal record back on his desk. "Good," he answered. "Very good. If you had given any other answer, I would have run you out of my control room. Now, do you want to tell me about it? Sit down."

So Max sat down and told him. All that he held back was Sam's name and such details as would have identified Sam. Naturally Dr. Hendrix noticed the omission and asked him point blank.

"I won't tell you, sir."

Hendrix nodded. "Very well. Let me add that I shall make no attempt to identify this, ah, friend of yours— if by chance he is in this ship."

"Thank you, sir."

There followed a considerable silence. At last Hendrix said, "Son, what led you to attempt this preposterous chicanery? Didn't you realize you would be caught?"

Max thought about it. "I guess I knew I would be, sir—eventually. But I wanted to space and there wasn't any other way to do it." When Hendrix did not answer Max went on. After the first relief of being

able to tell the truth, he felt defensive, anxious to justify himself—and just a little bit irked that Dr. Hendrix
did not see that he had simply done what he *had* to do
—so it seemed to Max. "What would you have done,
sir?"

"Me? How can I answer that? What you're really
asking is: do I consider your actions morally wrong, as
well as illegal?"

"Uh, I suppose so, sir."

"Is it wrong to lie and fake and bribe to get what
you want? It's worse than wrong, it's undignified!"

Dr. Hendrix chewed his lip and continued. "Perhaps
that opinion is the sin of the Pharisees . . . my own
weakness. I don't suppose that a young, penniless
tramp, such as you described yourself to be, can afford
the luxury of dignity. As for the rest, human personality is a complex thing, nor am I a judge. Admiral
Lord Nelson was a liar, a libertine, and outstandingly
undisciplined. President Abraham Lincoln was a vul-
garian and nervously unstable. The list is endless. No,
Jones, I am not going to pass judgment; you must do
that yourself. The authorities having jurisdiction will
reckon your offenses; I am concerned only with
whether or not you have the qualities I need."

Max's emotions received another shock. He had already resigned himself to the idea that he had lost his
chance. "Sir?"

"Don't misunderstand me." Hendrix tapped the
forged record. "I don't like this. I don't like it at all.
But perhaps you can live down your mistake. In the
meantime, I badly need another watch officer; if you
measure up, I can use you. Part of it is personal, too;
your uncle taught me, I shall try to teach you."

"Uh, I'll try, sir. Thank you."

"Don't thank me. I'm not even feeling particularly
friendly to you, at the moment. Don't talk with anyone. I'll ask the Captain to call a guild meeting and he
and Mr. Simes and I will vote on you. We'll make you
a probationary apprentice which will permit the Cap-

tain to appoint you to the temporary rank of merchant
cadet. The legalities are a bit different from those of
the usual route as you no doubt know."

Max did not know, though he was aware that
officers sometimes came up "through the cargo hatch"
—but another point hit him. "Mr. Simes, sir?"

"Certainly. By this procedure, all the astrogators
you serve with must pass on you."

"Uh, does it have to unanimous, sir?"

"Yes."

"Then— Well, sir, you might as well forget it. I
mean, I appreciate your willingness to, uh, but . . ."
His voice trailed off.

Dr. Hendrix smiled mirthlessly. "Hadn't you better
let me worry about that?"

"Oh. Sorry, sir."

"When it has been logged, I'll notify you. Or 'when
and if,' if you prefer."

"Yes, sir." Max stood up. "Sir? There were, uh, a
couple of other things I wondered about."

Hendrix had turned back to his desk. He answered,
"Well?" somewhat impatiently.

"Would you mind telling me—just for my curiosity
—how you caught me?"

"Oh, that. No doubt you've given yourself away to
several people. I'm sure Kelly knows, from the subjects
he avoided. For example, I once heard Lundy mention
to you Kiefer's Ritz on Luna. Your answer, though
noncommittal, implied that you did not really know
what dive he was talking about—and it is impossible
for a spaceman not to know that place, its entrance
faces the east lock to the space port."

"Oh."

"But the matter came to the top of my mind in con-
nection with this." He again indicated the false record.
"Jones, I deal in figures and my mind can no more
help manipulating them for all the information they
contain than I can help breathing. This record says
that you went to space a year before your uncle retired—I remember what year that was. But you told

me that your uncle had trained you at home and your
performance bore out that statement. Two sets of
alleged facts were contradictory; need I add that I
was fairly sure of the truth?"

"Oh. I guess I wasn't very smart."

"No, you weren't. Figures are sharp things, Jones.
Don't juggle them, you'll get cut. What was the other
matter?"

"Well, sir, I was kind of wondering what was going
to happen to me. I mean about *that.*"

"Oh," Hendrix answered indifferently, "that's up to
the Stewards & Clerks. My guild won't take action
concerning a disciplinary matter of another guild. Unless, of course, they call it 'moral turpitude' and make
it stick."

With that faint comfort Max left. Nevertheless he
felt easier than he had at any time since he had
signed on. The prospect of punishment seemed less a
burden than constantly worrying about getting
caught. Presently he forgot it and exulted in the opportunity—at last!—to take a crack at astrogator.

He wished he could tell Sam . . . or Ellie.

# 12

## HALCYON

The probationary appointment was logged later that same day. The Captain called him in, swore him in, then congratulated him and called him "Mister" Jones. The ceremony was simple, with no spectator but Hendrix and the Captain's secretary.

The commonplaces attendant on the change were, for a while, more startling to Max than the promotion itself. They started at once. "You had better take the rest of the day to shake down, Mr. Jones," the Captain said, blinking vaguely. "Okay, Doc?"

"Certainly, sir."

"Good. Bennett, will you ask Dumont to step in?"

The Chief Passengers' Steward was unblinkingly unsurprised to find the recent steward's mate third a ship's officer. To the Captain's query he said, "I was planning to put Mr. Jones in stateroom B-014, sir. Is that satisfactory?"

"No doubt, no doubt."

"I'll have boys take care of his luggage at once."

"Good. You trot along with Dumont, Mr. Jones. No, wait a moment. We must find you a cap." The Captain went to his wardrobe, fumbled around. "I had one that would do here somewhere."

Hendrix had been standing with his hands behind him. "I fetched one, Captain. Mr. Jones and I wear the same size, I believe."

"Good. Though perhaps his head has swelled a bit in the past few minutes. Eh?"

Hendrix grinned savagely. "If it has, I'll shrink it." He handed the cap to Max. The wide gold strap and sunburst the Astrogator had removed; substituted was a narrow strap with tiny sunburst surrounded by the qualifying circle of the apprentice. Max thought it must be old insignia saved for sentimental reasons by Hendrix himself. He choked up as he mumbled his thanks, then followed Dumont out of the Captain's cabin, stumbling over his feet.

When they reached the companionway Dumont stopped. "There is no need to go down to the bunk-room, sir. If you will tell me the combination of your locker, we'll take care of everything."

"Oh, gee, Mr. Dumont! I've got just a small amount of truck. I can carry it up myself."

Dumont's face had the impassivity of a butler's. "If I may make a suggestion, sir, you might like to see your stateroom while I have the matter taken care of." It was not a question; Max interpreted it correctly to mean: *"Look, dummy, I know the score and you don't. Do what I tell you before you make a terrible break!"*

Max let himself be guided. It is not easy to make the jump from crewman to officer while remaining in the same ship. Dumont knew this, Max did not. Whether his interest was fatherly, or simply a liking for correct protocol—or both—Dumont did not intend to allow the brand-new junior officer to go lower than "C" deck until he had learned to carry his new dignity with grace. So Max sought out stateroom B-014.

The bunk had a real foam mattress and a spread. There was a tiny wash basin with running water and a mirror. There was a bookshelf over the bunk and a wardrobe for his uniforms. There was even a shelf desk that let down for his convenience. There was a telephone on the wall, a buzzer whereby he could summon the steward's mate on watch! There was a movable chair all his own, a wastebasket, and—yes!—a little rug on the deck. And best of all, there was a door with a lock.

The fact that the entire room was about as large as a piano box bothered him not at all.

He was opening drawers and poking into things when Dumont returned. Dumont was not carrying Max's meager possessions himself; that task was delegated to one of his upper-decks staff. The steward's mate followed Dumont in and said, "Where shall I put this, sir?"

Max realized with sudden embarrassment that the man waiting on him had eaten opposite him for past months. "Oh! Hello, Jim. Just dump it on the bunk. Thanks a lot."

"Yes, sir. And congratulations!"

"Uh, thanks!" They shook hands. Dumont let that proper ceremony persist for a minimum time, then said, "That's all now, Gregory. You can go back to the pantry." He turned to Max. "Anything else, sir?"

"Oh, no, everything is fine."

"May I suggest that you probably won't want to sew insignia on these uniforms yourself? Unless you are better with a needle than I am," Dumont added with just the right chuckle.

"Well, I guess I could."

"Mrs. Dumont is handy with a needle, taking care of the lady passengers as she does. Suppose I take this one? It can be ready and pressed in time for dinner."

Max was happy to let him. He was suddenly appalled by a terrifying notion—he was going to have to eat in the Bifrost Lounge!

But there were further disturbances before dinner. He was completing the small task of stowing his possessions when there came a knock on the door, followed immediately by someone coming in. Max found himself nose to nose with Mr. Simes.

Simes looked at the cap on his head and laughed. "Take that thing off before you wear out your ears."

Max did not do so. He said, "You wanted me, sir?"

"Yes. Just long enough, Smart Boy, to give you a word of advice."

"Yes?"

Simes tapped himself on the chest. "Just this. There is only one assistant astrogator in this ship—and I'm it. Remember that. I'll still be it long after you've been busted back to sweeping up after cows. Which is where you belong."

Max felt a flush crawl up his neck and burn his cheeks. "Why," he asked, "if you think that, didn't you veto my appointment?"

Simes laughed again. "Do I look like a fool? The Captain says yes, the Astrogator says yes—should I stick my neck out? It's easier to wait and let you stick your neck out—which you will. I just wanted to let you know that a dinky piece of gold braid doesn't mean a thing. You're still junior to me by plenty. Don't forget it."

Max clenched his jaw and did not answer. Simes went on, "Well?"

"'Well' what?"

"I just gave you an order."

"Oh. Aye aye, Mr. Simes. I won't forget it. I certainly won't."

Simes looked at him sharply, said, "See that you don't," and left. Max was still facing his door, clenching his fists, when Gregory tapped on the door. "Dinner, sir. Five minutes."

Max delayed as long as he could, wishing mightily that he could slide down to Easy deck and take his usual place in the warm, noisy, relaxed comfort of the crew's mess. He hesitated in the lounge doorway, paralyzed with stage fright. The beautiful room was blazing with light and looked unfamiliar; he had never been in it save in early morning, to change the sandbox located down the pantry passage—at which times only standing lights were burning.

He was barely in time; some of the ladies were seated but the Captain was still standing. Max realized that he should be near his chair, ready to sit down when the Captain did—or as soon as the ladies were seated, he amended—but where should he go? He was still jittering when he heard his name shouted. "Max!"

Ellie came running up and threw her arms around his neck. "Max! I just heard. I think it's *wonderful!*" She looked at him, her eyes shining, then kissed him on both cheeks.

Max blushed to his ears. He felt as if every eye was turned on him—and he was right. To add to his embarrassment Ellie was dressed in formal evening dress of Hesperan high style, which not only made her look older and much more female, but also shocked his puritanical hillbilly standards.

She let go of him, which was well but left him in danger of collapsing at the knees. She started to babble something, Max did not know what, when Chief Steward Dumont appeared at her elbow. "The Captain is waiting, Miss," he said firmly.

"Bother to the Captain! Oh, well—see you after dinner, Max." She headed for the Captain's table. Dumont touched Max's sleeve and murmured, "This way, sir."

His place was at the foot of the Chief Engineer's table. Max knew Mr. Compagnon by sight but had never spoken to him. The Chief glanced up and said, "Evening, Mr. Jones. Glad to have you with us. Ladies and gentlemen, our new astrogation officer, Mr. Jones. On your right, Mr. Jones, is Mrs. Daigler. Mr. Daigler on her right, then—" and so on, around the table: Dr. and Mrs. Weberbauer and their daughter Rebecca, Mr. and Mrs. Scott, a Mr. Arthur, Senhor and Senhora Vargas.

Mrs. Daigler thought it was *lovely*, his being promoted. And so *nice* to have more young people at the table. She was much older than Max but young enough to be handsome and aware of it. She wore more jewels than Max had ever seen and her hair was lacquered into a structure a foot high and studded with pearls. She was as perfectly finished and as expensive as a precision machine and she made Max uncomfortable.

But he was not yet as uncomfortable as he could be. Mrs. Daigler produced a wisp of a handkerchief from her bosom, moistened it and said, "Hold still, Mr. Jones." She scrubbed his cheek. "Turn your head." Blushing, Max complied.

"There, that's better," Mrs. Daigler announced. "Mama fixed." She turned away and said, "Don't you think, Mr. Compagnon, that science, with all the wonderful things they do these days, could discover a lip paint that wouldn't come off?"

"Stop it, Maggie," her husband interrupted. "Pay no attention, Mr. Jones. She's got a streak of sadism as wide as she is."

"George, you'll pay for that. Well, Chief?"

The Chief Engineer patted his lips with snowy linen. "I think it must already have been invented, but there was no market. Women like to brand men, even temporarily."

"Oh, bosh!"

"It's a woman's world, ma'am."

She turned to Max. "Eldreth is a dear, isn't she? I suppose you knew her 'dirtside'?—as Mr. Compagnon calls it."

"No, ma'am."

"Then how? I mean, after all, there isn't much opportunity. Or is there?"

"Maggie, stop pestering him. Let the man eat his dinner."

Mrs. Weberbauer on his other side was as easy and motherly as Mrs. Daigler was difficult. Under her soothing presence Max managed to start eating. Then he noticed that the way he grasped a fork was not the way the others did, tried to change, made a mess of it, became aware of his untidy nails, and wanted to crawl under the table. He ate about three hundred calories, mostly bread and butter.

At the end of the meal Mrs. Daigler again gave her attention to him, though she addressed the Chief Engineer. "Mr. Compagnon, isn't it customary to toast a promotion?"

"Yes," the Chief conceded. "But he must pay for it. That's a requirement."

Max found himself signing a chit presented by Dumont. The price made him blink—his first trip might be a professional success, but so far it had been financial disaster. Champagne, iced in a shiny bucket, accompanied the chit and Dumont cut the wires and drew the cork with a flourish.

The Chief Engineer stood up. "Ladies and gentle-men—I give you Astrogator Jones. May he never mis-place a decimal point!"

"Cheers!"—"Bravo!"—"Speech, speech!"

Max stumbled to his feet and muttered, "Thank you."

His first watch was at eight o'clock the next morn-ing. He ate breakfast alone and reflected happily that as a watch stander he would usually eat either before or after the passengers. He was in the control room a good twenty minutes early.

Kelly glanced up and said, "Good morning, sir."

Max gulped. "Er—good morning, Chief!" He caught Smythe grinning behind the computer, turned his eyes hastily away.

"Fresh coffee, Mr. Jones. Will you have a cup?" Max let Kelly pour for him; while they drank Kelly quietly went over the details—acceleration schedule, position and vector, power units in use, sights taken, no special orders, etc. Noguchi relieved Smythe, and shortly be-fore the hour Dr. Hendrix appeared.

"Good morning, sir."

"Good morning, Doctor."

"Morning." Hendrix accepted coffee, turned to Max. "Have you relieved the officer of the watch?"

"Uh, why no, sir."

"Then do so. It lacks less than a minute of eight."

Max turned to Kelly and shakily saluted. "I relieve you, sir."

"Very well, sir." Kelly went below at once. Dr. Hen-drix sat down, took out a book and started to read. Max realized with a chilly feeling that he had been pushed in, to swim or not. He took a deep breath and went over to Noguchi. "Noggy, let's get the plates ready for the middle o' watch sights."

Noguchi glanced at the chronometer. "As you say, sir."

"Well . . . I guess it is early. Let's take a few dop-plers."

"Aye aye, sir." Noguchi climbed out of the saddle where he had been loafing.

Max said in a low voice, "Look, Noggy, you don't have to say 'sir' to me."

Noguchi answered just as quietly. "Kelly wouldn't like it if I didn't. Better let it ride."

"Oh." Max frowned. "Noggy? How does the rest of the Worry gang feel about it?"

Noguchi did not pretend not to understand. He answered, "Shucks, they're all rooting for you, if you can swing it."

"You're sure?"

"Certain. Just as long as you don't try to make a big hairy thing out of yourself like—well, like some I could mention." The computerman added, "Maybe Kovak isn't exactly cheering. He's been having a watch of his own, you know—for the first time."

"He's sore?"

"Not exactly. He couldn't expect to keep it long anyhow, not with a transition coming up. He won't go out of his way to give you trouble, he'll be fair."

Max made a mental note to see what he could do to swing Kovak over to his side. The two manned the dopplerscope, took readings on stars forward of vector, checked what they found by spectrostellograph, and compared both with standard plates from the chart safe. At first Max had to remember that he was in charge; then he got so interested in fussy details of measurements that he was no longer self-conscious. At last Noguchi touched his sleeve. "Pushing ten o'clock, sir. I'd better get set up."

"Huh? Sure, go ahead." He reminded himself not to help Noggy; the chartsman has his prerogatives, too. But he checked the set up just as Hendrix always did, as Simes rarely did, and as Kelly sometimes did, depending on who had made it.

After they had gotten the new data Max programmed the problem on paper (there being plenty of time), then called it off to Noguchi at the computer.

He thumbed the book himself, there being no "numbers boy" available. The figures were as clear in his recollection as ever, but he obeyed Hendrix's injunction not to depend on memory.

The result worried him. They were not "in the groove." Not that the *Asgard* was far out, but the discrepancy was measurable. He checked what he had done, then had Noguchi run the problem again, using a different programming method. The result came out the same.

Sighing, he computed the correction and started to take it to Hendrix for approval. But the Astrogator still paid no attention; he sat at the console, reading a novel from the ship's library.

Max made up his mind. He went to the console and said, "Excuse me, sir. I need to get there for a moment." Hendrix got up without answering and found another seat. Max sat down and called the power room. "Control officer speaking. I intend to increase boost at eleven o'clock. Stand by for time check."

Hendrix must have heard him, he thought, but the Astrogator gave no sign. Max fed in the correction, set the control chronometer to execute his wishes at eleven plus-or-minus nothing.

Shortly before noon Simes showed up. Max had already written his own log, based on Noguchi's log, and had signed it "M. Jones." He had hesitated, then added "C. O. o/W." Simes went to Dr. Hendrix, saluted, and said, "Ready to relieve you, sir."

Hendrix spoke his first word since eight o'clock. "He's got it."

Simes looked non-plussed, then went to Max. "Ready to relieve you." Max recited off the situation data while Simes read the log and the order book. Simes interrupted him while he was still listing minor ship's data. "Okay, I relieve you. Get out of my control room, Mister." Max got out. Dr. Hendrix had already gone down.

Noguchi had loitered at the foot of the ladder. He caught Max's eye, made a circle with thumb and finger and nodded. Max grinned at him, started to ask a question; he wanted to know if that discrepancy was a booby trap, intentionally left in by Kelly. Then he decided that it would not be fitting; he'd ask Kelly himself, or figure it from the records. "Thanks, Noggy."

That watch turned out to be typical only in the one respect that Dr. Hendrix continued to require Max to be officer of the watch himself. He did not again keep quiet but rode Max steadily, drilling him hour after hour, requiring him to take sights and set up problems continuously, as if the *Asgard* were actually close to transition. He did not permit Max to program on paper but forced him to pretend that time was too short and that data must immediately go into the computer, be acted on at once. Max sweated, with remote controls in each fist and with Hendrix himself acting as "numbers boy." The Astrogator kept pushing him for speed, speed, and more speed—never at the sacrifice of accuracy, for any error was unforgivable. But the goal was always greater speed.

Once Max objected. "Sir, if you would let me put it right into the machine, I could cut it down a lot."

Hendrix snapped, "When you have your own control room, you can do that, if you think it wise. Now you'll do it *my* way."

Occasionally Kelly would take over as his supervisor. The Chief Computerman was formal, using such phrases as, "May I suggest, sir—" or "I think I'd do it this way, sir." But once he broke out with, "Confound it, Max! Don't ever pull a dumb stunt like that!"

Then he started to amend his remarks. Max grinned. "Please, Chief. For a moment you made me feel at home. Thanks."

Kelly looked sheepish. "I'm tired, I guess. I could do with a smoke and some java."

While they were resting Max noted that Lundy was out of earshot and said, "Chief? You know more than I'll ever learn. Why didn't *you* buck for astrogator? Didn't you ever get a chance?"

Kelly suddenly looked bleak. "I once did," he said stiffly. "Now I know my limitations." Max shut up, much embarrassed. Thereafter Kelly reverted to calling him Max whenever they were alone.

Max did not see Sam for more than a week after he moved up to Baker deck. Even then the encounter was chance; he ran across him outside the Purser's office. "Sam!"

"Good morning, sir!" Sam drew up in a smart salute with a broad grin on his face.

"Huh? 'Good morning, sir' my foot! How's it going, Sam?"

"Aren't you going to return my salute? In my official capacity I can report you, you know. The Captain is very, very fussy about ship's etiquette."

Max made a rude noise. "You can hold that salute until you freeze, you clown."

Sam relaxed. "Kid, I've been meaning to get up and congratulate you—but every time I find you're on watch. You must live in the Worry Hole."

"Pretty near. Look, I'll be off this evening until midnight. What do you say I stop down to see you?"

Sam shook his head. "I'll be busy."

"Busy how? You expecting a jail break? Or a riot, maybe?"

Sam answered soberly, "Kid, don't get me wrong—but you stick to your end of the ship and I'll stick to mine. No, no, keep quiet and listen. I'm as proud as if I had invented you. But you can't fraternize in crew's quarters, not even with the Chief Master-at-Arms. Not yet."

"Who'll know? Who's to care?"

"You know blamed well that Giordano would love to tell Kuiper that you didn't know how to behave like an officer—and Old Lady Kuiper would pass it along to the Purser. Take my advice. Have I ever thrown you a curve?"

Max dropped the matter, though he badly wanted a chin with Sam. He needed to tell him that his faked record had been breached and to consult with him as to probable consequences.

Of course, he considered as he returned to his state-room, there wasn't a thing to keep him from carrying out his orginal intention of jumping ship with Sam at Nova Terra—except that it was now no longer possible to imagine it. He was an officer.

They were approaching the middle transition; the control room went on watch-and-watch. But still Dr. Hendrix did not take the watch; Simes and Jones alternated. The Astrogator stood every watch with Max but required him to do the work and carry the responsibility himself. Max sweated it out and learned that practice problems and study of theory were nothing like having it matter when he had no way and no time to check. You had to be *right*, every time—and there was always doubt.

When, during the last twenty-four hours, the Worry gang went on continuous watch, Max thought that Dr. Hendrix would push him aside. But he did not. Simes was pushed aside, yes, but Max took the worry seat, with Hendrix bending over him and watching everything he did, but not interfering. "Great heavens!" Max thought. "Surely he isn't going to let me make this transition? I'm not ready for it, not yet. I'll never keep up."

But data was coming too fast for further worry; he had to keep processing it, see the answers, and make decisions. It was not until twenty minutes before transition that Hendrix pushed him aside without a word and took over. Max was still recovering when they burst through into a new sky.

The last approach-and-transition before Halcyon was much like the second. There were a couple of weeks of easy watches, headed by Simes, Jones, and Kovak, with both Kelly and Hendrix getting a little rest. Max liked it, both on and off watch. On watch he continued to practice, trying to achieve the inhuman speed of Dr. Hendrix. Off watch he slept and enjoyed himself. The Bifrost Lounge no longer terrified him. He now played three-dee with Ellie there, with Chipsie on his shoulder, giving advice. Ellie had long since waved her eyes at Captain Blaine and convinced him that a pet so well behaved, so well house-broken, and in particular so well mannered (she had trained the spider puppy to say, "Good morning, Captain," whenever it saw Blaine)—in all respects so civilized should not be forced to live in a cage.

Max had even learned to swap feeble repartee with Mrs. Daigler, thinking up remarks and waiting for a chance. Ellie was threatening to teach him to dance, although he managed to stall her until resumption of watch-and-watch before transition made it impossible.

Again he found himself shoved into the worry seat for the last part of the approach. This time Dr. Hendrix did not displace him until less than ten minutes before burst through.

On the easy drop down to Halcyon Ellie's determination won out. Max learned to dance. He found that he liked it. He had good rhythm, did not forget her instructions, and Ellie was a fragrant, pleasant armful. "I've done all I can," she announced at last. "You're the best dancer with two left feet I've ever met." She required him to dance with Rebecca Weberbauer and with Mrs. Daigler. Mrs. Daigler wasn't so bad after all, as long as she kept her mouth shut—and Rebecca was cute. He began to look forward to the fleshpots of Halcyon, that being Ellie's stated reason for instructing him; he was to be conscripted as her escort.

Only one thing marred the final leg; Sam was in trouble. Max did not find out about it until after the trouble broke. He got up early to go on watch and found Sam cleaning decks in the silent passages of passenger quarters. He was in dungarees and wearing no shield. "Sam!"

Sam looked up, "Oh. Hi, kid. Keep your voice down, you'll wake people."

"But Sam, what in Ned are you doing?"

"Me? I seem to be manicuring this deck."

"But why?"

Sam leaned on his broom. "Well, kid, it's like this. The Captain and I had a difference of opinion. He won."

"You've been busted?"

"Your intuition is dazzling."

"What happened?"

"Max, the less you know about it the better. Don't fret. *Sic transit gloria mundi*—Tuesday is usually worse."

"But— See here, I've got to grab chow and go on watch. I'll look you up later."

"Don't."

Max got the story from Noguchi. Sam, it appeared, had set up a casino in an empty storeroom. He might have gotten away with it indefinitely had it remained a cards-and-dice set up, with a rake off for the house— the "house" being the Chief Master-at-Arms. But Sam had added a roulette wheel and that had been his downfall; Giordano had come to suspect that the wheel had less of the element of chance than was customary in better-run gambling halls—and had voiced his suspicion to Chief Clerk Kuiper. From there events took an inevitable course.

"When did he put in this wheel?"

"Right after we raised from Garson's Planet." Max thought uncomfortably of the "tea cozies" he had helped Sam bring aboard there. Noguchi went on, "Uh, didn't you know, sir? I thought you and him were pretty close before—you know, before you moved up decks."

Max avoided an answer and dug into the log. He found it under the previous day, added by Bennett to Simes' log. Sam was restricted to the ship for the rest of the trip, final disciplinary action postponed until return to Terra.

That last seemed to mean that Captain Blaine intended to give Sam a chance to show good behavior before making his recommendation to the guilds—the Captain was a sweet old guy, he certainly was. But "restricted"? Then Sam would never get his chance to run away from whatever it was he was running away from. He located Sam as soon as he was off watch, digging him out of his bunkroom and taking him out into the corridor.

Sam looked at him sourly. "I thought I told you not to look me up?"

"Never mind! Sam, I'm worried about you. This 'restricted' angle . . . it means you won't have a chance to—"

"*Shut up!*" It was a whisper but Max shut up. "Now look here," Sam went on, "Forget it. I got my stake and that's the important point."

"But . . ."

"Do you think they can seal this ship tight enough to keep me in when I decide to leave? Now stay away from me. You're teacher's pet and I want to keep it that way. I don't want you lectured about bad companions, meaning me."

"But I want to help, Sam. I . . ."

"Will you kindly get up above 'C' deck where you belong?"

He did not see Sam again that leg; presently he stopped worrying about it. Hendrix required him to compute the planetary approach—child's play compared with a transition—then placed Max at the conn when they grounded. This was a titulary responsibility since it was precomputed and done on radar-automatic. Max sat with the controls under his hands, ready to override the autopilot—and Hendrix stood behind him, ready to override him—but there was no need; the *Asgard* came down by the plotted curve as easy as descending stairs. The thrust beams bit in and Max reported, "Grounded, sir, on schedule.

"Secure."

Max spoke into the ship's announcers. "Secure power room. Secure all space details. Dirtside routine, second section."

Of the four days they were there he spent the first three nominally supervising, and actually learning from, Kovak in the routine ninety-day inspection and overhaul of control room instruments. Ellie was vexed with him, as she had had different plans. But on the last day he hit dirt with her, chaperoned by Mr. and Mrs. Mendoza.

It was a wonderful holiday. Compared with Terra, Halcyon is a bleak place and Bonaparte is not much of a city. Nevertheless Halcyon is an earth-type planet with breathable air, and the party from the *Asgard* had not set foot outdoors since Earthport, months of time and unthinkable light-years behind. The season was postaphelion, midsummer, Nu Pegasi burned warm and bright in blue sky. Mr. Mendoza hired a carriage and they drove out into green, rolling countryside behind four snuffling little Halcyon ponies. There they visited a native pueblo, a great beehive structure of mud, conoid on conoid, and bought souvenirs—two of which turned out to have "Made in Japan" stamped inconspicuously on them.

Their driver, Herr Eisenberg, interpreted for them. The native who sold the souvenirs kept swiveling his eyes, one after another, at Mrs. Mendoza. He twittered some remarks to the driver, who guffawed. "What does he say?" she asked.

"He was complimenting you."

"So? But how?"

"Well . . . he says you are for a slow fire and no need for seasoning; you'd cook up nicely. And he'd do it, too," the colonist added, "if you stayed here after dark."

Mrs. Mendoza gave a little scream. "You didn't tell us they were *cannibals.* Josie, take me back!"

Herr Eisenberg looked horrified. "Cannibals? Oh, no, lady! They don't eat each other, they just eat us—when they can get us, that is. But there hasn't been an incident in twenty years."

"But that's worse!"

"No, it isn't, lady. Look at it from their viewpoint.

They're civilized. This old fellow would never break one of their laws. But to them we are just so much prime beef, unfortunately hard to catch."

"Take us back at once! Why, there are hundreds of them, and only five of us."

"Thousands, lady. But you are safe as long as Gneeri is shining." He gestured at Nu Pegasi. "It's bad juju to kill meat during daylight. The spirit stays around to haunt."

Despite his reassurances the party started back. Max noticed that Eldreth had been unfrightened. He himself had wondered what had kept the natives from tying them up until dark.

They dined at the Josephine, Bonaparte's best (and only) hotel. But there was a real three-piece orchestra, a dance floor, and food that was at least a welcome change from the menus of the Bifrost Lounge. Many ship's passengers and several officers were there; it made a jolly party. Ellie made Max dance between each course. He even got up his nerve to ask Mrs. Daigler for a dance, once she came over and suggested it.

During the intermission Eldreth steered him out on the adjacent balcony. There she looked up at him. "You leave that Daigler hussy alone, hear me?"

"Huh? I didn't do anything."

She suddenly smiled warmly. "Of course not, you big sweet ninny. But Ellie has to take care of you." She turned and leaned on the rail. Halcyon's early night had fallen, her three moons were chasing each other. The sky blazed with more stars than can be seen in Terra's lonely neighborhood. Max pointed out the strange constellations and showed her the departure direction they would take tomorrow to reach transition for Nova Terra. He had learned four new skies so far, knew them as well as he knew the one that hung over the Ozarks—and he would learn many more. He was already studying, from the charts, other skies they would be in this trip.

"Oh, Max, isn't it *lovely!*"

"Sure is. Say, there's a meteor. They're scarce here, mighty scarce."

"Make a wish! Make a wish quick!"

"Okay." He wished that he would get off easy when it came to the showdown. Then he decided that wasn't right; he ought to wish old Sam out of his jam—not that he believed in it, either way.

She turned and faced him. "What did you wish?"

"Huh?" He was suddenly self-conscious. "Oh, mustn't tell, that spoils it."

"All right. But I'll bet you get your wish," she added softly.

He thought for a moment that he could have kissed her, right then, if he had played his cards right. But the moment passed and they went inside. The feeling stayed with him on the ride back, made him elated. It was a good old world, even if there were some tough spots. Here he was, practically a junior astrogator on his first trip—and it hadn't been more than weeks since he was borrowing McAllister's mules to work the crop and going barefooted a lot to save shoes.

And yet here he was in uniform, riding beside the best-dressed girl in four planets.

He fingered the insignia on his chest. Marrying Ellie wasn't such an impossible idea now that he was an officer—if he ever decided to marry. Maybe her old man wouldn't consider an officer—and an astrogator at that—completely ineligible. Ellie wasn't bad; she had spunk and she played a fair game of three-dee—most girls wouldn't even be able to learn the rules.

He was still in a warm glow when they reached the ship and were hoisted in.

Kelly met him at the lock. "Mr. Jones—the Captain wants to see you."

"Huh? Oh. G'night, Ellie—I'll have to run." He hurried after Kelly. "What's up?"

"Dr. Hendrix is dead."

# 13

# TRANSITION

Max questioned Kelly as they hurried up to the Captain's cabin.

"I don't know. I just don't know, Max." Kelly seemed close to tears. "I saw him before dinner—he came into the Hole to check what you and Kovak have been doing. He seemed all right. But the Purser found him dead in his bunk, the middle of the evening." He added worriedly, "I don't know what is going to happen now."

"What do you mean?"

"Well . . . if I was captain, I'd lay over and send for a relief. But I don't know."

For the first time Max realized that this change would make Mr. Simes the astrogator. "How long would it take to get a relief?"

"Figure it out. The *Dragon* is about three months behind us; she'd pick up our mail. A year about." In the contradictions of interstellar travel the ships themselves were the fastest method of communication; a radio message (had such a silly thing been attempted) would have taken more than two centuries to reach Earth, a like time for a reply.

Max found the Captain's cabin open and crowded with officers, all standing around, saying nothing, and looking solemn; he slipped inside without announcing himself and tried to be inconspicuous. Kelly did not go in. Captain Blaine sat at his desk with head bent. Several stragglers, members of the gay party at the Josephine, arrived after Max; First Officer Walther checked them off with his eyes, then said quietly to Blaine, "Ship's officers all present, sir."

Captain Blaine raised his head and Max was shocked to see how old he looked. "Gentlemen," he said in a low voice, "you know the sad news. Dr. Hendrix was found dead in his room this evening. Heart attack. The Surgeon tells me that he passed on about two hours before he was found—and that his death was probably almost painless."

His voice broke, then he continued. "Brother Hendrix will be placed in his last orbit two hours after we raise ship tomorrow. That is how he would have wished it, the Galaxy was his home. He gave unstintingly of himself that men should ride safely among the stars."

He paused so long that Max thought that the old man had forgotten that others were present. But when he resumed his voice was almost brisk. "That is all, gentlemen. Astrogators will please remain."

Max was not sure that he counted as an astrogator but the use of the plural decided him. First Officer Walther started to leave; Blaine called him back. When the four were alone, the Captain said, "Mr. Simes, you will take over head-of-department duties at once. Mr., uh . . ."; his eyes rested on Max.

"Jones, sir."

"Mr. Jones will assume your routine duties, of course. This tragedy leaves you short-handed; for the rest of this trip I will stand a regular watch."

Simes spoke up. "That isn't necessary, Captain. We'll make out."

"Perhaps. But those are my wishes."

"Aye aye, sir."

"Prepare to lift on schedule. Any questions?"

"No, sir."

"Goodnight, gentlemen. Dutch, stay a moment, please?"

Outside the door Simes started to turn away; Max stopped him. "Mr. Simes?"

"Huh? Yes?"

"Any instructions for me, sir?"

Simes looked him over. "You stand your watch, Mister. I'll handle everything else."

The next morning Max found a crepe armband on his desk and a notice from the First Officer that mourning would continue for one week. The *Asgard* raised

on schedule, with the Captain sitting quietly in his
chair, with Simes at the control console. Max stood
near the Captain, with nothing to do. Aside from the
absence of Hendrix all was routine—except that Kelly
was quite bad-tempered. Simes, Max admitted, handled the maneuver smartly—but it was precomputed,
anyone could have done it; shucks, Ellie could have
been sitting there. Or Chipsie.

Max had the first watch. Simes left him after en-
joining him not to deviate from schedule without
phoning him first. An hour later Kovak relieved Max
temporarily and Max hurried to the passenger lock.
There were five honorary pall bearers, the Captain,
Mr. Walther, Simes, Max, and Kelly. Behind them,
crowding the passageways, were officers and most of
the crew. Max saw no passengers.

The inner door of the lock was opened; two steward's mates carried the body in and placed it against
the outer door. Max was relieved to see that it had
been wrapped in a shroud covering it completely.
They closed the inner door and withdrew.

The Captain stood facing the door, with Simes and
the First Officer standing guard on one side of the
door and, on the other side facing them, Max and Kelly. The Captain flung one word over his shoulder:
"Pressure!"

Behind stood Bennett wearing a portable phone; he
relayed the word to the power room. The pressure
gauge over the lock door showed one atmosphere;
now it started to crawl upward. The Captain took a little book from his pocket and began to read the service
for the dead. Feeling that he could not stand to listen
Max watched the pressure gauge. Steadily it climbed.
Max reflected that the ship had already passed escape
speed for the Nu Pegasi system before he had been relieved; the body would take an open orbit.

The gauge reached ten atmospheres; Captain
Blaine closed his book. "Warn the passengers," he said
to Bennett.

Shortly the loudspeakers sounded: "All hands! All

passengers! The ship will be in free fall for thirty seconds. Anchor yourselves and do not change position."
Max reached behind him, found one of the many hand holds always present around an airlock and pulled down so that his grip would keep his feet in contact with the deck. A warning siren howled—then suddenly he was weightless as the ship's boost and the artificial anomalous gravity field were both cut out.

He heard the Captain say loudly and firmly, " 'Ashes to ashes, dust to dust.' Let the body be cast forth."

The pressure gauge dropped suddenly to zero and Dr. Hendrix was launched into space, there to roam the stars for all eternity.

Max felt weight again as the power room brought them back to ship-normal. The pressure gauge showed gradually building pressure. People turned away and left, their voices murmuring low. Max went up and relieved the watch.

The following morning Simes moved into Dr. Hendrix's cabin. There was trouble with First Officer Walther about it—Max heard only third-hand reports—but the Captain upheld Simes; he stayed in the Astrogator's quarters. The Worry Hole settled into routine not much different from what had gone before, except that Simes' personality spread through everything. There had never been a posted watch list before; Kelly had always assigned the crewmen and the Doctor had simply informed the top-watch standers orally of his wishes. Now a typed list appeared:

FIRST WATCH Randolph Simes, Astrogator
SECOND WATCH Captain Blaine
    ( M. Jones, acting apprentice, under instruction )
THIRD WATCH Kelly, Ch. Cmptrmn.
    *(signed)* Randolph Simes, Astrogator

Below was a four-watch list for crewmen, also signed by Simes.
Max looked at it and shrugged it off. It was obvious

that Simes had it in for him, though he could not figure out why. It was equally obvious that Simes did not intend to let him do any astrogation and that Max's chances of being accepted in time as a full-fledged brother had now, with the death of Dr. Hendrix, sunk to zero. Unless, of course, Captain Blaine overrode Simes and forced a favorable report, which was extremely unlikely. Max again began to think of going along with Sam at Nova Terra.

Well, in the meantime he'd stand his watches and try to stay out of trouble. That was that.

There was only one transition to be made between Halcyon and Nova Terra, a leap of ninety-seven light-years three weeks out from Halcyon at a boost of seventeen gravities—the boost always depended on the distance from the star to the gateway, since the purpose was to arrive there just under the speed of light. The Worry Hole stayed on a watch in three for the officers and one in four for crewmen for the first two weeks. Captain Blaine showed up each watch but seemed quite willing for Max to carry out the light duties of that portion of the leg. He gave little instruction—when he did, he was likely to wander off into anecdotes, amusing but not useful.

Max tried to continue his own drill, carrying out the routine middle o' watch computation as if it were the frantic matter it would have been near transition. Captain Blaine watched him, then said mildly, "Don't get yourself into a state, son. Always program on paper when possible—always. And take time to check. Hurrying causes mistakes." Max said nothing, thinking of Dr. Hendrix, but carried out the orders.

At the end of his first watch under the Captain Max signed the log as usual. When Simes came on watch four hours later, Max was dug out of bed and required to report to the control room. Simes pointed to the log. "What's the idea, Mister?"

"Of what, sir?"

"Signing the log. You weren't officer of the watch."

"Well, sir, the Captain seemed to expect it. I've

signed a lot of logs and he's always approved them in the past."

"Hmm— I'll speak to the Captain. Go below."

At the end of his next watch, having received no instructions, Max prepared the log and took it to the Captain. "Sir? Do you want to sign this? Or shall I?"

"Eh?" Blaine looked at it. "Oh, I suppose I had better. Always let a head of department do things his own way if possible. Remember that when you are a skipper, son." He signed it.

That settled it until the Captain started a habit of not being there, first for short periods, then for longer. The time came when he was absent at the end of the watch; Max phoned Mr. Simes. "Sir, the Captain isn't here. What do you want me to do?"

"So what? It's his privilege to leave the control room."

"But Kelly is ready to relieve and the log isn't signed. Shall I sign it? Or shall I phone him?"

"Phone him? Jumping jeepers, no! Are you crazy?"

"What are your orders, sir?"

Simes was silent, then answered, "Print his name, then sign under it 'By direction'—and after this use your head."

They changed to watch-and-watch for the last week. Max continued under the Captain; Kelly assisted Simes. Once the shift was made Blaine became meticulous about being present in the control room and, when Max started to make the first computation, gently pushed him aside. "I had better take over, lad. We're getting closer now."

So Max assisted him—and became horrifyingly aware that the Captain was not the man he must once have been. His knowledge of theory was sound and he knew all the short cuts—but his mind tended to wander. Twice in one computation Max had to remind him diplomatically of details. Yet the Old Man seemed unaware of it, was quite cheerful.

It went on that way. Max began to pray that the Captain would let the new Astrogator make the transi-

tion himself—much as he despised Simes. He wanted
to discuss his misgivings with Kelly—there was no one
else with whom it would have been possible—but Kelly was on the opposite watch with Simes. There was
nothing to do but worry.

When the last day arrived he discovered that Captain Blaine neither intended to take the ship through
himself nor to let Simes do it; he had a system of his
own. When they were all in the Worry Hole the Captain said, "I want to show you all a wrinkle that takes
the strain out of astrogating. With no reflections on
our dear brother, Dr. Hendrix, while he was a great
astrogator, none better—nevertheless he worked too
hard. Now here is a method taught me by my own
master. Kelly, if you will have the remote controls led
out, please."

He had them seat themselves in a half circle, himself, Simes, and Max, around the saddle of the computer, with Kelly in the saddle. Each of them was
armed with programming forms and Captain Blaine
held the remote-control switches in his lap. "Now the
idea is for us each to work a sight in succession, first
me, then Mr. Simes, then Mr. Jones. That way we
keep the data flowing without strain. All right, lads,
start pitching. Transition stations everyone."

They made a dry run, then the Captain stood up.
"Call me, Mr. Simes, two hours before transition. I believe you and Mr. Jones will find that this method
gives you enough rest in the meantime."

"Yes, sir. But Captain—may I make a suggestion?"

"Eh? Certainly, sir."

"This is a fine system, but I suggest that Kelly be
put in the astrogating group instead of Jones. Jones is
not experienced. We can put Kovak in the saddle and
Lundy on the book."

Blaine shook his head. "No. Accuracy is everything,
sir, so we must have our best operator at the computer. As for Mr. Jones, this is how he must get experience—if he gets rattled, you and I can always fill in
for him." He started to leave, then added, "But Kovak

can alternate with Kelly until I return. Mustn't have anyone getting tired, that way mistakes are made."

"Aye aye, sir."

Simes said nothing more to Max. They started working sights, alternately, using written programming on printed forms. The sights were coming in on a twenty-minute schedule, giving each of them forty minutes for a problem if he cared to take it. Max began to think that the Captain's method did have its points. Certainly Dr. Hendrix had worked himself to death—ships did not wear out but men did.

He had plenty of time to work not only his own problems, but those of Simes. The data came out orally and there was nothing to keep Max from programming Simes' sights in his head and checking on what went into the computer. So far as he could see Simes was doing all right—though of course there was no real strain involved, not yet.

They ate sandwiches and drank coffee where they sat, leaving their seats only for five minutes or so at a time. Captain Blaine showed up twenty minutes early. He smiled and said cheerily, "Everyone happy and relaxed? Now we really get down to it. I have just time for a cup of coffee."

A few minutes later he sat down and took over the control switches from Simes. The sights were coming through on a ten-minute schedule now, still ample time. Max continued to work them all, his own on paper and the others in his head. He was always through in time to catch the data for the next sight, program it mentally and check translations as Lundy thumbed the book. It gave him a running picture of how closely they were in the groove, how much hunting they were having to do in approaching their invisible target. It seemed to him that Simes tended to overcorrect and that the Captain was somewhat optimistically under-correcting, but neither was so far out as to endanger the ship.

Maybe he was wrong about the Captain—the Old Man seemed to steady down when it mattered. His own corrections, he was glad to see, the Captain applied without question.

After more than an hour with transition forty-five minutes away Captain Blaine looked up and said, "All right, boys, we're getting close. Slam them to us as fast as you can now."

Smythe and Kovak, with Noguchi and Bennett running for them, slipped into high gear; data poured out in a steady stream. Max continued to work every sight, programming his own in his head and calling off figures faster than he wrote them down. He noticed that Simes was sweating, sometimes erasing and starting over. But the figures Simes called out agreed with what Max thought they should be, from his own mental programming. Captain Blaine seemed relaxed, though he had not speeded up materially and sometimes was still using the computer when Max was ready to pour his sight into it.

At one point Simes spoke too rapidly, slurring his figures, Lundy promptly said, "Repeat, sir!"

"Confound it! Clean out your ears!" But Simes repeated. The Captain glanced up, then bent back to his own problem. As soon as the computer was free Captain Blaine called his own figures to Lundy. Max had already set up the Captain's sight in his mind, was subconsciously listening while watching Simes.

An alarm bell rang in his mind. "Captain! I don't check you!"

Captain Blaine stopped. "Eh?"

"That program is wrong, sir."

The Captain did not seem angry. He simply handed his programming board to Simes. "Check me, sir."

Simes glanced quickly at the figures. "I check you, sir!"

Blaine said, "Drop out, Jones. Mr. Simes and I will finish."

"But—"

"Drop out, Mister!"

Max got out of the circle, seething inside. Simes'

check of the Captain's set up hadn't meant anything, unless Simes had listened to and remembered (as Max had) the data as it came in. The Captain had transposed an eight and a three in the fifth and sixth decimal places—the set up would look okay unless one knew the correct figures. If Simes had even bothered to check it, he added bitterly.

But Max could not keep from noting and processing the data in his mind. Simes' next sight should catch the Captain's error; his correction should repair it. It would be a big correction, Max knew; traveling just under the speed of light the ship clipped a million miles in less than six seconds.

Max could see Simes hesitate as the lights from his next sight popped up on the computer and Lundy translated them back. Why, the man looked frightened! The correction called for would push the ship extremely close to critical speed—Simes paused, then ordered less than half the amount that Max believed was needed.

Blaine applied it and went on with his next problem. When the answer came out the error, multiplied by time and unthinkable velocity, was more glaring than ever. The Captain threw Simes a glance of astonishment, then promptly made a correction. Max could not tell what it was, since it was done without words by means of the switch in his lap.

Simes licked the dryness from his lips. "Captain?"

"Time for just one more sight," Blaine answered. "I'll take it myself, Mr. Simes."

The data were passed to him, he started to lay his problem out on the form. Max saw him erase, then look up; Max followed his gaze. The pre-set on the chronometer above the computer showed the seconds trickling away. "Stand by!" Blaine announced.

Max looked up. The stars were doing the crawling together that marked the last moments before transition. Captain Blaine must have pressed the second switch, the one that would kick them over, while Max was watching, for the stars suddenly blinked out and were replaced instantaneously by another starry firmament, normal in appearance.

The Captain lounged back, looked up. "Well," he said happily, "I see we made it again." He got up and headed for the hatch, saying over his shoulder, "Call me when you have laid us in the groove, Mr. Simes." He disappeared down the hatch.

Max looked up again, trying to recall from the charts he had studied just what piece of this new sky they were facing. Kelly was looking up, too. "Yes, we came through," Max heard him mutter. "But *where?*"

Simes also had been looking at the sky. Now he swung around angrily. "What do you mean?"

"What I said," Kelly insisted. "That's not any sky I ever saw before."

"Nonsense, man! You just haven't oriented yourself. Everybody knows that a piece of sky can look strange when you first glance at it. Get out the flat charts for this area; we'll find our landmarks quickly enough."

"They are out, sir. Noguchi."

It took only minutes to convince everyone else in the control room that Kelly was right, only a little longer to convince even Simes. He finally looked up from the charts with a face greenish white. "Not a word to anybody," he said. "That's an order—and I'll bust any man who slips. Kelly, take the watch."

"Aye aye, sir."

"I'll be in the Captain's cabin." He went below to tell Blaine that the *Asgard* had come out in unknown space—was lost.

# 14

## ANYWHERE

Two hours later Max climbed wearily up into the Worry Hole. He had just had a bad half hour, telling the truth as he saw it. Captain Blaine had been disinclined to blame anyone but himself, but had seemed stunned and bewildered. Simes had been nasty. His unstated logic seemed to be that, since it could not possibly be his fault and since it was unthinkable to blame the Captain, it must be Max's fault. Since Max had been relieved some minutes before transition, his theory seemed to be that Max had caused it by making a disturbance as they were approaching the critical instant—joggled their elbows, so to speak.

Mr. Walther had been present, a mute judge. They spoke of matters outside his profession; he had seemed to be studying their faces. Max had stuck doggedly to his story.

He found Kelly still on watch. Kovak and Smythe were taking spectrograms; Noguchi and Lundy were busy with papers. "Want to be relieved?" he said to Kelly.

Kelly looked troubled. "I'm sorry, but you can't."

"Huh?"

"Mr. Simes phoned while you were on your way up. He says you are not to stand duty until further notice."

"He did? Well, I'm not surprised."

"He also said that you were to stay out of the control room."

Max made a violent statement about Simes. He added, "Well, it was nice while it lasted. Be seeing you."

He turned away but Kelly stopped him. "Don't be in a hurry, Max. He won't be up for a while. I want to know what happened. From the computer I can't tell what goes on."

Max told him, drawing on his memory for the figures. Kelly nodded at last. "That confirms what I've been able to dig out. The Captain flubbed with a transposition—easy to do. Then Simes didn't have the guts to make a big correction when it came around to him. But one more thing you don't know. Neither do they—yet."

"Huh? What?"

"The power room recorder shows it. Guenther had the watch down there and gave it to me over the phone. No, I didn't tell him anything was wrong. I just asked for the record; that's not unusual. By the way, any excitement down below? Passengers blowing their tops?"

"Not when I came up."

"Won't be long. They can't keep this quiet forever. Back to my story—things were already sour but the Captain had one last chance. He applied the correction and a whopping big one. But he applied it with the wrong sign, just backwards."

Profanity was too weak. All Max could say was, "Oh, my!"

"Yeah. Well, there's the devil to pay and him out to lunch."

"Any idea where we are?"

Kelly pointed to Kovak and Smythe at the spectro-stellograph. "They're fishing, but no bites. Bright stars first, B-types and O's. But there is nothing that matches the catalogues so far."

Noguchi and Lundy were using a hand camera. Max asked, "What are *they* doing?"

"Photographing the records. All of 'em—programming sheets, the rough data from the chartsmen, the computer tape, everything."

"What good will that do?"

"Maybe none. But sometimes records get lost. Sometimes they even get changed. But not this time. I'm going to have a set of my own."

The unpleasant implications of Kelly's comments were sinking into Max's mind when Noguchi looked up. "That's all, Boss."

"Good." Kelly turned to Max. "Do me a favor. Stick

those films in your pocket and take them with you. I want them out of here. I'll pick them up later."

"Well . . . all right." While Noguchi was unloading the camera Max added to Kelly, "How long do you think it will take to figure out where we are, checking spectra?"

Kelly looked more troubled than ever. "Max, what makes you think there is anything to find?"

"I don't follow you."

"Why should anything out there . . ." He made a sweeping gesture. ". . . match up with any charts we've got here?"

"You mean," Max said slowly, "that we might not be in our own galaxy at all? Maybe in another, like the Andromeda Nebula, say?"

"Maybe. But that's not all. Look, Max, I'm no theoretical physicist, that's sure, but so far as I know all that theory says is that when you pass the speed of light you have to go out of your own space, somewhere else. You've become irrelevant and it won't hold you. But *where* you go, unless you are set just right for a Horst congruency, that's another matter. The theory doesn't say. Does it?"

Max's head started to ache. "Gee, I don't know."

"Neither do I. But since we weren't set to duck back into our own space at another point, we may be anywhere. And I mean *anywhere*. We may be in some other space-time totally unconnected with our own." He glanced up at the strange stars.

Max went below feeling worse than ever. He passed Simes going up; the Astrogator scowled at him but did not say anything. When Max reached his stateroom he put the films in a drawer—then thought about it, removed the drawer and cached them in dead space behind the drawer.

Max stayed in his room and worried. He fretted over being kept out of the control room, wanting very badly himself to check the sky for known stars. B- and O-type stars—well, that was all right, but there were

half a dozen other ways. Globular star clusters, now—
they'd be easy to identify; snag four of them and you'd
know where you were as clear as reading a street
sign. Then it would be just a case of fining it down,
because you'd know what to look for and where. After
which you'd high-tail it for the nearest charted congruency, whether it took you a week or a year. The
ship couldn't *really* be lost.

But suppose they weren't even in the right galaxy?

The thought dismayed him. If that were the case,
they'd never get home before the end of time. It was
chased out by another thought—suppose Kelly's suspicion had been correct, that this was an entirely
different universe, another system of space and time?
What then? He had read enough philosophical fancies
to know that there was no theoretical reason for such
to be impossible; the Designer might have created an
infinity of universes, perhaps all pretty much alike—or
perhaps as different as cheese and Wednesday. Mil-
lions, billions of them, all side by side from a multi-
dimensional point of view.

Another universe might have different laws, a
different speed of light, different gravitational ballis-
tics, a different time rate—why they might get back to
find that ten million years had passed and Earth burnt
to a cinder!

But the light over his desk burned steadily, his heart
pumped as always, obeying familiar laws of hydrau-
lics, his chair pressed up against him—if this was a
different sort of space the differences weren't obvious.
And if it *was* a different universe, there was nothing to
be done about it.

A knock came at the door, he let Kelly in and gave
him the chair, himself sitting on the bed. "Any news?"

"No. Golly I'm tired. Got those pix?"

Max took out the drawer, fished around behind it,
gave them to Kelly. "Look, Chief, I got an idea."

"Spill it."

"Let's assume that we're in the right galaxy, because—"

"Because if we ain't, there isn't any point in trying!"

"Well, yes. All right, we're in the Milky Way. So we look around, make quick sample star counts and estimate the distance and direction of the center. Then we try to identify spectra of stars in that direction, after deciding what ones we ought to look for and figuring apparent magnitudes for estimated distance. That would . . ."

"—save a lot of time," Kelly finished wea. ily. "Don't teach your grandpop how to suck eggs. What the deuce do you think I've been doing?"

"Oh. Sorry."

"Don't be. It's more than our revered boss thought of. While I been trying to work he's been bellyachin' around, finding fault, and trying to get me to say that he was dead right in everything—worrying about himself instead of worrying about his ship. Pfui! By the way, he grabbed the records just like I thought he would—'to show the Captain.' *He* says." Kelly stood up. "I'd better go."

"Don't rush. I'll ring for coffee."

"Running out of my ears now." Kelly took the films from his pocket and looked at them dutifully. "I had Noggy make two shots of everything; this is a double set. That's a good hidey-hole you've got. What say we stick one set in there and let it cool? Never can tell."

"Kelly, you aren't really expecting trouble over those records? Seems to me we've got trouble enough with the ship being lost."

"Huh? Max, you're going to make a good officer some day. But you're innocent. Now I'm a suspenders *and* belt man. I like to take as few chances as possible. Doc Hendrix—rest his soul!—was the same way." Kelly waited until Max had returned the spare set to the space back of the drawer, then started to leave. He paused.

"One thing I forgot to tell you, Max. We happened to come out pretty close to a star and a G-type at that."

"Oh." Max considered it. "Not one we know?"

"Of course not, or I would have said so. Haven't sized it yet, but figuring normal range in the G's we could reach it in not less than four weeks, not more than a year, at high boost. Thought you'd like to know."

"Well, yes. Thanks. But I can't see that it makes much difference."

"No? Doesn't it seem like a good idea to have a Sol-type star, with maybe Earth-type planets around it, not far off?"

"Well . . ."

"It does to me. The Adam-and-Eve business is rugged at best—and we might be in for a long stay." With that he left.

No steward's mate came to tell Max it was time for dinner; when he noticed that it was past time, he went to the lounge. Most of the passengers were already seated, although some were standing around talking. It was impossible to miss the feeling of unrest in the room. Max saw that the Captain was not at his table, nor was Mr. Walther at his. As he headed for his own table a Mr. Hornsby tried to grab his arm. Max shook him off. "Sorry, sir. I'm in a hurry."

"Wait a minute! I want to ask you . . ."

"Sorry." He hurried on and sat down. Chief Engineer Compagnon was not at the table, but the usual passengers were present. Max said, "Good evening," and reached for his soup spoon, just to keep busy.

There was no soup to be toyed with, nor were there rolls and butter on the table, although it was ten minutes past the hour. Such things simply did not happen in Chief Steward Dumont's jurisdiction. Come to think about it, Dumont was not in sight.

Mrs. Daigler put a hand on his arm. "Max? Tell me, dear—what is this silly rumor going around?"

Max tried to maintain a poker face. "What rumor, ma'am?"

"You must have heard it! After all, you're in astroga-tion. They say that the Captain turned the wrong corner or something and that we're falling into a star."

Max tried to give a convincing chuckle. "Who told you that? Whoever it was probably couldn't tell a star from his elbow."

"You wouldn't fool your Aunt Maggie?"

"I can assure you positively that the *Asgard* is not falling into a star. Not even a small star." He turned in his chair. "But it does look like something's fallen into the galley. Dinner is awfully late."

He remained turned, trying to avoid further questions. It did not work. Mr. Arthur called out sharply, "Mr. Jones!"

He turned back. "Yes?"

"Why stall us? I have been informed authoritatively that the ship is lost."

Max tried to look puzzled. "I don't follow you. We seem to be in it."

Mr. Arthur snorted. "You know what I mean! Something went wrong with that whatyoumucallit—transition. We're lost."

Max put on a school-teacherish manner, ticking off points on his fingers. "Mr. Arthur, I assure you that the ship is in absolutely no danger. As for being lost, I assure you just as firmly that if we are, the Captain neglected to tell me so. I was in the control room at transition and he seemed quite satisfied with it. Would you mind telling me who has been spreading this story? It's a serious thing, starting such rumors. People have been known to panic."

"Well . . . it was one of the crew. I don't know his name."

Max nodded. "I thought so. Now in my experience in space . . ." He went on, quoting from his uncle. ". . . I have learned that the only thing faster than light is the speed with which a story can spread through a ship. It doesn't have to have any foundation, it spreads just the same." He looked around again. "I wonder what has happened to dinner? I'd hate to go on watch hungry."

Mrs. Weberbauer said nervously, "Then we are all right, Maxie?"

"We're all right, ma'am."

Mrs. Daigler leaned toward him again and whispered, "Then why are you sweating, Max?"

He was saved by a steward's mate rushing up to the table and starting to deal out plates of soup. Max stopped him when he came around and said quietly, "Jim, where's Dumont?"

Out of the corner of his mouth the waiter said, "Cooking."

"Huh? Where's the chef?"

The steward's mate leaned down and whispered, "Frenchy is boiled as a judge. I guess he couldn't take it. You know."

Max let him go. Mr. Arthur said sharply, "What did he tell you?"

"I was trying to find out what went wrong in the galley," Max answered. "Seems the cook incapacitated himself." He spooned up a mouthful of the soup. "From the taste I'd say he had burned his thumb in this so-called chowder. Pretty bad, isn't it?"

Max was saved from further evasions by the arrival of the First Officer. Mr. Walther went to the Captain's table and banged on a glass with a spoon. "Your attention, please!"

He waited for quiet, then took a paper from his pocket. "I have an announcement to make on behalf of the Captain. Those of you who are familiar with the theory of astrogation are aware that space is changing constantly, due to the motions of the stars, and that consequently no two trips are exactly alike. Sometimes it is necessary, for this reason, to make certain changes in a ship's routing. Such a circumstance has arisen in this present trip and the *Asgard* will be somewhat delayed in reaching her next destination. We regret this, but we can't change the laws of nature. We hope that you will treat it as a minor inconvenience—or even as additional vacation, in the friendly and comfortable atmosphere of our ship. Please remember, too, that the insurance policy accompanying your ticket covers you completely against loss or damage you may be cost through the ship being behind schedule."

He put away the paper; Max had the impression that he had not actually been reading from it. "That is all that the Captain had to say, but I want to add something myself. It has come to my attention that someone has been spreading silly rumors about this minor change in schedule. I am sorry if any of you have been alarmed thereby and I assure you that I will take very strict measures if the originator can be identified." He risked a dignified smile. "But you know how difficult it is to trace down a bit of gossip. In any case, I want to assure you all that the *Asgard* is in no danger of any sort. The old girl was plying space long before any of us were born, she'll still be going strong after we all die of old age—bless her sturdy bones!" He turned and left at once.

Max had listened in open-mouthed admiration. He came from country where the "whopper" was a respected literary art and it seemed to him that he had never heard a lie told with more grace, never seen one interwoven with truth with such skill, in his life. Piece by piece, it was impossible to say that anything the First Officer had said was untrue; taken as a whole it was a flat statement that the *Asgard* was not lost—a lie if he ever heard one. He turned back toward his table mates. "Will someone pass the butter, please?"

Mr. Arthur caught his eye. "And you told us," he said sharply, "that nothing was wrong!"

Mr. Daigler growled, "Lay off him, Arthur. Max did pretty well, under the circumstances."

Mrs. Weberbauer looked bewildered. "But Mr. Walther said that everything was all right?"

Daigler looked at her with compassion. "We're in trouble, Mama Weberbauer. That's obvious. But all we can do is keep calm and trust the ship's officers. Right, Max?"

"I guess that's right, sir."

# 15

## "THIS ISN'T A PICNIC"

Max kept to his room that evening and the next day, wishing neither to be questioned by passengers nor to answer questions about why he had been relieved of duty. In consequence he missed the riot, having slept through it. He first heard of it when the steward's mate who tended his room showed up with a black eye. "Who gave you the shiner, Garcia?"

"I'm not sure, sir. It happened in the ruckus last night."

"Ruckus? What ruckus?"

"You mean you don't know?"

"This is the first I've heard ot it. What happened?"

Garcia Lopez stared at the overhead. "Well—I wouldn't want to say too much. You know how it is—nobody wants to testify against a mate. No?"

"Who asked you to peach on a mate? You don't have to mention names—but what happened?"

"Well, sir. Some of those chicos, they ain't got much sense." Slowly Max learned that the unrest among the crew had been greater than that among the passengers, possibly because they understand more clearly the predicament. Some of them had consulted with Giordano's poor-man's vodka, then had decided to call on the Captain in a body and demand straight talk. The violence had taken place when the master-at-arms had attempted to turn them back at the companionway to "C" deck.

"Anybody hurt?"

"Not what you'd call hurt. Cut up a little. I picked this up . . ." He touched his eye tenderly. ". . . from being too anxious to see what was going on. Slats Kovak busted an ankle."

"Kovak! Why would *he* be in it?" It did not make sense that a member of the Worry gang should take part in anything so unreasonable.

"He was coming down, coming off watch, I guess. Maybe he was backing up the constable. Or maybe he just got caught in the swinging doors. Your friend Sam Anderson was sure in the thick of it."

Sam! Max felt sick at heart—Sam in trouble *again!* "You're sure?"

"I was there."

"Uh, he wasn't leading it, was he?"

"Oh, you got me wrong, M— Mr. Jones. He settled it. I never see a man who could use his hands like that. He'd grab two of 'em . . . *clop!* their heads would come together. Then he would grab two more."

Max decided to come out of hiding and do two things; look up Kovak, find out how he was and what he might need or want, and second, look up Sam. But before he could leave Smythe arrived with a watch list to initial. He found that he was assigned watch-and-watch with Simes—and that he himself was due on watch immediately. He went up, wondering what had caused Simes to relent.

Kelly was in the control room; Max looked around, did not see Simes. "You got it, Chief?"

"Until you relieve me. This is my last watch."

"How's that? Are you his pet peeve now?"

"You could say so. But not the way you think, Max. He drew up a watch list with him and me heel-and-toe. I politely pointed out the guild rules, that I wasn't being paid to take the responsibility of top watch."

"Oh, brother! What did he say?"

"What could he say? He could order me in writing and I could accept in writing, with my objection to the orders entered in the log—and his neck is out a yard. Which left him his choice of putting you back on the list, asking the Captain to split it with him, or turning his cap around and relieving himself for the next few weeks. With Kovak laid up it didn't leave him much choice. You heard about Kovak?"

"Yes. Say, what was that?" Max glanced over where Noguchi was loafing at the computer and lowered his voice. "Mutiny?"

Kelly's eyes grew round. "Why, as I understand it, sir, Kovak slipped and fell down a companionway."

"Oh. Like that, huh?"

"That's what it says in the log."

"Hmm . . . well, I guess I had better relieve you. What's the dope?"

They were in orbit under power for the nearby G-type star; the orders were entered in the Captain's order book . . . in Simes' handwriting but with Captain Blaine's signature underneath. To Max it looked shaky, as if the Old Man had signed it under emotional stress. Kelly had already placed them in the groove. "Have we given up trying to find out where we are?" Max asked.

"Oh, no. Orders are to spend as much time as routine permits on it. But I'll lay you seven to two you don't find anything. Max, this is somewhere else entirely."

"Don't give up. How do you know?"

"I feel it."

Nevertheless Max spent the watch "fishing." But with no luck. Spectrograms, properly taken and measured, are to stars what fingerprints are to men; they can be classified and comparisons made with those on file which are most nearly similar. While he found many which matched fairly closely with catalogued spectra, there was always the difference that makes one identical twin not quite like his brother.

Fifteen minutes before the end of the watch he stopped, and made sure that he was ready to be relieved. While waiting he thought about the shenanigan Kelly had pulled to get him back on duty. Good old Kelly! He knew Kelly well enough to know that he must not thank him; to do so would be to attribute to the Chief Computerman a motive which was "improper"—just wink the other eye and remember it.

Simes stomped in five minutes past the hour. He said nothing but looked over the log and records of observations Max had made. Max waited several minutes while growing more and more annoyed. At last he said, "Are you ready to relieve me, sir?"

"All in good time. I want to see first what you've loused up this time." Max kept his mouth shut. Simes pointed at the log where Max had signed it followed by "C.O. o/W." "That's wrong, to start with. Add 'under instruction.'"

Max breathed deeply. "Whose instruction, sir?"

"Mine."

Max hesitated only momentarily before answering, "No, sir. Not unless you are present during my watch to supervise me."

"Are you defying me?"

"No, sir. But I'll take written orders on that point . . . entered in the log."

Simes closed the log book and looked him slowly up and down. "Mister, if we weren't short-handed you wouldn't be on watch. You aren't ready for a top watch—and it's my opinion that you won't ever be."

"If that's the way you feel, sir, I'd just as lief go back to chartsman. Or steward's mate."

"That's where you belong!" Simes' voice was almost a scream. Noguchi had hung around after Lundy had relieved him; they both looked up, then turned their heads away.

Max made no effort to keep his answer private. "Very good, sir. Will you relieve me? I'll go tell the First Officer that I am surrendering my temporary appointment and reverting to my permanent billet."

Max expected a blast. But Simes made a visible effort to control himself and said almost quietly, "See here, Jones, you don't have the right attitude."

Max thought to himself, "What have I got to lose?" Aloud he said, "You're the one who doesn't have the right attitude, sir."

"Eh? What's that?"

"You've been riding me ever since I came to work in the Hole. You've never bothered to give me any instruction and you've found fault with everything I did. Since my probationary appointment it's been four times worse. You came to my room and told me that you were opposed to my appointment, that you didn't want me . . ."

"You can't prove that!"

"I don't have to. Now you tell me that I'm not fit to stand the watch you've just required me to stand. You've made it plain that you will never recommend me for permanent appointment, so obviously I'm wasting my time. I'll go back to the Purser's gang and do what I can there. Now, will you relieve me, sir?"

"You're insubordinate."

"No, sir, I am not. I have spoken respectfully, stating facts. I have requested that I be relieved—my watch was over a good half hour ago—in order that I may see the First Officer and revert to my permanent billet. As allowed by the rules of both guilds," Max added.

"I won't let you."

"It's my option, sir. You have no choice."

Simes' face showed that he indeed had no choice. He remained silent for some time, then said more quietly, "Forget it. You're relieved. Be back up here at eight o'clock."

"Not so fast, sir. You have stated publicly that I am not competent to take the watch. Therefore I can't accept the responsibility."

"Confound it! What are you trying to do? Blackmail me?"

Max agreed in his mind that such was about it, but he answered, "I wouldn't say so, sir. You can't have it both ways."

"Well—I suppose you are competent to stand this sort of watch. There isn't anything to do, actually."

"Very good, sir. Will you kindly log the fact?"

"Huh?"

"In view of the circumstances, sir, I insist on the letter of the rules and ask you to log it."

Simes swore under his breath, then grabbed the stylus and wrote quickly. He swung the log book around. "There!"

Max read: "M. Jones is considered qualified to stand a top watch in space, not involving anomaly. (s) R. Simes, Astrogator."

Max noted the reservation, the exception that would allow Simes to keep him from ever reaching permanent status. But Simes had stayed within the law. Besides, he admitted to himself, he didn't want to leave the Worry gang. He comforted himself with the thought that since they were all lost together it might never matter what Simes recommended.

"Quite satisfactory, sir."

Simes grabbed the book. "Now get out. See that you're back here on time."

"Aye aye, sir." Max could not refrain from having the last word, standing up to Simes had gone to his head. "Which reminds me, sir: will you please relieve me on time after this?"

"*What?*"

"Under the law a man can't be worked more than four hours out of eight, except for a logged emergency."

"Go below!"

Max went below, feeling both exultant and sick. He had no taste for fights, never had; they left him with a twisted lump inside. He burst into his room, and almost fell over Sam.

"Sam!"

"The same. What's eating you, boy? You look like the goblins had been chasing you."

Max flopped on his bunk and sighed. "I feel that way, too." He told Sam about the row with Simes.

Sam nodded approval. "That's the way to deal with a jerk like that—insult him until he apologizes. Give him lumps enough times and he'll eat out of your hand."

Max shook his head dolefully. "Today was fun, but he'll find some way to take it out on me. Oh, well!"

"Not so, my lad. Keep your nose clean and wait for the breaks. If a man is stupid and bad-tempered—

which he is, I sized him up long ago—if you are smart and keep *your* temper, eventually he leaves himself wide open. That's a law of nature."

"Maybe." Max swung around and sat up. "Sam—you're wearing your shield again."

Sam stuck his thumb under the badge of office of Chief Master-at-Arms. "Didn't you notice?"

"I guess I was spinning too fast. Tell me about it—did the First decide to forgive and forget?"

"Not precisely. You know about that little excitement last night?"

"Well, yes. But I understand that officially nothing happened?"

"Correct. Mr. Walther knows when to pull his punches."

"What did happen? I heard you cracked some skulls together."

"Nothing much. And not very hard. I've seen ships where it would have been regarded as healthy exercise to settle your dinner. Some of the lads got scared and that made them lap up happy water. Then a couple with big mouths and no forehead got the inspiration that it was their right to talk to the Captain about it. Being sheep, they had to go in a flock. If they had run into an officer, he could have sent them back to bed with no trouble. But my unfortunate predecessor happened to run into them and told them to disperse. Which they didn't. He's not the diplomatic type, I'm afraid. So he hollered, 'Hey, Rube!' in his quaint idiom and the fun began."

"But where do you figure? You came to help him?"

"Hardly. I was standing at a safe distance, enjoying the festivities, when I noticed Mr. Walther's bedroom slippers coming down the ladder. Whereupon I waded in and was prominent in the ending. The way to win a medal, Max, is to make sure the general is watching, then act."

Max grinned. "Somehow I hadn't figured you for the hero type."

"Heaven forbid! But it worked out. Mr. Walther

sent for me, ate me out, told me that I was a scoundrel and a thief and a nogoodnick—then offered me my shield back if I could keep order below decks. I looked him in the eye, a sincere type look, and told him I would do my best. So here I am."

"I'm mighty pleased, Sam."

"Thanks. Then he looked me in the eye and told me that he had reason to suspect—as if he didn't know!—that there might be a still somewhere in the ship. He ordered me to find it, and then destroy any liquor I found."

"So? How did Mr. Gee take that?"

"Why, Fats and I disassembled his still and took the pieces back to stores, then we locked up his stock in trade. I pleaded with him not to touch it until the ship was out of its mess. I explained that I would break both his arms if he did."

Max chuckled. "Well, I'm glad you're back in good graces. And it was nice of you to come tell me about it." He yawned. "Sorry. I'm dead for sleep."

"I'll vamoose. But I didn't come to tell you, I came to ask a question."

"Huh? What?"

"Have you seen the Skipper lately?"

Max thought back. "Not since transition. Why?"

"Nor has anyone else. I thought he might be spending his time in the Worry Hole."

"No. Come to think, he hasn't been at his table either—at least when I've been in the lounge."

"He's been eating in his cabin." Sam stood up. "Very, very interesting. Mmm . . . I wouldn't talk about it, Max."

Simes was monosyllabic when Max relieved him. Thereafter they had no more words; Simes acted as if Max did not exist except for the brief formalities in relieving. The Captain did not show up in the control room. Several times Max was on the point of asking Kelly about it, but each time decided not to. But there were rumors around the ship—the Captain was sick, the Captain was in a coma, Walther and the Surgeon had relieved him of duty, the Captain was constantly at his desk, working out a new and remarkable way to get the ship back to where it belonged.

By now it was accepted that the ship was lost, but the time for hysteria had passed; passengers and crew were calm and there seemed to be general consent that the decision to put down around the solar-type star toward which they were headed was the only reasonable decision. They were close enough now that it had been determined that the star did have planets— no G-class star had ever been found to be without planets, but to pick them up on a stereoplate was consoling.

It came to a choice between planet #3 and planet #4. Bolometric readings showed the star to have a surface temperature slightly over 6000° Kelvin, consistent with its spectrum; it was not much larger than Father Sol; calculated surface temperatures for the third and fourth planets gave a probability that the third might be uncomfortably hot whereas number four might be frigid. Both had atmospheres.

A fast hyperboloid swing past both settled the matter. The bolometer showed number three to be too hot and even number four to be tropical. Number four had a moon which the third did not—another advantage for four, for it permitted, by examining the satellite's period, an easy calculation of its mass; from that and its visible diameter its surface gravity was a matter of substitution in classic Newtonian formula . . . ninety-three percent of Earth-normal, comfortable and rather low in view of its over ten-thousand-mile diameter. Absorption spectra showed oxygen and several inert gases.

Simes assisted by Kelly placed the *Asgard* in a pole-to-pole orbit to permit easy examination—Max, as usual, was left to chew his nails.

The Captain did not come to the control room even to watch this maneuver.

They hung in parking orbit while their possible future home was examined from the control room and stared at endlessly from the lounge. It was in the lounge that Ellie tracked Max down. He had hardly seen her during the approach, being too busy and too tired with a continuous heel-and-toe watch and in the second place with much on his mind that he did not want to have wormed out of him. But, once the orbit was established and power was off, under standard doctrine Simes could permit the watch to be taken by crewmen—which he did and again told Max to stay out of the control room.

Max could not resist the fascination of staring at the strange planet; he crowded into the lounge along with the rest. He was standing back and gazing over heads when he felt his arm grabbed. "Where have you been?"

"Working." He reached out and caressed Chipsie; the spider puppy leaped to his shoulders and started searching him.

"Hmmmph! You don't work all the time. Do you know that I sent *nine* notes to your room this past week?"

Max knew. He had saved them but had not answered. "Sorry."

"Sorry he says. Never mind— Max, tell me all about it." She turned and looked out. "What have they named it? Is there anybody on it? Where are we going to land? *When* are we going to land? Max, aren't you *excited?*"

"Whew! They haven't named it yet—we just call it 'the planet' or 'number four.' Kelly wants to name it 'Hendrix.' Simes is hedging; I think he wants to name it after himself. The Captain hasn't made any decision that I know of."

"They ought to name it 'Truth' or 'Hope' or something like that. Where is the Captain, Max? I haven't seen the old dear for *days*."

"He's working. This is a busy time for him, of course." Max reflected that his evasion might be true. "About your other questions, we haven't seen any signs of cities or towns or anything that looks like civilization."

"What do you mean by 'civilization'? Not a lot of dirty old cities surely?"

Max scratched his head and grinned. "You've got me. But I don't see how you could have it, whatever it is, without cities."

"Why not? Bees have cities, ants have cities, challawabs have cities. None of them is civilized. I can think of a lovely civilization that would just sit around in trees and sing and think beautiful thoughts."

"Is that what you want?"

"No, it would bore me to death. But I can think about it, can't I? You didn't say when we were going to land?"

"I don't know. When they decide it's safe."

"I wish they would hurry. Isn't it thrilling? Just like Robinson Crusoe, or Swiss Family Robinson—I can't keep those two straight. Or the first men on Venus."

"They died."

"So they did. But we won't, not on—" She waved her hand at the lovely green and blue and cloudy-white globe. "—not on, uh, I'm going to call it 'Charity' because that's what it looks like."

Max said soberly, "Ellie, don't you realize this is serious?" He kept his voice low in order not to alarm others. "This isn't a picnic. If this place doesn't work out, it might be pretty awful."

"Why?"

"Look, don't quote me and don't talk about it. But I don't think any of us will ever get home again."

She sobered momentarily, then shrugged and smiled. "You can't frighten me. Sure, I'd like to go home—but if I can't, well, Charity is going to be good to us. I know it."

Max shut up.

# 16

## "—OVER A HUNDRED YEARS—"

The *Asgard* landed on Charity the following day. El-dreth affixed her choice by the statistical process of referring to the planet by that name, assuming that it was official, and repeating it frequently.

When word was passed that landing would commence at noon, ship's time, Max went to the control room and simply assumed that it was his right to be present. Simes looked at him sourly but said nothing—for an evident reason: Captain Blaine was present.

Max was shocked at his appearance. The Captain seemed to have aged ten to fifteen years since the bad transition. In place of his habitual cheerful expression was one that Max had trouble tagging—until he recalled that he had seen it on horses, on horses too old to work but still working—head bent, eyes dull, mute and resigned against a fate both inescapable and unbearable. The old man's skin hung loose, as if he had not eaten for days or weeks. He seemed hardly interested in what was going on around him.

He spoke only once during the maneuver. Just before the chronometer showed noon Simes straightened up from the console and looked at his skipper. Blaine lifted his head and said in a hoarse whisper, "Take her down, Mister."

An Imperial military ship in landing on a strange spot would normally guide a radar-beacon robot down first, then home in on the beacon. But the *Asgard* was a merchant liner; she expected to land nowhere but at ports equipped with beams and beacons and other aids. Consequently the landing was made blind by precomputed radar-automatic and was planned for an open valley selected by photograph. The planet was densely wooded in most areas, choice was limited.

Simes presented a picture of the alert pilot, hands poised at the controls, eyes on the radar screen portraying the view below them, while racked in front of him were comparison photographs, radar and visual. The let down was without incident; starry black sky gave way to deep purple, then to blue. There was not even a jar as the ship touched, for its private gravity inside its Horstian field kept them from feeling impressed acceleration. Max knew they were down when he saw Simes cut in the thrust beams to cradle the ship upright.

Simes said to the microphone, "Power room, start auxiliaries and secure. All hands, dirtside routine, first section." He turned to Blaine. "Grounded, Captain."

Blaine's lips shaped the words, "Very good, sir." He got up and shuffled toward the hatch. When he had gone Simes ordered, "Lundy, take stand-by watch. The rest of you clear the control room."

Max went down with Kelly. When they reached "A" deck Max said grudgingly, "It was a smart landing I'll have to admit."

"Thanks," said Kelly.

Max glanced at him. "So you calculated it?"

"I didn't say that. I just said, 'Thanks.'"

"So? Well, you're welcome." Max felt his weight pulse and suddenly he was a trifle lighter. "They cut the field. Now we're really down."

He was about to invite Kelly into his room for the inevitable coffee when the ship's speakers sounded: "All hands! All passengers! Report to Bifrost Lounge for an important announcement. Those on watch are ordered to listen in by phone."

"What's up?" asked Max.

"Why wonder? We'll go see."

The lounge was crowded with passengers and crew. First Officer Walther stood near the Captain's table, counting the crowd with his eyes. Max saw him speak to Bennett, who nodded and hurried away. The large view port was across the lounge from Max; he stretched on his toes and tried to see out. All he could see was hilltops and blue sky.

There was a lessening of the murmur of voices; Max looked around to see Bennett preceding Captain Blaine through the crowd. The Captain went to his table and sat down; the First Officer glanced at him, then cleared his throat loudly. "Quiet, please."

He went on, "I've called you together because Captain Blaine has something he wants to say to you." He stopped and stepped back respectfully.

Captain Blaine slowly stood up, looked uncertainly around. Max saw him square his thin shoulders and lift his head. "Men," he said, his voice suddenly firm and strong. "My guests and friends—" he went on, his voice sinking. There was a hush in the lounge, Max could hear the Captain's labored breathing. He again asserted control of himself and continued, "I have brought you . . . I have brought you as far as I can. . . ." His voice trailed off. He looked at them for a long moment, his mouth trembling. It seemed impossible for him to continue. The crowd started to stir.

But he did continue and they immediately quieted. "I have something else to say," he began, then paused. This pause was longer, when he broke it his voice was a whisper. "I'm sorry. God keep you all." He turned and started for the door.

Bennett slipped quickly in front of him. Max could hear him saying quietly and firmly: "Gangway, please. Way for the Captain." No one said anything until he was gone, but a woman passenger at Max's elbow was sobbing softly.

Mr. Walther's sharp, clear voice rang out. "Don't go away, anyone! I have additional announcements to make." His manner ignored what they had all just seen. "The time has come to sum up our present situation. As you can see, this planet is much like our Mother Earth. Tests must be made to be sure that the atmosphere is breathable, and so forth; the Surgeon and the Chief Engineer are making them now. But it

seems likely that this new planet will prove to be emi-
nently suitable for human beings, probably even more
friendly than Earth.

"So far, we have seen no indications of civilized life.
On the whole, that seems a good thing. Now as to our
resources— The *Asgard* carries a variety of domestic
animals, they will be useful and should be conserved
as breeding stock. We have an even wider variety of
useful plants, both in the ship's hydroponic gardens
and carried as seeds. We have a limited but adequate
supply of tools. Most important of all the ship's library
contains a fair cross-section of our culture. Equally important, we ourselves have our skills and tradi-
tions . . ."

"Mr. Walther!"

"Yes, Mr. Hornsby?"

"Are you trying to tell us that you are dumping us
here?"

Walther looked at him coldly. "No. Nobody is being
'dumped' as you put it. You can stay in the ship and
you will be treated as a guest as long as the *Asgard*—
or you yourself—is alive. Or until the ship reaches the
destination on your ticket. If it does. No, I have been
trying to discuss reasonably an open secret; this ship is
lost."

A voiceless sigh went through the room. All of them
knew it, but up till now it had not been admitted
officially. The flat announcement from a responsible
officer echoed like the sentence of a court.

"Let me state the legal position," Mr. Walther went
on. "While this ship was in space you passengers were
subject to the authority of the Captain, as defined by
law, and through him you were subject to me and the
other ship's officers. Now we have landed. You may go
freely . . . or you may stay. Legally this is an unsched-
uled stopover; if the ship ever leaves here you may
return to it and continue as passengers. That is my responsibility to you and it will be carried out. But I tell
you plainly that at present I have no hope to offer that

we will ever leave here—which is why I spoke of colonizing. We are lost."

In the rear of the room a woman began to scream hysterically, with incoherent sounds of, ". . . home! I want to go home! Take me . . ."

Walther's voice cut through the hubbub. "Dumont! Flannigan! Remove her. Take her to the Surgeon."

He continued as if nothing had happened. "The ship and the ship's crew will give every assistance possible, consistent with my legal responsibility to keep the ship in commission, to aid any of you who wish to colonize. Personally I think . . ."

A surly voice cut in, "Why talk about 'law'? There is no law here!"

Walther did not even raise his voice. "But there is. As long as this ship is in commission, there is law, no matter how many light-years she may be from her home port. Furthermore, while I have no authority over any who choose to leave the ship, I strongly advise you to make it your first act dirtside to hold a town meeting, elect officers, and found a constitutional government. I doubt that you can survive otherwise."

"Mr. Walther."

"Yes, Mr. Daigler?"

"This is obviously no time for recriminations . . ."

"Obviously!"

Daigler grinned wryly. "So I won't indulge, though I could think of some. But it happens that I know something professionally about the economics of colonizing."

"Good! We'll use your knowledge."

"Will you let me finish? A prime principle in maintaining a colony out of touch with its supply base is to make it large enough. It's a statistical matter, too small a colony can be overwhelmed by a minor setback. It's like going into a dice game with too little money: three bad rolls and you're sunk. Looking around me, it's evident that we have much less than optimal minimum. In fact—"

"It's what we have, Mr. Daigler."

"I see that. I'm not a wishful thinker. What I want to know is, can we count on the crew as well?"

Mr. Walther shook his head. "This ship will not be decommissioned as long as there are men capable of manning it. There is always hope, no matter how small, that we may find a way home. It is even possible that an Imperial survey ship might discover us. I'm sorry—no."

"That isn't quite what I asked. I was two jumps ahead of you, I figured you wouldn't let the crew colonize. But can we count on their help? We seem to have about six females, give or take one, who will probably help to carry on the race. That means that the next generation of our new nation is going to be much smaller. Such a colony would flicker and die, by statistical probability—*unless* every man jack of us works ten hours a day for the rest of his life, just to give our children a better chance of making it. That's all right with me, if we all make an all-out try. But it will take all the manpower we have to make sure that some young people who aren't even born yet get by thirty years from now. Will the crew help?"

Mr. Walther said quietly, "I think you can count on it."

"Good enough."

A small, red-faced man whose name Max had never learned interrupted. "Good enough, my eye! I'm going to sue the company, I'm going to sue the ship's officers individually. I'm going to shout it from the . . ." Max saw Sam slipping through the crowd to the man's side, the disturbance stopped abruptly.

"Take him to the Surgeon," Mr. Walther said wearily. "He can sue us tomorrow. The meeting is adjourned."

Max started for his room. Eldreth caught up with him. "Max! I want to talk with you."

"All right." He started back toward the lounge.

"No, I want to talk privately. Let's go to your room."

"Huh? Mrs. Dumont would blow her top, then she'd tell Mr. Walther."

"Bother with all that! Those silly rules are dead. Didn't you listen at the meeting?"

"You're the one who didn't listen."

He took her firmly by the arm, turned her toward the public room. They ran into Mr. and Mrs. Daigler coming the other way. Daigler said, "Max? Are you busy?"

"Yes," answered Eldreth.

"No," said Max.

"Hmm . . . you two had better take a vote. I'd like to ask Max some questions. I've no objection to your being with us, Eldreth, if you will forgive the intrusion."

She shrugged. "Oh, well, maybe you can handle him. I can't."

They went to the Daiglers' stateroom, larger and more luxurious than Max's and possessing two chairs. The two women perched on the bed, the men took the chairs. Daigler began, "Max, you impress me as a man who prefers to give a straight answer. There are things I want to know that I didn't care to ask out there. Maybe you can tell me."

"I will if I can."

"Good. I've tried to ask Mr. Simes, all I get is a snottily polite brush off. I haven't been able to get in to see the Captain—after today I see that there wouldn't have been any point anyhow. Now, can you tell me, with the mathematics left out, what chance we have to get home? Is it one in three, or one in a thousand—or what?"

"Uh, I couldn't answer it that way."

"Answer it your own way."

"Well, put it this way. While we don't know where we are, we know positively where we aren't. We aren't within, oh, say a hundred light-years of any explored part of the Galaxy."

"How do you know? It seems to me that's a pretty

big space to be explored in the weeks since we got off the track."

"It sure is. It's a globe twelve hundred trillion miles thick. But we didn't have to explore it, not exactly."

"Then how?"

"Well, sir, we examined the spectra of all first magnitude stars in sight—and a lot more. None of them is in our catalogues. Some are giants that would be first magnitude anywhere within a hundred light-years of them—they'd be certain to be in the catalogues if a survey ship had ever been that close to them. So we are absolutely certain that we are a long, long way from anywhere that men have ever been before. Matter of fact, I spoke too conservatively. Make it a globe twice as thick, eight times as big, and you'd still be way over on the conservative side. We're *really* lost."

"Mmm . . . I'm glad I didn't ask those questions in the lounge. Is there any possibility that we will ever know where we are?"

"Oh, sure! There are thousands of stars left to examine. Chief Kelly is probably shooting one this minute."

"Well, then, what are the chances that we will eventually find ourselves?"

"Oh, I'd say they were excellent—in a year or two at the outside. If not from single stars, then from globular star clusters. You realize that the Galaxy is a hundred thousand light-years across, more or less, and we can see only stars that are fairly close. But the globular clusters make good landmarks, too." Max added the mental reservation, *if we aren't in the wrong galaxy*. There seemed no point in burdening them with that dismaying possibility.

Daigler relaxed and took out a cigar. "This is the last of my own brand, but I'll risk smoking it now. Well, Maggie, I guess you won't have to learn how to make soap out of wood ashes and hog drippings after all. Whether it's one year or five, we can sweat it out and go home."

"I'm glad." She patted her ornate coiffure with soft,

beautifully manicured hands. "I'm hardly the type for it."

"But you don't understand!"

"Eh? What's that, Max?"

"I didn't say we could get back. I just said I thought it was fairly certain we would find out where we are."

"What's the difference? We find out, then we go home."

"No, because we *can't* be less than a hundred light-years from explored space."

"I don't see the hitch. This ship can do a hundred light-years in a split second. What was the longest leap we made this cruise? Nearly five hundred light-years, wasn't it?"

"Yes, but—" Max turned to Eldreth. "You understand? Don't you?"

"Well, maybe. That folded-scarf thing you showed me?"

"Yes, yes. Mr. Daigler, sure the *Asgard* can transit five hundred light-years in no time—or any other distance. But *only* at calculated and surveyed congruencies. We don't know of any within a hundred light-years, at least . . . and we won't know of any even if we find out where we are because we know where we *aren't*. Follow me? That means that the ship would have to travel at top speed for something over a hundred years and maybe much longer, just for the first leg of the trip."

Mr. Daigler stared thoughtfully at his cigar ash, then took out a pen knife and cut off the burning end. "I'll save the rest. Well, Maggie, better study up on that homemake soap deal. Thanks, Max. My father was a farmer, I can learn."

Max said impulsively, "I'll help you, sir."

"Oh yes, you did tell us that you used to be a farmer, didn't you? You should make out all right." His eyes swung to Eldreth. "You know what I would do, if I were you kids? I'd get the Captain to marry you right away. Then you'd be all set to tackle colonial life right."

Max blushed to his collar and did not look at Ellie. "I'm afraid I can't. I'm a crew member, I'm not eligible to colonize."

Mr. Daigler looked at him curiously. "Such devotion to duty. Well, no doubt Ellie can take her pick among the single men passengers."

Eldreth smoothed her skirt demurely. "No doubt."

"Come, Maggie. Coming, Eldreth?"

# 17

# CHARITY

"Charityville" was a going concern within a week. It had a mayor, Mr. Daigler, a main street, Hendrix Avenue, even its first wedding, performed by the mayor in the presence of the villagers—Mr. Arthur and little Becky Weberbauer. The first cottage, now building, was reserved for the newlyweds. It was a log cabin and a very sloppy job, for, while there were those among them who had seen pictures or had even seen log cabins, there was no one who had ever built one before.

There was an air of hope, of common courage, even of gaiety in the new community. The place was fragrant with new starts, forward-looking thoughts. They still slept in the ship and breakfasted there, then carried their lunches and labored mightily, men and women alike, through the short day—Charity spun on her axis in twenty-one-plus hours. They returned at nightfall, dined in the ship, and some found energy to dance a bit before going to bed.

Charity seemed to be all that her name implied. The days were balmy, the nights were mild—and beautiful beyond anything yet found in the Galaxy. Its star (they simply called it "the Sun") was accompanied by more comets than had yet been seen around any star. A giant with a wide tail stretched from zenith to western horizon, diving at their Sun. Another, not yet so grand but awesome enough to have caused watchers for the end of the world on Earthly hilltops, approached from the north, and two more decorated the southern sky with lace of icy fire.

Concomitant with comets was, necessarily, an equal abundance of meteors. Every night was a shower of falling stars, every day ended like Solar Union Day with a display of fireworks.

They had seen no dangerous animals. Some of the settlers reported seeing centaurlike creatures about the size of Shetland ponies, but they seemed timid and had scurried away when discovered. The prevalent life form appeared to be marsupial mammals in various sizes and shapes. There were no birds, but there was another sort of flying life not found elsewhere—jellyfishlike creatures four or five feet high with dangling tendrils, animated balloons. They appeared to have muscular control over their swollen bladders for they could rise and fall, and could even, by some not evident means, go upwind against a gentle breeze—in higher winds they anchored to treetops, or floated free and let the wind carry them.

They seemed curious about Charityville and would hang over a work site, turning slowly around as if to see everything. But they never got within reach. Some of the settlers wanted to shoot one down and examine it; Mayor Daigler forbade it.

There was another animal too—or might be. They were called "peekers" because all that anyone had seen was something that ducked quickly behind a rock or tree when anyone tried to look. Between the possibly mythical peeker and the ubiquitous balloons the colonists felt that their new neighbors took a deep but not unfriendly interest in what they were doing.

Maggie Daigler—she was "Maggie" to everyone now—had put away her jewels, drawn dungarees from ship's stores, and chopped off her hair. Her nails were short and usually black with grime. But she looked years younger and quite happy.

In fact, everyone seemed happy but Max.

Ellie was avoiding him. He cursed himself and his big mouth thrice daily and four times at night. Sure, Daigler had spoken out of turn—but was that any reason for him to open his mouth and put his foot in it? Of course, he had never figured on marrying Ellie—but shucks, maybe they were stuck here forever. "Probably," not "maybe," he corrected. The ban on joining the colony would be let up in time—in which case, what was the sense in getting in bad with the only eligible girl around?

An astrogator ought to be a bachelor but a farmer needed a wife. Mighty nice to have some one cooking the turnip greens and jointing a chicken while a man was out in the fields. He ought to know—Maw had let it slide often enough. Ellie wouldn't be like Maw. She was strong and practical and with just a little teaching would do all right.

Besides she was about the prettiest thing he ever saw, if you looked at her right.

When Mr. and Mrs. Dumont, by special dispensation, joined the colony it caused him to act. Since the steward and stewardess would have no duties in a ship without passengers no one could reasonably object—but it gave Max an approach. He went to see the First Officer.

"Probationary Apprentice Jones, sir."

Walther glanced up. "I think I'd say 'Assistant Astrogator Jones' if I were you. Closer to the facts. Come in."

"Uh, that's what I wanted to speak with you about, sir."

"So? How?"

"I want to revert to my billet."

"Eh? Why would you rather be a chartsman than an astrogator? And what difference does it make—now?"

"No, sir. I'm electing to resume my permanent appointment, steward's mate third."

Walther looked amazed. "There must be more to this. Explain yourself."

With much stammering Max explained his trouble with Simes. He tried to be fair and finished with the dismal feeling that he had sounded childish. Walther said, "You're sure about this? Mr. Simes has said nothing to me about you."

"He wouldn't, sir. But it's true. You can ask Kelly."

Walther thought for a while. "Mr. Jones, I wouldn't attach too much importance to this. At your age these

conflicts of personality often seem more serious than
they are. My advice is to forget it and do your work.
I'll speak to Mr. Simes about his keeping you out of
the control room. That isn't proper and I am surprised
to hear it."

"No, sir."

" 'No, sir' what?"

"I want to return to steward's mate."

"Eh? I don't understand you."

"Because, sir, I want to join the colony. Like Chief
Steward Dumont."

"Oh. . . . A light begins to dawn." Walther slapped
the desk emphatically. "Absolutely no! Under no circumstances."

"Sir?"

"Please understand me. This is not discrimination. If
you were a steward's mate and nothing else, I would
consider your request—under the special circumstances which I believe pertain. But you are an astrogator. You know our situation. Dr. Hendrix is dead. Captain Blaine—well, you have seen him. He may recover,
I cannot plan on it. Mr. Jones, as long as there is any
faint hope that this ship will ever lift again, as long as
we have crew to work her, no astrogator, no chartsman, no computerman will be relieved from duty for
any reason whatsoever. You see that, don't you?"

"I guess so, sir. Uh, aye aye, sir."

"Good. By the way, keep this to yourself, but as
soon as the colony can get along without us temporarily, I want the ship placed in a parking orbit so that
you specialists can maintain a search. You can't work
very well through this atmosphere, can you?"

"No, sir. Our instruments were designed for open
space."

"So we must see that you get it." The First Officer
sat silent, then added, "Mr. Jones—Max, isn't it? May
I speak to you man to man?"

"Uh? Certainly, sir."

"Mmm . . . Max, this is none of my business, but
treat it as fatherly advice. If you have an opportunity

to marry—and want to—you don't have to join the
colony to do it. If we stay, it won't matter in the long
run whether you are crew or a charter member of the
village. If we leave, your wife goes with you."

Max's ears burned. He could think of nothing to say.

"Hypothetical question, of course. But that's the
proper solution." Walther stood up. "Why don't you
take the day off? Go take a walk or something. Fresh
air will do you good. I'll speak to Mr. Simes."

Instead, Max went looking for Sam, did not find him
in the ship, discovered that he had gone dirtside. He
followed him down and walked the half mile to Charityville.

Before he reached the building that was being
worked on he saw a figure separate itself from the
gang. He soon saw that it was Eldreth. She stopped in
front of him, a sturdy little figure in dirty dungarees.
She planted her feet and set fists on her hips.

"Uh, howdy, Ellie."

"Up to your old tricks! Avoiding me. Explain yourself."

The injustice of it left him stuttering. "But . . . Now
see here, Ellie, it's not that way at all. You've been . . ."

"A likely story. You sound like Chipsie caught with
her hand in a candy dish. I just wanted to tell you,
you reluctant Don Juan, that you have nothing to worry about. I'm not marrying anyone this season. So you
can resume the uneven tenor of your ways."

"But, Ellie . . ." he started desperately.

"Want me to put it in writing? Put up a bond?" She
looked fiercely at him, then began to laugh, wrinkling
her nose. "Oh, Max, you large lout, you arouse the
eternal maternal in me. When you are upset your face
gets as long as a mule's. Look, forget it."

"But, Ellie . . . Well, all right."

"Pals?"

"Pals."

She sighed. "I feel better. I don't know why, but I
don't like to be on the outs with you. Where were you
going?"

"Uh, nowhere. Taking a walk."

"Fine. I'll go too. Half a sec while I gather in Chipsie." She turned and called, "Mister Chips! Chipsie!"

"I don't see her."

"I'll get her." She ran off, to return quickly with the spider puppy on her shoulder and a package in her hand. "I picked up my lunch. We can split it."

"Oh, we won't be gone that long. Hi, Chipsie baby."

"Hi, Max. Candy?"

He dug into a pocket, found a sugar cube that he had saved several days ago for the purpose; the spider puppy accepted it gravely and said, "Thank you."

"Yes, we will," Ellie disagreed, "because some of the men saw a herd of those centaur ponies the other side of that ridge. It's quite a hike."

"I don't think we ought to go that far," he said doubtfully. "Won't they miss you?"

"I've been doing my share. See my callouses?" She stuck out a grimy paw. "I told Mr. Hornsby that I was suddenly come down with never-get-overs and he would have to find somebody else to hold while he hammered."

He was pleased to give in. They went up rising ground and into an arroyo and soon were in a grove of primitive conifers. Mr. Chips jumped down from Ellie's shoulders and scurried up a tree. Max stopped. "Hadn't we better catch her?"

"You worry too much. Chipsie wouldn't run away. She'd be scared to death. Chipsie! Here, honey!"

The spider puppy hustled through branches, got directly above them, dropped a cone on Max. Then she laughed, a high giggle. "See? She just wants to play."

The ridge was high and Max found that his hillbilly's wind had been lost somewhere among the stars. The arroyo meandered slowly upwards. He was still woodsman enough to keep a sharp eye out for landmarks and directions. At weary last they topped the crest. Ellie paused. "I guess they're gone," she said disappointedly, staring out over flatter country below them. "No! Look over there. See them! About two dozen little black dots."

"Uh huh. Yeah."

"Let's go closer. I want a good look."

"I wonder if that's smart? We're a far piece from the ship and I'm not armed."

"Oh, they're harmless."

"I was thinking of what else might be in these woods."

"But we're already in the woods, and all we've seen are the hobgoblins." She referred to the balloonlike creatures, two of which had trailed them up the arroyo. The humans had grown so used to their presence that they no longer paid them any attention.

"Ellie, it's time we went back."

"No."

"Yes. I'm responsible for you. You've seen your centaurs."

"Max Jones, I'm a free citizen. You may be starting back; I'm going to have a close look at those underslung cow ponies." She started down.

"Well— Wait a moment. I want to get my bearings." He took a full look around, fixed the scene forever in his mind, and followed her. He was not anxious to thwart her anyhow; he had been mulling over the notion that this was a good time to explain why he had said what he had said to Mr. Daigler—and perhaps lead around to the general subject of the future. He wouldn't go so far as to talk about marriage—though he might bring it up in the abstract if he could figure out an approach.

How did you approach such a subject? You didn't just say, "There go the hobgoblins, let's you and me get married!"

Ellie paused. "There go the hobgloblins. Looks as if they were heading right for the herd."

Max frowned. "Could be. Maybe they talk to them?"

She laughed. "Those things?" She looked him over

carefully. "Maxie, I've just figured out why I bother with you."

Huh? Maybe she was going to lead up to it for him. "Why?"

"Because you remind me of Putzie. You get the same puzzled look he does."

" 'Putzie?' Who is Putzie?"

"Putzie is the man my father shipped me off to Earth to get me away from—and the reason I crushed out of three schools to get back to Hespera. Only Daddy will probably have shipped him off, too. Daddy is tricky. Come here, Chipsie. Don't go so far."

She continued, "You'll love Putzie. He's nice. Stop it, Chipsie."

Max despised the man already. "I don't like to fret you," he said, "but it's a long way to Hespera."

"I know. Let's not borrow trouble." She looked him over again. "I might keep you in reserve, if you weren't so jumpy."

Before he could think of the right answer she had started down.

The centaurs—it seemed the best name, though the underparts were not much like horses and the parts that stuck up were only vaguely humanoid—clustered near the foot of the hill, not far out from the trees. They weren't grazing, it was hard to tell what they were doing. The two hobgoblins were over the group, hovering as if in interest just as they did with humans. Ellie insisted on going to the edge of the clearing to see them better.

They reminded Max of clowns made up to look like horses. They had silly, simple expressions and apparently no room for a brain case. They appeared to be marsupials, with pouches almost like bibs. Either they were all females or with this species the male had a pouch too. Several little centaurs were cavorting around, in and out the legs of their elders.

One of the babies spied them, came trotting toward them, sniffling and bleating. Behind it the largest adult pulled out of the herd to watch the young one. The colt scampered up and stopped about twenty feet away.

"Oh, the darling!" Ellie said and ran out a few feet, dropped to one knee. "Come here, pet. Come to mama."

Max started for her. "Ellie! Come back here!"

The large centaur reached into its pouch, hauled out something, swung it around its head like a gaucho's throwing rope. "Ellie!"

He reached her just as it let go. The thing struck them, wound around and held them. Ellie screamed and Max struggled to tear it loose—but they were held like Laocoön.

Another line came flying through the air, clung to them. And another.

Mr. Chips had followed Ellie. Now she skittered away, crying. She stopped at the edge of the clearing and shrilled, "Max! Ellie! Come *back. Please* back!"

# 18

# CIVILIZATION

Ellie did not faint nor grow hysterical. After that involuntary scream, her next remark was simply, "Max, I'm sorry. My fault."

The words were almost in his ear, so tightly were they tied together by the clinging ropes. He answered, "I'll get us loose!" and continued to strain at their bonds.

"Don't struggle," she said quietly, "It just makes them tighter. We'll have to talk our way out of this."

What she said was true; the harder he strained the tighter the pythonlike bonds held them. "Don't," Ellie pleaded. "You're making it worse. It's hurting me." Max desisted.

The largest centaur ambled up and looked them over. Its broad simple face was still more ludicrous close up and its large brown eyes held a look of gentle astonishment. The colt approached from the other side and sniffed curiously, bleated in a high voice. The adult bugled like an elk; the colt shied sideways, then rejoined the herd on a dead run.

"Take it easy," Ellie whispered. "I think they were scared that we would hurt the baby. Maybe they'll just look us over and let us go."

"Maybe. But I wish I could get at my knife."

"I'm glad you can't. This calls for diplomacy."

The rest of the herd came up, milled around and looked them over, while exchanging calls that combined bugling, whinnying, and something between a cough and a snort. Max listened. "That's language," he decided.

"Of course. And how I wish I had studied it at Miss Mimsey's."

The largest centaur leaned over them, smoothed at their bonds; they became looser but still held them.

Max said sharply, "I think they are going to untie us. Get ready to run."

"Yes, boss."

Another centaur reached into its built-in pouch, took out another of the ropelike things. It dropped to its fore knees, flipped the end so that it curled around Max's left ankle. The end seemed to weld into a loop, hobbling Max as effectively as a bowline knot; Ellie was treated the same way. The biggest centaur then patted their bonds, which fell off and writhed gently on the ground. It picked them up and stuffed them into its pouch.

The centaur which had hobbled them wrapped the ends of their tethers around its upright trunk, they merged into a belt. After an exchange of sour bugle calls with the leader, it patted the leashes, . . . which then stretched like taffy, becoming quite twenty feet long and much more slender. Max pressed his knife on Ellie and said, "Try to cut yourself loose. If you can, then run for it. I'll keep them busy."

"No, Max."

"Yes! Dawggone it, quit being a brat! You've made enough trouble."

"Yes, Max." She took the knife and tried to saw through the strange rope near her ankle. The centaurs made no attempt to stop her, but watched with the same air of gentle astonishment. It was as if they had never seen a knife, had no notion of what one was. Presently she gave up. "No good, Max. It's like trying to slice duraplastic."

"Why, I keep that knife like a razor. Let me try."

He had no better luck. He was forced to stop by the herd moving out—walk or be dragged. He managed to close the knife while hopping on one foot to save his balance. The group proceeded at a slow walk for a few steps, then the leader bugled and the centaurs broke into a trot, exactly like ancient cavalry.

Ellie stumbled at once and was dragged. Max sat down, managed to grab his hobble and hang on while shouting, "Hey! Stop!"

Their captor stopped and looked around almost
apologetically. Max said, "Look, stupid. We can't keep
up. We're not horses," while helping Ellie to her feet.
"Are you hurt, kid?"

"I guess not." She blinked back tears. "If I could lay
hands on that hay-burning oaf, he'd be hurt—plenty!"

"You skinned your hand."

"It won't kill me. Just tell him to slow down, will
you?"

Seeing them on their feet the monster immediately
started to trot again. Down they went again, with Max
trying to drag them to a halt. This time the leader trotted back from the main herd and consulted their custodian. Max took part, making up in vehemence what
he lacked in semantic efficiency.

Perhaps he was effective; their keeper slowed to a
fast walk, letting the others go ahead. Another centaur
dropped back and became a rear guard. One of the
animated balloons, which had continued to hover over
the herd, now drifted back and remained over Max
and Ellie.

The pace was just bearable, between a fast walk
and a dogtrot. The route led across the open, flat floor
of the valley and through knee-high grass. The grass
saved them somewhat, as the centaur leading them
seemed to feel that a fall or two every few hundred
yards represented optimum efficiency. He never
seemed impatient and would stop and let them get up,
but always started off again at a clip brisk for humans.
Max and Ellie ceased trying to talk, their throats being
burned dry by their panting efforts to keep up. A tiny
stream meandered through the bottom of the valley;
the centaur jumped easily across it. It was necessary
for the humans to wade. Ellie paused in midstream,
leaned down and started to drink. Max objected, "Ellie! Don't drink that—you don't know that it's safe."

"I hope it poisons me so I can lie down and die.
Max, I can't go much farther."

"Chin up, kid. We'll get out of this. I've been keeping track of where we've gone." He hesitated, then drank also, being terribly thirsty. The centaur let them, then tugged them on.

It was as far again to the rising ground and forest on the other side. They had thought that they were as tired as they could be before they started up hill; they were mistaken. The centaur was agile as a goat and seemed surprised that they found it difficult. Finally Ellie collapsed and would not get up; the centaur came back and stirred her roughly with a three-toed hoof.

Max struck him with both fists. The centaur made no move to retaliate but looked at him with that same stupid astonishment. Their rear guard came up and conversed with it, after which they waited for perhaps ten minutes. Max sat down beside Ellie and said anxiously, "Feeling any better?"

"Don't talk."

Presently the guard edged between them and drove Max back by stepping on him, whereupon the other centaur tugged on Ellie's leash. It contracted and she was forced to scramble to her feet. The centaurs let them rest twice after that. After an endless time, when the local sun was dropping low in the west, they came out on flat table land, still heavily wooded. They continued through trees for a distance which Max's count of paces told him was under a mile but seemed like ten, then stopped.

They were in a semi-clearing, a space carpeted with fallen needles. Their guard came up to the other centaur and took from him the end of Max's leash, flipped it around the base of a tree, to which it clung. The other centaur did the same with Ellie's leash to another tree about forty feet away. Having done so, they roughly urged the two together, while stopping to stroke their bonds until they were stretched out very thin. It allowed Max and Ellie enough slack that they might have passed each other.

This did not seem to please the centaurs. One of them shifted Max's leash farther back into the surrounding bushes, dragging him with it. This time at the extreme limit allowed by their bonds they were about six feet apart. "What are they doing?" asked Ellie.

"Looks like they don't want us to combine forces."

Finished, the centaurs trotted away. Ellie looked after them, began to sob, then cried openly, tears running down her dirty face and leaving tracks. "Stow it," Max said harshly. "Sniffling will get us nowhere."

"I can't help it," she bawled. "I've been brave all day—at least I've tried to be. I . . ." She collapsed face down and let herself go.

By getting down prone and stretching Max could just reach her head. He patted her tangled hair. "Take it easy, kid," he said softly. "Cry it out, if you'll feel better."

"Oh, Maxie! Tied up . . . like a dog."

"We'll see about that." He sat up and examined his tether.

Whatever the ropelike leash was, it was not rope. It had a smooth shiny surface which reminded him more of a snake, though the part that wound around his ankle showed no features; it simply flowed around his ankle and merged back into itself.

He lifted the bight and detected a faint throbbing. He stroked it as he had seen the centaurs do and it responded with flowing pulsations, but it neither shrank nor grew longer, nor did it loosen its grip. "Ellie," he announced, "This thing is *alive*."

She lifted a woebegone face. "What thing?"

"This rope."

"Oh, that! Of course."

"At least," he went on, "if it isn't, it's not really dead." He tried his knife again, there was no effect. "I'll bet if I had a match I could make it cry 'Uncle.' Got an Everlite, Ellie?"

"I don't smoke."

"Neither do I. Well, maybe I can make a fire some other way. Rubbing two sticks together, or something."

"Do you know how?"

"No." He continued stroking and patting the living rope, but, though he always got a response in pulsations, he did not seem to have the right touch; the bond stayed as before. He was continuing this fruitless attempt when he heard his name called. "Max! Ellie!"

Ellie sat up with a jerk. "Chipsie! Oh, Max, she followed us. Come here, darling!"

The spider puppy was high above them in a tree. She looked carefully around, then scurried down, making the last ten feet a flying leap into Ellie's arms. They cuddled and made soft noises, then Ellie straightened up, her eyes shining. "Max, I feel so much better."

"So do I." He added, "Though I don't know why."

The spider puppy announced gravely, "Chipsie follow."

Max reached across and petted her. "Yes, Chipsie did. Good girl!"

Ellie hugged the spider puppy. "I don't feel deserted now, Max. Maybe everything will come out all right."

"Look, Ellie, we're not in too bad a spot. Maybe I'll find the combination to tickle these ropes or snakes or whatever so they'll give up. If I do, we'll sneak back tonight."

"How would we find our way?"

"Don't worry. I watched every foot of the way, every change of direction, every landmark."

"Even in the dark?"

"Easier in the dark. I know these stars—I sure ought to. But suppose we don't get loose; we still aren't licked."

"Huh? I don't relish spending my life tied to a tree."

"You won't. Look—I think these things are just curious about us. They won't eat us, that's sure—they probably live on grass. Maybe they'll get bored and turn us loose. But if they don't, it'll be rough on them."

"Huh? Why?"

"Because of Mr. Walther and George Daigler—and Sam, Sam Anderson; that's why. They're probably beating the bushes for us right now. We are less than ten miles from the ship—five by a straight line. They'll find us. Then if these silly-looking centaurs want to get tough, they'll learn about modern weapons. They and their fool throwing ropes!"

"It might take a long time to find us. Nobody knows where we went."

"Yes," he admitted. "If I had a pocket radio. Or some way to signal. Or even a way to build a fire. But I don't."

"I never thought. It just seemed like going for a stroll in the park."

Max thought darkly that he had tried to warn her. Why, even the hills around home weren't safe if a body didn't keep his eyes peeled . . . you could run into a mean old bobcat, or even a bear. Person like Ellie never 'ud had enough hard knocks to knock sense into her, that was her trouble.

Presently he admitted that he himself hadn't looked for grief from anything as apparently chuckled-headed and harmless as these centaur things. Anyhow, as Sam would say, no use cryin' over spilt milk when the horse was already stolen.

"Ellie."

"Huh?"

"Do you suppose Chipsie could find her way back?"

"Why, I don't know."

"If she could, we could send a message."

Chipsie looked up. "Back?" she inquired. "Please back. Go home."

Ellie frowned. "I'm afraid Chipsie doesn't talk that well. She'd probably just hiccup and get incoherent."

"I don't mean that. I know Chipsie is no mental giant. I . . ."

"Chipsie is smart!"

"Sure. But I want to send a written message and a map." He fumbled in a pocket, pulled out a stylus. "Do you have any paper?"

"I'll see." She found a folded paper in a dungaree pocket. "Oh, dear! I was supposed to take this to Mr. Giordano. Mr. Hornsby will be so vexed with me."

"What is it?"

"A requisition for number-ten wire."

"It doesn't matter now." He took the paper, scratched out the memorandum, turned it over and began to draw, stopping to consult the pictures filed in his mind for distances, which way the local sun lay, contours, and other details.

"Max?"

"Quiet, can't you?" He continued to sketch, then added: "URGENT—to First Officer Walther: Eldreth Coburn and self captured by centaurs. Be careful and watch out for their throwing ropes. Respectfully, M. Jones." He handed it to Ellie. "That ought to do it. Is there any way to fasten it to her? I sure don't want her to drop it."

"Mmm . . . let me see. Turn your back, Max."

"Why?"

"Don't be difficult. Turn your back."

He did so, shortly she said, "All right now." He faced her and she handed him a ribbon. "How's this?"

"Swell!" They managed to tie the ribbon, with the note folded and firmly attached, around Mr. Chips' waist, anchoring it to a middle limb . . . not too easy as the spider puppy seemed to think it was a game and was ticklish as well.

"There! Stop squirming, Chipsie, and listen. Ellie wants you to go home."

"Home?"

"Yes, home. Go back to the ship."

"Ellie go home?"

"Ellie can't go home."

"No."

"Honey, you've *got* to."

"No."

"Look, Chipsie. You find Maggie and tell her Ellie said to give you some candy. You give Maggie this." She tugged at the tied note.

"Candy?"

"Go home. Find Maggie. Maggie will give you candy."

"Ellie go home."

"Please, Chipsie."

"Ellie," Max said urgently, "something is coming."

Eldreth looked up, saw a centaur coming through the trees. She pointed. "Look, Chipsie! They're coming! They'll catch Chipsie! Go home! Run!"

The spider puppy squealed in terror and scurried for the trees. Once on a branch she looked back and whimpered. "Go home!" screamed Ellie. "Find Maggie!"

Mr. Chips shot a glance at the centaur, then disappeared. They had no time to worry further, the centaur was almost up to them. He glanced at them and went on by; it was what followed the centaur that grabbed their attention. Ellie suppressed a shriek. "Max! They've caught everybody."

"No," he corrected grimly. "Look again." The gathering gloom had caused him to make the same mistake; it seemed that the entire ship's company trotted after the centaur in single file, ankle leashed to ankle by living ropes. But only the first glance gave such an impression. These creatures were more than humanoid —but such degraded creatures had never sailed between the stars.

They shuffled quickly along like well-trained animals. One or two looked at Ellie and Max in passing, but their stares were bovine, incurious. Small children not on leash trotted with their mothers, and once Max was startled to see a wrinkled little head peeping out of a pouch—these man-creatures were marsupials, too.

Max controlled a desire to retch and as they passed out of sight he turned to Ellie. "Gosh!"

"Max," Eldreth said hoarsely, "do you suppose we've died and gone to our punishment?"

"Huh? Don't be silly. Things are bad enough."

"I mean it. That was something right out of Dante's Inferno."

Max was swallowing uneasily and not feeling good-tempered. "Look, you can pretend you're dead if you want to. Me, I'm alive and I mean to stay so. Those things weren't men. Don't let it throw you."

"But they *were* men. Men and women and children."

"No, they weren't. Being shaped like us doesn't make them men. Being a man is something else entirely." He scowled. "Maybe the centaurs are 'men.'"

"Oh, no—"

"Don't be too sure. They seem to run things in this country."

The discussion was cut short by another arrival. It was almost dark and they did not see the centaur until he entered their clearing. He was followed by three of the—Max decided to call them 'men' though he resented the necessity—followed by three men. They were not on leashes. All three were bearing burdens. The centaur spoke to them; they distributed what they carried.

One of them set down a large clay bowl filled with water in the space separating Max and Ellie. It was the first artifact that any human had seen on Charity and did not indicate a high level of mechanical culture, being crudely modeled and clearly not thrown on a potter's wheel; it held water, no more could be said for it. A second porter dumped a double armful of small fruits beside the bowl. Two of them splashed into the bowl, he did not bother to fish them out.

Max had to look twice to see what the third slave was carrying. It looked as if he had three large ovoid balls slung by ropes in each of his hands; second inspection showed them to be animals about the size of opossums which he carried by their tails. He went

around the clearing, stopping every few feet and lift-
ing one of his burdens to a lower branch. When he
had finished they were surrounded by six small creatures, each hanging by its tail. The centaur followed
the slave, Max saw him stroke each animal and press a
spot on its neck. In each case the entire body of the little animal lit up, began to shine like a firefly with soft
silvery light.

The clearing was softly illuminated thereby—well
enough, Max thought, to read large print. One of the
hobgoblins balloons came sailing silently between
trees and anchored to a point thirty feet above them;
it seemed to settle down for the night.

The centaur came over to Max and prodded him
with a hoof, snorting inquiringly. Max listened carefully, then repeated the sound. The centaur answered
and again Max mimicked. This useless exchange continued for a few phrases, then the centaur gave up and
left, his train trotting after him.

Ellie shivered. "Phew!" she exclaimed, "I'm glad
they're gone. I can stand the centaurs, a little, but
those men . . . ugh!"

He shared her disgust; they looked less human close
up, having hair lines that started where their eyebrows
should have been. They were so flat-headed that their
ears stuck up above their skulls. But it was not this
that had impressed Max. When the centaur had spoken to him Max had gotten his first good look into a
centaur's mouth. Those teeth were never meant for
munching grain, they were more like the teeth of a ti-
ger—or a shark.

He decided not to mention this. "Say, wasn't that
the same one that was leading the herd that caught
us?"

"How would I know? They all look alike."

"But they don't, any more than two horses look
alike."

"Horses all look alike."

"But . . ." He stopped, baffled by a city viewpoint at

which communication failed. "I think it was the same one."

"I can't see that it matters."

"It might. I'm trying to learn their language."

"I heard you swallowing your tonsils. How did you do that?"

"Oh, you just remember what a sound sounds like, then do it." He threw his head back and made a very plaintive sound.

"What was *that?*"

"A shote stuck in a fence. Little shote by the name of Abner I had once."

"It sounds tragic."

"It was, until I helped him loose. Ellie, I think they've bedded us down for the night." He gestured at the bowl and the fruit beside it. "Like feeding the hogs."

"Don't put it that way. Room service. Room service and maid service and lights. Food and drink." She picked up one of the fruits. It was about the size and shape of a cucumber. "Do you suppose this is fit to eat?"

"I don't think you ought to try it. Ellie, it would be smart not to eat or drink anything until we are rescued."

"Well, maybe we could go hungry but we certainly can't go without water. You die of thirst in a day or two."

"But we may be rescued before morning."

"Maybe." She peeled the fruit. "It smells good. Something like a banana."

He peeled one and sniffed it. "More like a pawpaw."

"Well?"

"Mmm— Look here, I'll eat one. If it hasn't made me sick in a half hour, then you can try one."

"Yes, sir, boss man." She bit into the one she held.

"Mind the seeds."

"Ellie, you're a juvenile delinquent."

She wrinkled her nose and smiled. "You say the

sweetest things! I try to be."

Max bit into his. Not bad—not as much flavor as a pawpaw, but not bad. Some minutes later he was saying, "Maybe we should leave some for breakfast?"

"All right. I'm full anyway." Ellie leaned over and drank. Without words they had each concluded that the cloying meal required them to risk the water. "There, I feel better. At least we'll die comfortably. Max? Do you think we dare sleep? I'm dead."

"I think they are through with us for the night. You sleep, I'll sit up."

"No, that's not fair. Honest, what good would it do to keep watch? We can't get away."

"Well . . . here, take my knife. You can sleep with it in your hand."

"All right." She reached across the bowl and accepted it. "Good night, Max. I'm going to count sheep."

"Good night." He stretched out, shifted and got a tree cone out of his ribs, then tried to relax. Fatigue and a full stomach helped, the knowledge of their plight hindered—and that hobgoblin hanging up there. Maybe *it* was keeping watch—but not for their benefit.

"Max? Are you asleep?"

"No, Ellie."

"Hold my hand? I'm *scared*."

"I can't reach it."

"Yes, you can. Swing around the other way."

He did so, and found that he could reach over his head past the water bowl and clasp her hand. "Thanks, Max. Good night some more."

He lay on his back and stared up through the trees. Despite the half light given by the luminiferous animals he could see stars and the numerous meteor trails crisscrossing the sky. To avoid thinking he started counting them. Presently they started exploding in his head and he was asleep.

The light of the local sun through the trees awakened him. He raised his head. "I wondered how long you would sleep," Eldreth announced. "Look who's here."

He sat up, wincing with every move, and turned around. Mr. Chips was sitting on Ellie's middle and peeling one of the papaya-like fruits. " 'Lo, Maxie."

"Hello, Chipsie." He saw that the note was still tied to her. "Bad girl!"

Mr. Chips turned to Ellie for comfort. Tears started to leak out. "No, no," corrected Ellie. "Good girl. She's promised to go find Maggie as soon as she finishes breakfast. Haven't you, dear?"

"Go find Maggie," the spider puppy agreed.

"Don't blame her, Max. Spider puppies aren't nocturnal back home. She just waited until we were quiet, then came back. She couldn't help it. I found her sleeping in my arm."

The spider puppy finished eating, then drank daintily from the bowl. Max decided that it didn't matter, considering who had probably used it before they had. This thought he suppressed quickly. "Find Maggie," Mr. Chips announced.

"Yes, dear. Go straight back to the ship as fast as you can and find Maggie. Hurry."

"Find Maggie. Hurry fast. 'Bye, Maxie." The spider puppy took to the trees and scampered away in the right direction.

"Do you think she'll get there?" asked Max.

"I think so. After all, her ancestors found their way through forests and such for a lot of generations. She knows it's important; we had a long talk."

"Do you really think she understands that much?"

"She understands about pleasing me and that's enough. Max, do you suppose they can possibly reach us today? I don't want to spend another night here."

"Neither do I. If Chipsie can move faster than we can . . ."

"Oh, she can."

"Then maybe—if they start quickly."

"I hope so. Ready for breakfast?"

"Did Chipsie leave anything?"

"Three apiece. I've had mine. Here."

"Sure you're lying? There were only five when we went to sleep." She looked sheepish and allowed him to split the odd one. While they were eating he noticed a change. "Hey, what became of the over-sized lightning bugs?"

"Oh. One of those awful creatures came at dawn and carried them away. I was set to scream but he didn't come close to me, so I let you sleep."

"Thanks. I see our chaperone is with us." The hobgoblin still hung in the tree tops.

"Yes, and there have been peekers around all morning, too."

"Did you get a look at one?"

"Of course not." She stood up, stretched and winced. "Now to see what beautiful surprises this lovely day brings forth." She made a sour face. "The program I would pick is to sit right here and never lay eyes on anything until George Daigler shows up with about a dozen armed men. I'd kiss him. I'd kiss all of them."

"So would I."

Until well past noon Eldreth's chosen schedule prevailed, nothing happened. They heard from time to time the bugling and snorting of centaurs but saw none. They talked in desultory fashion, having already disposed of both hopes and fears, and were dozing in the sunshine, when they suddenly came alert to the fact that a centaur was entering the clearing.

Max felt sure that it was the leader of the herd, or at least that it was the one who had fed and watered them. The creature wasted no time, making it clear with kicks and prods that they were to allow themselves to be leashed for travel.

Never once were they free of the living ropes. Max thought of attacking the centaur, perhaps leaping on his back and cutting his throat. But it seemed most unlikely that he could do it quietly enough; one snort might bring the herd down on them. Besides which he knew no way to get free of their bonds even if he killed the centaur. Better wait—especially with a messenger gone for help.

They were led, falling and being dragged occasionally, along the route taken by the party of slaves. It became apparent that they were entering a large centaur settlement. The path opened out into a winding, well-tended road with centaurs going both directions and branching off onto side roads. There were no buildings, none of the outward marks of a civilized race—but there was an air of organization, of custom, of stability. Little centaurs scampered about, got in the way, and were ordered aside. There was activity of various sorts on both sides of the road and grotesque human slaves were almost as numerous as centaurs, carrying burdens, working in unexplained fashions—some with living-rope bonds, some allowed to run free. They could not see much because of the uncomfortable pace they were forced to maintain.

Once Max noted an activity on his side of the road that he wished to see better. He did not mention it to Ellie, not only because talking was difficult but because he did not wish to worry her—but it had looked like an outdoor butcher shop to him. The hanging carcasses were not centaurs.

They stopped at last in a very large clearing, well filled with centaurs. Their master patted the lines that bound them and thereby caused them to shorten until they were fetched close to his sides. He then took his place in a centaur queue.

A large, grizzled, and presumably elderly centaur was holding court on one side of the "square." He stood with quiet dignity as single centaurs or groups came in succession before him. Max watched with interest so great that he almost lost his fear. Each case would be the cause of much discussion, then the centaur chieftain would make a single remark and the case would be over. The contestants would leave quietly. The conclusion was inescapable that law or custom was being administered, with the large centaur as arbiter.

There was none of the travesties of men in the clearing but there were underfoot odd animals that looked like flattened-out hogs. Their legs were so short that they seemed more like tractor treads. They were mostly mouth and teeth and snuffling snouts, and whatever they came to, if it was not a centaur's hoof, they devoured. Max understood from watching them how the area, although thickly inhabited, was kept so clean; these scavengers were animated street cleaners.

Their master gradually worked up toward the head of the line. The last case before theirs concerned the only centaur they had seen which did not seem in vibrant health. He was old and skinny, his coat was dull and his bones stuck pitifully through his hide. One eye was blind, a blank white; the other was inflamed and weeping a thick ichor.

The judge, mayor, or top herd leader discussed his case with two younger healthy centaurs who seemed to be attending him almost as nurses. Then the boss centaur moved from his position of honor and walked around the sick one, inspecting him from all sides. Then he spoke to him.

The old sick one responded feebly, a single snorted word. The chief centaur spoke again, got what seemed to Max the same answer. The chief backed into his former position, set up a curious whinnying cry.

From all sides the squatty scavengers converged on the spot. They formed a ring around the sick one and his attendants, dozens of them, snuffling and grunting. The chief bugled once; one attendant reached into its pouch and hauled forth a creature curled into a knot, the centaur stroked it and it unwound. To Max it looked unpleasantly like an eel.

The attendant extended it toward the sick centaur. It made no move to stop him, but waited, watching with his one good eye. The head of the slender thing was suddenly touched to the neck of the sick centaur; he jerked in the characteristic convulsion of electric shock and collapsed.

The chief centaur snorted once—and the scavengers

waddled forward with surprising speed, swarming over the body and concealing it. When they backed away, still snuffling, there were not even bones.

Max called out softly, "Steady, Ellie! Get a grip on yourself, kid."

She answered faintly, "I'm all right."

# 19

# A FRIEND IN NEED

For the first time they were turned loose. Their master tickled their bonds, which dropped from their ankles. Max said softly to Ellie, "If you want to run for it, I'll keep them busy."

Ellie shook her head. "No good. They'd have me before I went fifty feet. Besides—I can't find my way back."

Max shut up, knowing that she was right but having felt obliged to offer. The chief centaur inspected them with the characteristic expression of gentle surprise, exchanged bugling comments with their captor. They were under discussion for some time, there appeared to be some matter to be decided. Max got out his knife. He had no plan, other than a determination that no centaur would approach either one of them with that electric-shock creature, or any other menace, without a fight.

The crisis faded away. Their captor flicked their leashes about their ankles and dragged them off. Fifteen minutes later they were again staked out in the clearing they had occupied. Ellie looked around her after the centaur had gone and sighed. " 'Be it ever so humble . . .' Max, it actually feels good to get back here."

"I know."

The monotony that followed was varied by one thing only: fading hope and mounting despair. They were not treated unkindly; they were simply domestic animals—fed and watered and largely ignored. Once a day they were given water and plenty of the native papayas. After the first night they no longer had the luxury of "artificial" light, nor did the hobgoblin hang over their clearing. But there was no way of escape, short of gnawing off a leg and crawling away.

For two or three days they discussed the possibility

of rescue with mounting anxiety, then, having beaten the subject to death they dropped it; it simply added to their distress. Ellie rarely smiled now and she had quit her frivolous back talk; it seemed that it had finally gotten through her armor that this could happen to Eldreth Coburn, only daughter of the rich and almost all-powerful Mr. Commissioner Coburn—a chattel, a barnyard animal of monsters themselves suitable only for zoos.

Max took it a little more philosophically. Never having had much, he did not expect much—not that he enjoyed it. He kept his worst fear secret. Ellie referred to their status as "animals in a zoo" because most of their visitors were small centaurs who came sniffling and bleating around with a curiosity that their elders seemed to lack. He let her description stand because he believed their status worse than that—he thought that they were being fattened for the table.

One week after their capture Eldreth declined to eat breakfast and stayed silent all morning. All that Max could think of to say evoked only monosyllables. In desperation he said, "I'll beat you at three-dee and spot you two starships."

That roused her. "You and who else?" she said scornfully. "And with what?"

"Well, we could play it in our heads. You know—blindfold."

She shook her head. "No good. You'd claim your memory was better than mine and I wouldn't be able to prove you were cheating."

"Nasty little brat."

She smiled suddenly. "That's better. You've been too gentle with me lately—it depresses me. Max, we could make a set."

"How?"

"With these." She picked up one of many tree cones that littered the clearing. "A big one is a flagship. We can pick various sizes and break the thingamajigs off and such."

They both got interested. The water bowl was

moved aside so that it no longer occupied the center of the space marked by the limits of their tethers and the no-man's-land between them was brushed free of needles and marked with scratches as boards. The boards had to be side by side; they must stack them in their minds, but that was a common expedient for players with good visualization when using an unpowered set—it saved time between moves.

Pebbles became robots; torn bits of cloth tied to cones distinguished sides and helped to designate pieces. By midafternoon they were ready. They were still playing their first game when darkness forced them to stop. As they lay down to sleep Max said, "I'd better not take your hand. I'd knock over men in the dark."

"I won't sleep if you don't—I won't feel safe. Besides, that gorilla messed up one board changing the water."

"That's all right. I remember where they were."

"Then you can just remember where they all are. Stretch out your arm."

He groped in the darkness, found her fingers. "Night, Max. Sleep tight."

"Good night, Ellie."

Thereafter they played from sunup to sundown. Their owner came once, watched them for an hour, went away without a snort. Once when Ellie had fought him to a draw Max said, "You know, Ellie, you play this game awfully well—for a girl."

"Thank you too much."

"No, I mean it. I suppose girls are probably as intelligent as men, but most of them don't act like it. I think it's because they don't have to. If a girl is pretty, she doesn't have to think. Of course, if she can't get by on her looks, then—well, take you for example. If you . . ."

"*Oh!* So I'm ugly, Mr. Jones!"

"Wait a minute. I didn't say that. Let's suppose that you were the most beautiful woman since Helen of Troy. In that case, you would . . ." He found that he was talking to her back. She had swung round, grabbed her knees, and was ignoring him.

He stretched himself to the limit of his tether, bound leg straight out behind him, and managed to touch her shoulder. "Ellie?"

She shook off his hand. "Keep your distance! You smell like an old goat."

"Well," he said reasonably, "you're no lily yourself. You haven't had a bath lately either."

"I know it!" she snapped, and started to sob. "And I hate it. I just . . . h- h- *hate* it. I look *awful*."

"No, you don't. Not to me."

She turned a tear-wet and very dirty face. "Liar."

"Nothing wrong that some soap and water won't fix."

"Oh, if only I had some." She looked at him. "You aren't at your best yourself, Mr. Jones. You need a haircut and the way your beard grows in patches is ghastly."

He fingered the untidy stubble on his chin. "I can't help it."

"Neither can I." She sighed. "Set up the boards again."

Thereafter she beat him three straight games, one with a disgraceful idiot's mate. He looked at the boards sadly when it was over. "And you are the girl who flunked improper fractions?"

"Mr. Jones, has it ever occurred to you, the world being what it is, that women sometimes prefer not to appear too bright?" He was digesting this when she added, "I learned this game at my father's knee, before I learned to read. I was junior champion of Hespera before I got shanghaied. Stop by sometime and I'll show you my cup."

"Is that true? Really?"

"I'd rather play than eat—when I can find competition. But you're learning. Someday you'll be able to give me a good game."

"I guess I don't understand women."

"That's an understatement."

Max was a long time getting to sleep that night.
Long after Eldreth was gently snoring he was still
staring at the shining tail of the big comet, watching
the shooting star trails, and thinking. None of his
thoughts was pleasant.

Their position was hopeless, he admitted. Even
though Chipsie had failed (he had never pinned much
hope on her), searching parties should have found
them by now. There was no longer any reason to think
that they would be rescued.

And now Ellie was openly contemptuous of him. He
had managed to hurt her pride again—again with his
big, loose, flapping jaw! Why, he should have told her
that she was the prettiest thing this side of paradise, if
it would make her feel good—she had mighty little to
feel good about these days!

Being captive had been tolerable because of her, he
admitted—now he had nothing to look forward to but
day after day of losing at three-dee while Ellie grimly
proved that girls were as good as men and better. At
the end of it they would wind up as an item in the diet
of a thing that should never have been born.

If only Dr. Hendrix hadn't died!

If only he had been firm with Ellie when it mattered.

To top it off, and at the moment almost the worst of
all, he felt that if he ate just one more of those blasted
pawpaws it would gag him.

He was awakened by a hand on his shoulder and a
whisper in his ear. "Max!"

"What the—?"

"*Quiet!* Not a sound."

It was Sam crouching over him—Sam!

As he sat up, sleep jarred out of him by adrenalin
shock, he saw Sam move noiselessly to where Ellie
slept. He squatted over her but did not touch her.
"Miss Eldreth," he said softly.

Ellie's eyes opened and stared. She opened her
mouth, Max was terrified that she might cry out. Sam

hastily signed for silence; she looked at him and nodded. Sam knelt over her, seemed to study something in the shadow-laced moonlight, then took out a hand gun. There was the briefest of low-energy discharges, entirely silent, and Ellie stood up—free. Sam returned to Max. "Hold still," he whispered. "I don't want to burn you." He knelt over Max's bound ankle.

When the gun flared Max felt an almost paralyzing constriction around his ankle, then the thing fell off. The amputated major part contracted and jerked away into the shadows. Max stood up. "How—"

"Not a word. Follow me." Sam led off into the bushes with Ellie behind him and Max following closely. They had gone only twenty yards when there was a whimpering cry of "Ellie!" and the spider puppy landed in Eldreth's arms. Sam turned suddenly.

"Keep her quiet," he whispered, "for your life."

Ellie nodded and started petting the little creature, crooning to it voicelessly. When Chipsie tried to talk, she silenced it, then stuffed it inside her shirt. Sam waited these few moments, now started on without speaking.

They proceeded for several hundred yards as near silently as three people who believe their lives hang on it can manage. Finally Sam stopped. "This is as far as we dare go," he said in a low voice. "Any farther in the dark and I'd be lost. But I'm pretty sure we are outside their sleeping grounds. We'll start again at the first light."

"How did you get here in the dark, then?"

"I didn't. Chips and I have been hiding in thick bushes since midafternoon, not fifty feet from you."

"Oh." Max looked around, looked up at the stars. "I can take us back in the dark."

"You can? It 'ud be a darn good thing. These babies don't stir out at night—I think."

"Let me get in the lead. You get behind Ellie."

It took more than an hour to get to the edge of the tableland. The darkness, the undergrowth, the need for absolute silence, and the fact that Max had to take it slowly to keep his bearings despite his photographic memory all slowed them down. The trip downhill into the valley was even slower.

When they reached the edge of the trees with comparatively flat grassland in front Sam halted them and surveyed the valley by dim moonlight. "Mustn't get caught in the open," he whispered. "They can't throw those snakes too well among trees, but out in the open —oh, brother!"

"You know about the throwing ropes?"

"Sure."

"Sam," whispered Ellie. "Mr. Anderson, why did . . ."

"Sssh!" he cautioned. "Explanations later. Straight across, at a dogtrot. Miss Eldreth, you set the pace. Max, pick your bearings and guide us. We'll run side by side. All set?"

"Just a minute." Max took the spider puppy from Eldreth, zipping it inside his shirt as she had done. Mr. Chips did not even wake up, but moaned softly like a disturbed baby. "Okay."

They ran and walked and ran again for a half hour or more, wasting no breath on words, putting everything into gaining distance from the centaur community. Knee-high grass and semi-darkness made the going hard. They were almost to the bottom of the valley and Max was straining to spot the stream when Sam called out, "Down! Down flat!"

Max hit dirt, taking it on his elbows to protect Chips; Ellie flopped beside him. Max turned his head cautiously and whispered, "Centaurs?"

"No. Shut up."

A hobgoblin balloon, moving at night to Max's surprise, was drifting across the valley at an altitude of about a hundred feet. Its course would take it past them, missing them by perhaps a hundred yards. Then it veered and came toward them.

It lost altitude and hovered almost over them. Max saw Sam aim carefully, steadying his pistol with both hands. There was momentarily a faint violet pencil from gun to hobgoblin; the creature burst and fell so close by that Max could smell burned meat. Sam returned his weapon and got to his feet. "One less spy," he said with satisfaction. "Let's get going, kids."

"You think those things spy?"

" 'Think'? We know. Those polo ponies have this place *organized*. Pipe down and make miles."

Ellie found the stream by falling into it. They hauled her out and waded across, stopping only to drink. On the other bank Sam said, "Where's your left shoe, Miss Eldreth?"

"It came off in the brook."

Sam stopped to search but it was useless; the water looked like ink in the faint light. "No good," he decided. "We could waste the whole night. You're due for sore feet—sorry. Better throw away your other shoe."

It did not slow them until they reached the far ridge beyond which lay Charityville and the ship. Soon after they started up Ellie cut her right foot on a rock. She did her best, setting her jaw and not complaining, but it handicapped them. There was a hint of dawn in the air by the time they reached the top. Max started to lead them down the arroyo that he and Ellie had come up so many year-long days ago. Sam stopped him. "Let me get this straight. This isn't the draw that faces the ship, is it?"

"No, that one is just north of this." Max reconstructed in his mind how it had looked from the ship and compared it with his memory of the photomap taken as the ship landed. "Actually a shoulder just beyond the next draw faces the ship."

"I thought so. This is the one Chips led me up, but I want us to stay in the trees as long as possible. It'll be light by the time we'd be down to the flat."

"Does it matter? There have never been any centaurs seen in the valley the ship is in."

"You mean you never saw any. You've been away, old son. We're in danger now—and in worse danger the closer we get to the ship. Keep your voice down—and lead us to that shoulder that sticks out toward the ship. If you can."

Max could, though it meant going over strange terrain and keeping his bearings from his memory of a small-scale map. It involved "crossing the furrows," too, instead of following a dry water course—which led to impasses such as thirty-foot drops that had to be gone painfully around. Sam grew edgy as the light increased and urged them to greater speed and greater silence even as Ellie's increasingly crippled condition made his demands harder to meet.

"I really am sorry," he whispered after she had to slide and scramble down a rock slope, checking herself with bare and bloody feet. "But it's better to get there on stumps than to let them catch you."

"I know." Her face contorted but she made no sound. It was daylight by the time Max led them out on the shoulder. Silently he indicated the ship, a half mile away. They were about level with its top.

"Down this way, I think," he said quietly to Sam.

"No."

"Huh?"

"Chilluns, it's Uncle Sam's opinion that we had better lie doggo in those bushes, holding still and letting the beggar flies bite us, until after sundown."

Max eyed the thousand yard gap. "We could run for it."

"And four legs run faster than two legs. We've learned that lately."

The bushes selected by Sam grew out to the edge of the shoulder. He crawled through them until he reached a place where he could spy the valley below while still hidden. Ellie and Max wriggled after him. The ground dropped off sharply just beyond them. The ship faced them, to their left and nearer was Charityville.

"Get comfortable," Sam ordered, "and we'll take turns keeping guard. Sleep if you can, this will be a long watch."

Max tried to shift Mr. Chips around so that he might lie flat. A little head poked out of his collar.

"Good morning," the spider puppy said gravely. "Breakfast?"

"No breakfast, hon," Ellie told her. "Sam, is it all right to let her out?"

"I guess so. But keep her quiet." Sam was studying the plain below. Max did the same.

"Sam? Why don't we head for the village? It's closer."

"Nobody there. Abandoned."

"What? Look, Sam, can't you tell us now what's happened?"

Sam did not take his eyes off the plain. "Okay. But hold it down to whispers. What do you want to know?"

That was a hard one—Max wanted to know everything. "What happened to the village?"

"Gave it up. Too dangerous."

"Huh? Anybody caught?"

"Not permanently. Daigler had a gun. But then the fun began. We thought that all they had were those throwing snakes and that we had scared them off. But they've got lots more than that. Things that burrow underground, for example. That's why the village had to be abandoned."

"Anybody hurt?"

"Well . . . the newlyweds were already in residence. Becky Weberbauer is a widow."

Ellie gasped and Sam whispered sharply to be quiet. Max mulled it over before saying, "Sam, I don't see why, after they got my message, they didn't . . ."

"What message?"

Max explained. Sam shook his head. "The pooch got back all right. By then we knew you were missing and were searching for you—armed, fortunately. But there was no message."

"Huh? How did you find us?"

"Chips led me, I told you. But that was all. Somebody stuffed her into her old cage and that's where I found her yesterday. I stopped to pet her, knowing

you were gone, Miss Eldreth—and found the poor little thing nearly out of her mind. I finally got it
through my head that she knew where you two were.
So . . ." He shrugged.

"Oh. But I can't see," Max whispered, "why you
risked it alone. You already knew they were dangerous; you should have had every man in the ship with
you, armed."

Sam shook his head. "And we would have lost every
man. A sneak was possible; the other wasn't. And we
had to get you back."

"Thanks. I don't know how to say it, Sam. Anyhow,
thanks."

"Yes," added Ellie, "and stop calling me 'Miss Eldreth.' I'm Ellie to my friends."

"Okay, Ellie. How are the feet?"

"I'll live."

"Good." He turned his head to Max. "But I didn't
say we *wanted* to get you back, I said we *had* to. You,
Max. No offense, Ellie."

"Huh? Why me?"

"Well . . ." Sam seemed reluctant. "You'll get the
details when you get back. But it looks like you'll be
needed if they take the ship off. You're the only astrogator left."

"Huh? What happened to Simes?"

"*Quiet!* He's dead."

"For Pete's sake." Max decided that, little as he
liked Simes, death at the hands of the centaurs he
would not have wished on any human; he said so.

"Oh, no, it wasn't that way. You see, when Captain
Blaine died . . ."

"The Captain, *too?*"

"Yes."

"I knew he was sick, I didn't know he was that
sick."

"Well, call it a broken heart. Or honorable hara-kiri.
Or an accident. I found an empty box for sleeping
pills when I helped pack his things. Maybe he took

them, or maybe your pal Simes slipped them in his tea. The Surgeon certified 'natural causes' and that's how it was logged. What is a natural cause when a man can't bear to live any longer?"

Ellie said softly, "He was a good man."

"Yes," agreed Sam. "Too good, maybe."

"But how about Simes?"

"Well, now, that was another matter. Simes seemed to feel that he was crown prince, but the First wouldn't stand for it. Something about some films the Chief Computerman had. Anyhow, he tried to get tough with Walther and I sort of broke his neck. There wasn't time to be gentle," Sam added hastily. "Simes pulled a gun."

"Sam! You aren't in trouble?"

"None, except here and now. If we—quiet, kids!" He peered more sharply through the bushes. "Not a sound, not a movement," he whispered. "It may miss us."

A hobgoblin was drifting down from north, paralleling the ridge above and out from it, as if it were scouting the high land. Max said in Sam's ear, "Hadn't we better scrunch back?"

"Too late. Just hold still."

The balloon drifted abreast of them, stopped, then moved slowly toward them. Max saw that Sam had his gun out. He held his fire until the hobgoblin hovered above them. The shot burned needles and branches but it brought down the thing.

"Sam! There's another one!"

"Where?" Sam looked where Max pointed. The second hobgoblin apparently had been covering the first, higher and farther out. Even as they watched it veered away and gained altitude.

"Get it, Sam!"

Sam stood up. "Too late. Too far and too late. Well, kids, away we go. No need to keep quiet. Sit down and slide, Ellie; it'll save your feet some."

Down they went, scattering rocks and tearing their

clothes, with Mr. Chips on her own and enjoying it. At the bottom Sam said, "Max, how fast can you do a half mile?"

"I don't know. Three minutes."

"Make it less. Get going. I'll help Ellie."

"No."

"You get there! You're needed."

"No!"

Sam sighed. "Always some confounded hero. Take her other arm."

They made a couple of hundred yards half carrying Eldreth, when she shook them off. "I can go faster alone," she panted.

"Okay, let's go!" Sam rasped.

She proved herself right. Ignoring her injured feet she pumped her short legs in a fashion which did not require Max's best speed to keep up, but nevertheless kept him panting. The ship grew larger ahead of them. Max saw that the cage was up and wondered how long it would take to attract attention and get it lowered.

They were half way when Sam shouted, "Here comes the cavalry! Speed it up!"

Max glanced over his shoulder. A herd of centaurs —a dozen, two dozen, perhaps more—was sweeping toward them from the hills on a diagonal plainly intended to cut them off. Ellie saw them too and did speed up, with a burst that momentarily outdistanced Max.

They had cut the distance to a few hundred yards when the cage swung free of the lock and sank lazily toward the ground. Max started to shout that they were going to make it when he heard the drum of hooves close behind. Sam yelled, "Beat it, kids! Into the ship." He stopped.

Max stopped too, while shouting, "*Run*, Ellie!"

Sam snarled, "Run for it, I said! What can *you* do? Without a gun?"

Max hesitated, torn by an unbearable decision. He

saw that Ellie had stopped. Sam glanced back, then backhanded Max across the mouth. "Get moving! Get her inside!"

Max moved, gathering Ellie in one arm and urging her on. Behind them Sam Anderson turned to face his death . . . dropping to one knee and steadying his pistol over his left forearm in precisely the form approved by the manual.

# 20

# "—A SHIP IS NOT JUST STEEL—"

The cage hit the ground, four men swarmed out as Max stumbled inside and dumped Ellie on the floor. The door clanged shut behind them, but not too quickly for Mr. Chips. The spider puppy ran to Ellie, clutched her arm and wailed. Eldreth tried to sit up.

"You all right?" Max demanded.

"Uh, sure. But . . ." She shut up as Max whirled around and tried to open the cage door.

It would not open. It was not until then that he realized that the lift was off the ground and rising slowly. He punched the "stop" control.

Nothing happened, the car continued upward. About ten feet off the ground it stopped. Max looked up through the grille roof and shouted, "Hey! In the lock, there! Lower away!"

He was ignored. He tried the door again—uselessly, as its safety catch prevented it being opened when the cage was in the air. Frustrated and helpless, he grabbed the bars and looked out. He could see nothing of Sam. The centaurs were milling around in the middle distance. He saw one stumble and go down and then another. Then he saw the four men who had passed him. They were on their bellies in fair skirmish line not far from the cage, each with a shoulder gun and each firing carefully. The range was not great, about three hundred yards; they were taking steady toll. Each silent, almost invisible bolt picked off a centaur.

Max counted seven more centaur casualties—then the monsters broke and ran, scattering toward the hills. The firing continued and several more dropped before distance made firing uncertain.

Somebody shouted, "Hold your fire!" and one of the men stumbled to his feet and ran toward the center of the battle. The others got up and followed him.

When they came back they were carrying something that looked like a bundle of clothing. The cage lowered to the ground, they came inside and laid it gently on the floor. One of them glanced at Eldreth, then quickly removed his jacket and laid it over Sam's face. Not until then did Max see that it was Mr. Walther.

The other three were Mr. Daigler, a power man whom Max knew only by sight, and Chief Steward Giordano. The fat man was crying openly. "The filthy vermin!" he sobbed. "He never had a chance. They just rode him down and tromped him." He choked, then added, "But he got at least five of 'em." His eyes rested on Max without recognition. "He made 'em pay."

Eldreth said gently, "Is he dead?"

"Huh? Of course. Don't talk silly." The steward turned his face away.

The car bumped to a stop. Walther looked in through the lock and said angrily, "Get those bystanders out of the way. What is this? A circus?" He turned back. "Let's get him in, men."

As he was bending to help, Max saw Eldreth being led away by Mrs. Dumont. Tenderly they carried Sam in and deposited him on the deck where the Surgeon was waiting. Walther straightened up and seemed to notice Max for the first time. "Mr. Jones? Will you see me in my stateroom as quickly as possible, please?"

"Aye aye, sir. But . . ." Max looked down at his friend. "I'd like to . . ."

Walther cut him short. "There's nothing you can do. Come away." He added more gently, "Make it fifteen minutes. That will give you time for a wash and a change."

Max presented himself on time, showered, his face hastily scraped, and in clean clothes—although lacking a cap. His one cap was somewhere in the far valley, lost on capture. He found Chief Engineer Compagnon and Mr. Samuels, the Purser, with the First

Officer. They were seated around a table, having coffee. "Come in, Mr. Jones," Walther invited. "Sit down. Coffee?"

"Uh, yes, sir." Max discovered that he was terribly hungry. He loaded the brew with cream and sugar.

They sat for a few minutes, talking of unimportant matters, while Max drank his coffee and steadied down. Presently Walther said, "What shape are you in, Mr. Jones?"

"Why, all right, I guess, sir. Tired, maybe."

"I imagine so. I'm sorry to have to disturb you. Do you know the situation now?"

"Partly, sir. Sam told me . . . Sam Anderson . . ." His voice broke.

"We're sorry about Anderson," Mr. Walther said soberly. "In many ways he was one of the best men I ever served with. But go on."

Max recounted what Sam had had time to tell him, but shortened the statements about Simes and Captain Blaine to the simple fact that they were dead. Walther nodded. "Then you know what we want of you?"

"I think so, sir. You want to raise the ship, so you want me to astrogate." He hesitated. "I suppose I can."

"Mmm . . . yes. But that's not all."

"Sir?"

"You must be Captain."

All three had their eyes fixed on him. Max felt lightheaded and for a moment wondered what was wrong. Their faces seemed to swell and then recede. He realized vaguely that he had had little to eat and almost no sleep for many hours and had been running on nerve—yes, that must be what was wrong with him. From a long distance away he heard Walther's voice: ". . . utterly necessary to leave this planet without delay. Now our legal position is clear. In space, only an astrogation officer may command. You are being asked to assume command responsibility while very young but you are the only qualified person— therefore you *must* do it."

Max pulled himself together, the wavering figures came into focus. "Mr. Walther?"

"Yes?"

"But I'm not an astrogator. I'm just a probationary apprentice."

Chief Engineer Compagnon answered him. "Kelly says you're an astrogator," he growled.

"Kelly is more of an astrogator than I am!"

Compagnon shook his head. "You can't pass judgment on yourself." Samuels nodded agreement.

"Let's dispose of that," Walther added. "There is no question of the Chief Computerman becoming captain. Nor does your rank in your guild matter. Line of command, underway, necessarily is limited to astrogators. You are senior in that line, no matter how junior you feel. At this moment, I hold command—until I pass it on. But I can't take a ship into space. If you refuse . . . well, I don't know what we will have to do. I don't know."

Max gulped and said, "Look, sir, I'm not refusing duty. I'll astrogate—shucks, I suppose it's all right to call me the astrogator, under the circumstances. But there is no reason to pretend that I'm captain. You stay in command while I conn the ship. That's best, sir —I wouldn't know how to *act* like a captain."

Walther shook his head. "Not legally possible."

Compagnon added, "I don't care about the legalities. But I know that responsibility can't be divided. Frankly, young fellow, I'd rather have Dutch as skipper than you—but he can't astrogate. I'd be delighted to have Doc Hendrix—but he's gone. I'd rather hold the sack myself than load it on you—but I'm a physicist and I know just enough of the math of astrogation to know that I couldn't in a lifetime acquire the speed that an astrogator *has* to have. Not my temperament. Kelly says you've got it already. I've shipped with Kelly a good many years, I trust him. So it's your pidgin, son; you've got to take it—and the authority that goes with it. Dutch will help—we'll all help—but you can't duck out and hand him the sack."

Mr. Samuels said quietly, "I don't agree with the Chief Engineer about the unimportance of legal aspects; most of these laws have wise reasons behind them. But I agree with what else he says. Mr. Jones, a ship is not just steel, it is a delicate political entity. Its laws and customs cannot be disregarded without inviting disaster. It will be far easier to maintain morale and discipline in this ship with a young captain—with all his officers behind him—than it would be to let passengers and crew suspect that the man who *must* make the crucial decisions, those life-and-death matters involving the handling of the ship, that this all-powerful man nevertheless can't be trusted to command the ship. No, sir, such a situation would frighten me; that is how mutinies are born."

Max felt his heart pounding, his head was aching steadily. Walther looked at him grimly and said, "Well?"

"I'll take it." He added, "I don't see what else I can do."

Walther stood up. "What are your orders, Captain?"

Max sat still and tried to slow his heart. He pressed his fingers to throbbing temples and looked frightened. "Uh, continue with routine. Make preparations to raise ship."

"Aye aye, sir." Walther paused, then added, "May I ask when the Captain plans to raise ship?"

He was having trouble focusing again. "When? Not before tomorrow—tomorrow at noon. I've got to have a night's sleep." He thought to himself that Kelly and he could throw it into a parking orbit, which would get them away from the centaurs—then stop to figure out his next move.

"I think that's wise, sir. We need the time."

Compagnon stood up. "If the Captain will excuse me, sir, I'll get my department started."

Samuels joined him. "Your cabin is ready, sir—I'll have your personal effects moved in in a few minutes."

Max stared at him. He had not yet assimilated the

side implications of his new office. Use Captain Blaine's holy of holies? Sleep in his bed? "Uh, I don't think that's necessary. I'm comfortable where I am."

Samuels glanced at the First Officer, then said, "If you please, Captain, this is one of the things I was talking about when I said that a ship is a delicate political entity."

"Eh?" Max thought about it, then suddenly felt both the burden descend on him and the strength to meet it. "Very well," he answered, his voice deepening. "Do it."

"Yes, sir." Samuels looked at him. "Also, Captain—if you wish it—I'll have Lopez stop in and trim your hair."

Max pushed locks back of his ear. "It *is* shaggy, isn't it? Very well."

The Purser and the Chief Engineer left. Max stood for a moment uncertainly, not sure what his next cue was in this new role. Walther said, "Captain? Can you spare me a few more minutes?"

"Oh, certainly." They sat down and Walther poured more coffee. Max said, "Mr. Walther? Do you suppose we could ring the pantry and get some toast? I haven't eaten today."

"Why, surely! Sorry, sir." Instead of ringing, the First Officer phoned and ordered a high tea. Then he turned to Max. "Captain, I didn't give you all the story —nor did I wish to until we were alone."

"So?"

"Don't misunderstand me. My turning over command to you did not depend on these other matters— nor is it necessary for your officers to know everything that the Captain knows . . . even your department heads."

"Uh, I suppose not."

Walther stared at his coffee. "Have you heard how Mr. Simes happened to die?"

Max told him what little he had learned from Sam. Walther nodded. "That is essentially correct. Mmmm . . . It is not good to speak ill of the dead, but Simes was an unstable character. When Captain Blaine passed on, he took it for granted that he was immediately captain of this ship."

"Well—I suppose it looked that way to him, from the legal standpoint."

"Not at all! Sorry to correct you, Captain, but that is one hundred percent wrong."

Max frowned. "I guess I'm dumb—but I thought that was the argument that was used on me?"

"No, sir. The ship being on the ground, command devolved on me, the senior. I am not required to turn command over to an astrogator until—and *unless*— the ship goes into space. Even then it is not automatically a matter of turning it over to the senior astrogating officer. I have a clearly defined responsibility, with numerous adjudicated cases in point: I must turn command over only to a man I believe can handle it.

"Now I have long had doubts about Mr. Simes, his temperament, I mean. Nevertheless, in this emergency, I would have found it terribly hard *not* to turn command over to him, once it was decided to raise ship. But before we lost the Captain I had had occasion to dig into Mr. Simes' ability as an astrogator—partly as a result of a conversation with you. I talked with Kelly —as you have gathered, Kelly is *very* well thought of. I believe I know now how that last transition went sour; Kelly took pains to show me. That and the fact that Kelly told me bluntly that there wasn't a member of the Worry gang willing to go into space under Mr. Simes made me decide that, if it ever came up, I'd let this ship sit here forever before I would let Simes be captain. That was just thinking ahead; the Captain was sick and prudence forced me to consider possibilities.

"Then the Captain did die—and Simes announced that he was captain. The fool even moved into the cabin and sent for me. I told him he was not in command and never would be. Then I left, got witnesses and took my chief of police along to eject him. You know what happened. Your life isn't the only one that Anderson saved; I owe him mine, too."

Walther abruptly changed the subject. "That phenomenal trick of memory you do—computing without tables or reference books. Can you do it all the time?"

"Uh? Why, yes."

"Do you know all the tables? Or just some of them?"

"I know all the standard tables and manuals that are what an astrogator calls his 'working tools.'" Max started to tell about his uncle, Walther interrupted gently.

"If you please, sir. I'm glad to hear it. I'm *very* glad to hear it. Because the only such books in this ship are the ones in your head."

Kelly had missed the books, of course—not Walther. When he disclosed his suspicions to Walther the two conducted a search. When that failed, it was announced that one (but only one) set was missing; Walther had offered a reward, and the ship had been combed from stern to astrodome—no manuals.

"I suppose he ditched them dirtside," Walther finished. "You know where that leaves us—we're in a state of seige. And we'd find them only by accident if we weren't. So I'm very glad you have the same confidence in your memory that Kelly has."

Max was beginning to have misgivings—it is one thing to do something as a stunt, quite another to do it of necessity. "It isn't that bad," he answered. "Perhaps Kelly never thought of it, but logarithms and binary translation tables can probably be borrowed from engineering—with those we could fudge up methods for any straight hop. The others are needed mostly for anomalous transitions."

"Kelly thought of that, too. Tell me, Captain, how does a survey ship go back after it penetrates a newly located congruency?"

"Huh? So *that* is what you want me to do with the ship?"

"It is not for me," Walther said formally, "to tell the Captain where to take his ship."

Max said slowly, "I've thought about it. I've had a lot of time to think lately." He did not add that he had dwelt on it nights in captivity to save his reason. "Of course, we don't have the instruments that survey ships carry, nor does applied astrogation go much into the theory of calculating congruencies. And even some survey ships don't come back."

"But . . ." They were interrupted by a knock on the door. A steward's mate came in and loaded the table with food. Max felt himself starting to drool.

He spread a slice of toast with butter and jam, and took a big bite. "My, this is good!"

"I should have realized. Have a banana, sir? They look quite good—I believe hydroponics has had to thin them out lately."

Max shuddered. "I don't think I'll ever eat bananas again. Or pawpaws."

"Allergic, Captain?"

"Not exactly. Well . . . yes."

He finished the toast and said, "About that possibility. I'll let you know later."

"Very well, Captain."

Shortly before the dinner hour Max stood in front of the long mirror in the Captain's bedroom and looked at himself. His hair was short again and two hours sleep had killed some of his fatigue. He settled a cap on his head at the proper angle—the name in the sweat band was "Hendrix"; he had found it laid out with one of his own uniforms to which captain's insignia had been added. The sunburst on his chest bothered him—that he was indeed captain he conceded, even though it seemed like a wild dream, but he had felt that he was not entitled to anything but the smaller sunburst and circle, despite his four stripes.

Walther and Samuels had been respectful but firm, with Samuels citing precedents that Max could not check on. Max had given in.

He looked at himself, braced his shoulders, and sighed. He might as well go face them. As he walked down the companionway to the lounge he heard the speakers repeating, "All hands! All passengers! Report to Bifrost Lounge!"

The crowd made way for him silently. He went to the Captain's table—*his* table!—and sat down at its head. Walther was standing by the chair. "Good evening, Captain."

"Evening, Mr. Walther."

Ellie was seated across from him. She caught his eye and smiled. "Hello, Ellie." He felt himself blushing.

"Good evening, Captain," she said firmly. She was dressed in the same high style she had worn the first time he had ever seen her in the lounge; it did not seem possible that this lady could be the same girl whose dirty face had looked at him over three-dee boards scratched in dirt.

"Uh, how are your feet?"

"Bandages and bedroom slippers. But the Surgeon did a fine job. I'll be dancing tomorrow."

"Don't rush it."

She looked at his stripes and his chest. "*You* should talk."

Before he could answer the unanswerable Walther leaned over and said quietly, "We're ready, Captain."

"Oh. Go ahead." Walther tapped on a water glass.

The First Officer explained the situation in calm tones that made it seem reasonable, inevitable. He concluded by saying, ". . . and so, in accordance with law and the custom of space, I have relinquished my temporary command to your new captain. Captain Jones!"

Max stood up. He looked around, swallowed, tried to speak, and couldn't. Then, as effectively as if it had been a dramatic pause and not desperation, he picked up his water tumbler and took a sip. "Guests and fellow crewmen," he said, "we can't stay here. You know that. I have been told that our Surgeon calls the system we are up against here 'symbiotic enslavement'—

like dog to man, only more so, and apparently covering the whole animal kingdom on this planet. Well, men aren't meant for slavery, symbiotic or any sort. But we are too few to win out now, so we must leave."

He stopped for another sip and Ellie caught his eye, encouraging him. "Perhaps someday other men will come back—better prepared. As for us, I am going to try to take the *Asgard* back through the . . . uh, 'hole' you might call it, where we came out. It's a chancy thing. No one is forced to come along—but it is the only possible way to get home. Anyone who's afraid to chance it will be landed on the north pole of planet number three—the evening star we have been calling 'Aphrodite.' You may be able to survive there, although it is pretty hot even at the poles. If you prefer that alternative, turn your names in this evening to the Purser. The rest of us will try to get home." He stopped, then said suddenly, "That's all," and sat down.

There was no applause and he felt glumly that he had muffed his first appearance. Conversation started up around the room, crewmen left, and steward's mates quickly started serving. Ellie looked at him and nodded quietly. Mrs. Mendoza was on his left; she said, "Ma—I mean 'Captain'—is it really so dangerous? I hardly like the thought of trying anything *risky*. Isn't there something else we can do?"

"No."

"But surely there must be?"

"No. I'd rather not discuss it at the table."

"But . . ." He went on firmly spooning soup, trying not to tremble. When he looked up he was caught by a glittering eye across the table, a Mrs. Montefiore, who preferred to be called "Principessa"—a dubious title. "Dolores, don't bother him. We want to hear about his adventures—don't we, Captain?"

"No."

"Come now! I hear that it was terribly *romantic*." She drawled the word and gave Ellie a sly, sidelong look. She looked back at Max with the eye of a predatory bird and showed her teeth. She seemed to have more teeth than was possible. "Tell us *all* about it!"

"No."

"But you simply *can't* refuse!"

Eldreth smiled at her and said, "Princess darling—your mouth is showing."

Mrs. Montefiore shut up.

After dinner Max caught Walther alone. "Mr. Walther?"

"Oh—yes, Captain?"

"Am I correct in thinking that it is my privilege to pick the persons who sit at my table?"

"Yes, sir."

"In that case—that Montefiore female. Will you have her moved, please? Before breakfast?"

Walther smiled faintly. "Aye aye, sir."

# 21

# THE CAPTAIN OF THE ASGARD

They took Sam down and buried him where he had fallen. Max limited it to himself and Walther and Giordano, sending word to Ellie not to come. There was a guard of honor but it was armed to kill and remained spread out around the grave, eyes on the hills. Max read the service in a voice almost too low to be heard—the best he could manage.

Engineering had hurriedly prepared the marker, a pointed slab of stainless metal. Max looked at it before he placed it and thought about the inscription. "Greater love hath no man"?—no, he had decided that Sam wouldn't like that, with his cynical contempt of all sentimentality. He had considered, "He played the cards he was dealt"—but that didn't fit Sam either; if Sam didn't like the cards, he sometimes slipped in a whole new deck. No, this was more Sam's style; he shoved it into the ground and read it:

IN MEMORY OF
SERGEANT SAM ANDERSON
LATE OF THE
IMPERIAL MARINES
*"He ate what was set before him."*

Walther saw the marker for the first time. "So that's how it was? Somehow I thought so."

"Yes. I never did know his right name. Richards. Or maybe Roberts."

"Oh." Walther thought over the implication. "We could get him reinstated, sir, posthumously. His prints will identify him."

"I think Sam would like that."

"I'll see to it, sir, when we get back."

"*If* we get back."

"If you please, Captain—*when* we get back."

Max went straight to the control room. He had been up the evening before and had gotten the first shock of being treated as captain in the Worry Hole over with. When Kelly greeted him with, "Good morning, Captain," he was able to be almost casual.

"Morning, Chief. Morning, Lundy."

"Coffee, sir?"

"Thanks. About that parking orbit—is it set up?"

"Not yet, sir."

"Then forget it. I've decided to head straight back. We can plan it as we go. Got the films?"

"I picked them up earlier." They referred to the films cached in Max's stateroom. Simes had managed to do away with the first set at the time of Captain Blaine's death; the reserve set was the only record of when and where the *Asgard* had emerged into this space, including records of routine sights taken immediately after transition.

"Okay. Let's get busy. Kovak can punch for me."

The others were drifting in, well ahead of time, as was customary in Kelly's gang. "If you wish, sir. I'd be glad to compute for the Captain."

"Kovak can do it. You might help Noguchi and Lundy with the films."

"Aye aye, sir." Data flowed to him presently. He had awakened twice in the night in cold fright that he had lost his unique memory. But when the data started coming, he programmed without effort, appropriate pages opening in his mind. The problem was a short departure to rid themselves of the planet's influence, an adjustment of position to leave the local sun "behind" for simpler treatment of its field, then a long, straight boost for the neighborhood in which they had first appeared in this space. It need not be precise, for transition would not be attempted on the first pass; they must explore the area, taking many more photographic sights and computing from them, to establish a survey that had never been made.

Departure was computed and impressed on tape for the autopilot and the tape placed in the console long

before noon. The ship had been keeping house on local time, about fifty-five standard minutes to the hour;
now the ship would return to Greenwich, the time always kept in the control room—dinner would be late
and some of the "beasts" would as usual reset their
watches the wrong way and blame it on the government.

They synchronized with the power room, the tape
started running, there remained nothing to do but
press the button a few seconds before preset time and
thereby allow the autopilot to raise ship. The phone
rang, Smythe took it and looked at Max. "For you,
Captain. The Purser."

"Captain?" Samuels sounded worried. "I dislike to
disturb you in the control room."

"No matter. What is it?"

"Mrs. Montefiore. She wants to be landed on Aphrodite."

Max thought a moment. "Anybody else change his
mind?"

"No, sir."

"They were all notified to turn in their names last
night."

"I pointed that out to her, sir. Her answers were not
entirely logical."

"Nothing would please me more than to dump her
there. But after all, we are responsible for her. Tell her
'no.'"

"Aye aye, sir. May I have a little leeway in how I express it?"

"Certainly. Just keep her out of my hair."

Max flipped off the phone, found Kelly at his elbow.
"Getting close, sir. Perhaps you will take the console
now and check the set up? Before you raise?"

"Eh? No, you take her up, Chief. You'll have the first
watch."

"Aye aye, Captain." Kelly sat down at the console,
Max took the Captain's seat, feeling self-conscious. He
wished that he had learned to smoke a pipe—it looked
right to have the Captain sit back, relaxed and smok-

ing his pipe, while the ship maneuvered.

He felt a slight pulsation and was pressed more firmly into the chair cushions; the *Asgard* was again on her own private gravity, independent of true accelerations. Moments later the ship raised, but with nothing to show it but the change out the astrodome from blue sky to star-studded ebony of space.

Max got up and found that he was still holding an imaginary pipe, he hastily dropped it. "I'm going below, Chief. Call me when the departure sights are ready to compute. By the way, what rotation of watches do you plan on?"

Kelly locked the board, got up and joined him. "Well, Captain, I had figured on Kovak and me heel-and-toe, with the boys on one in three. We'll double up later."

Max shook his head. "No. You and me and Kovak. And we'll stay on one in three as long as possible. No telling how long we'll fiddle around out there before we take a stab at it."

Kelly lowered his voice. "Captain, may I express an opinion?"

"Kelly, any time you stop being frank with me, I won't have a chance of swinging this. You know that."

"Thank you, sir. The Captain should not wear himself out. You have to do all the computing as it is." Kelly added quietly, "The safety of your ship is more important than—well, perhaps 'pride' is the word."

Max took a long time to reply. He was learning, without the benefit of indoctrination, that a commanding officer is not permitted foibles commonplace in any other role; he himself is ruled more strongly by the powers vested in him than is anyone else. The Captain's privileges—such as chucking a tiresome female from his table—were minor, while the penalties of the inhuman job had unexpected ramifications.

"Chief," he said slowly, "is there room to move the coffee mess over behind the computer?"

Kelly measured the space with his eye. "Yes, sir. Why?"

"I was thinking that would leave room over here to install a cot."

"You intend to sleep up here, sir?"

"Sometimes. But I was thinking of all of us—you shave up here half the time, as it is. The watches for the next few weeks do not actually require the O.W. to be awake most of the time, so we'll all doss off when we can. What do you think?"

"It's against regulations, sir. A bad precedent . . . and a bad example." He glanced over at Noguchi and Smythe.

"You would write it up formal and proper, for my signature, citing the regulation and suspending it on an emergency basis 'for the safety of the ship.'"

"If you say so, sir."

"You don't sound convinced, so maybe I'm wrong. Think it over and let me know."

The cot appeared and the order was posted, but Max never saw either Kelly or Kovak stretched out on the cot. As for himself, had he not used it, he would have had little sleep.

He usually ate in the control room as well. Although there was little to do on their way out to rendezvous with nothingness but take sights to determine the relations of that nothingness with surrounding sky, Max found that when he was not computing he was worrying, or discussing his worries with Kelly.

How did a survey ship find its way back through a newly calculated congruency? And what had gone wrong with those that failed to come back? Perhaps Dr. Hendrix could have figured the other side of an uncharted congruency using only standard ship's equipment—or perhaps not. Max decided that Dr. Hendrix could have done it; the man had been a fanatic about his profession, with a wide knowledge of the theoretical physics behind the routine numerical computations—much wider, Max was sure, than most astrogators.

Max knew that survey ships calculated congruencies from both sides, applying to gravitational field theory data gathered on the previously unknown side. He made attempts to rough out such a calculation, then gave up, having no confidence in his results—he was sure of his mathematical operations but unsure of theory and acutely aware of the roughness of his data. There was simply no way to measure accurately the masses of stars light-years away with the instruments in the *Asgard*.

Kelly seemed relieved at his decision. After that they both gave all their time to an attempt to lay out a "groove" to the unmarked point in the heavens where their photosights said that they had come out—in order that they might eventually scoot down that groove, arriving at the locus just below the speed of light, then kick her over and hope.

A similar maneuver on a planet's surface would be easy—but there is no true parallel with the situation in the sky. The "fixed" stars move at high speeds and there are no other landmarks; to decide what piece of featureless space corresponds with where one was at another time requires a complicated series of calculations having no "elegant" theoretical solutions. For each charted congruency an astrogator has handed to him a table of precalculated solutions—the "Critical Tables for Charted Anomalies." Max and Kelly had to fudge up their own.

Max spent so much time in the control room that the First Officer finally suggested that passenger morale would be better if he could show himself in the lounge occasionally. Walther did not add that Max should wear a smile and a look of quiet confidence, but he implied it. Thereafter Max endeavored to dine with his officers and passengers.

He had of course seen very little of Eldreth. When he saw her at the first dinner after Walther's gentle suggestion she seemed friendly but distant. He decided that she was treating him with respect, which made him wonder if she were ill. He recalled that she had originally come aboard in a stretcher, perhaps she was not as rugged as she pretended to be. He made a mental note to ask the Surgeon—indirectly, of course!

They were dawdling over coffee and Max was beginning to fidget with a desire to get back to the Worry Hole. He reminded himself sharply that Walther expected him not to show anxiety—then looked around and said loudly, "This place is like a morgue. Doesn't anyone dance here these days? Dumont!"

"Yes, Captain?"

"Let's have some dance music. Mrs. Mendoza, would you honor me?"

Mrs. Mendoza tittered and accepted. She turned out to be a disgrace to Argentina, no sense of rhythm. But he piloted her around with only minor collisions and got her back to her chair, so timed that he could bow out gracefully. He then exercised the privilege of rank by cutting in on Mrs. Daigler. Maggie's hair was still short but her splendor otherwise restored.

"We've missed you, Captain."

"I've been working. Short-handed, you know."

"I suppose so. Er . . . Captain, is it pretty soon now?"

"Before we transit? Not long. It has taken this long because we have had to do an enormous number of fiddlin' calculations—to be safe, you know."

"Are we *really* going home?"

He gave what he hoped was a confident smile. "Absolutely. Don't start any long book from the ship's library; the Purser won't let you take it dirtside."

She sighed. "I feel better."

He thanked her for the waltz, looked around, saw Mrs. Montefiore and decided that his obligation to maintain morale did not extend that far. Eldreth was seated, so he went to her. "Feet still bothering you, Ellie?"

"No, Captain. Thank you for asking."

"Then will you dance with me?"

She opened her eyes wide. "You mean the Captain has time for po' li'l ole me?"

He leaned closer. "One more crack like that, dirty face, and you'll be tossed into irons."

She giggled and wrinkled her nose. "Aye aye, Captain, sir."

For a while they danced without talking, with Max a little overpowered by her nearness and wondering why he had not done this sooner. Finally she said, "Max? Have you given up three-dee permanently?"

"Huh? Not at all. After we make this transit I'll have time to play—if you'll spot me two starships."

"I'm sorry I ever told you about that. But I do wish you would say hello to Chipsie sometimes. She was asking this morning, 'Where Maxie?'"

"Oh, I *am* sorry. I'd take her up to the control room with me occasionally, except that she might push a button and lose us a month's work. Go fetch her."

"The crowd would make her nervous. We'll go see her."

He shook his head. "Not to your room."

"Huh? Don't be silly. I've got no reputation left anyhow, and a captain can do as he pleases."

"That shows you've never been a captain. See that vulture watching us?" He indicated Mrs. Montefiore with his eyes. "Now go get Chipsie and no more of your back talk."

"Aye aye, Captain."

He scratched Chipsie's chin, fed her sugar cubes, and assured her that she was the finest spider puppy in that part of the sky. He then excused himself.

He was feeling exhilarated and oddly reassured. Seeing Mr. Walther disappearing into his room, he paused at the companionway and on impulse followed him. A matter had been worrying him, this was as good a time as any.

"Dutch? Are you busy?"

The First Officer turned. "Oh. No, Captain. Come in."

Max waited during the ceremonial coffee, then broached it. "Something on my mind, Mr. Walther—a personal matter."

"Anything I can do?"

"I don't think so. But you're a lot more experienced than I am; I'd like to tell you about it."

"If the Captain wishes."

"Look, Dutch, this is a 'Max' matter, not a 'Captain' matter."

Walther smiled. "All right. But don't ask me to change my form of address. I might pick up a bad habit."

"Okay, okay." Max had intended to sound out Walther about his phony record: had Dr. Hendrix reported it? Or hadn't he?

But he found it impossible to follow that line; being a captain had forced him into a different mold. "I want to tell you how I got into this ship." He told it all, not suppressing Sam's part now that it no longer could hurt Sam. Walther listened gravely.

"I've been waiting for you to mention this, Captain," he said at last. "Dr. Hendrix reported it to me, in less detail, when he put you up for apprentice astrogator. We agreed that it was a matter that need not be raised inside the ship."

"It's what happens after we get back that frets me. If we get back."

"When we get back. Are you asking for advice? Or help? Or what?"

"I don't know. I just wanted to tell you."

"Mmmm . . . there are two alternatives. One we could handle here, by altering a not very important report. In which . . ."

"No, Dutch. I won't have phony reports going out of the *Asgard*."

"I was fairly certain you would say that. I feel the same way, except that I would feel obligated for—well, various reasons—to cover up for you if you asked it."

"I once intended to arrange a phony on it. I even felt justified. But I can't do it now."

"I understand. The remaining alternative is to report it and face the music. In which case I'll see it through with you—and so will the Chief Engineer and the Purser, I feel sure."

Max sat back, feeling warm and happy. "Thanks, Dutch. I don't care what they do to me . . . just as long as it doesn't keep me out of space."

"I don't think they'll try to do that, not if you bring this ship in. But if they do—well, they'll know they've been in a fight. Meantime try to forget it."

"I'll try." Max frowned. "Dutch? Tell me the truth, what do *you* think about the stunt I pulled?"

"That's a hard question, Captain. More important is, how do you feel about it?"

"Me? I don't know. I know how I used to feel—I felt belligerent."

"Eh?"

"I was always explaining—in my mind of course—why I did it, justifying myself, pointing out that the system was at fault, not me. Now I don't want to justify myself. Not that I regret it, not when I think what I would have missed. But I don't want to duck out of paying for it, either."

Walther nodded. "That sounds like a healthy attitude. Captain, no code is perfect. A man must conform with judgment and commonsense, not with blind obedience. I've broken rules; some violations I paid for, some I didn't. This mistake you made could have turned you into a moralistic prig, a 'Regulation Charlie' determined to walk the straight and narrow and to see that everyone else obeyed the letter of the law. Or it could have made you a permanent infant who thinks rules are for everyone but him. It doesn't seem to have had either effect; I think it has matured you."

Max grinned. "Well, thanks, Dutch." He stood up. "I'll get back up to the Hole and mess up a few figures."

"Captain? Are you getting enough sleep?"

"Me? Oh, sure, I get a nap almost every watch."

"Minus four hours, Captain." Max sat up on the cot

in the control room, rubbing sleep out of his eyes. The *Asgard* was in the groove, had been boosting along it for days, working up to that final burst that would squeeze them out of this space and into another—one they knew or some other, depending on how well their "fudging" had conformed to the true structure of the universe.

Max blinked at Kelly. "How long have you been up here?"

"Not long, Captain."

"Did you get *any* sleep?"

"Well, now, Captain . . ."

"Forget it, you're incorrigible. Got one ready?"

"Yes, sir."

"Shoot." Max sat on the cot while they passed data to him, eyes closed while he programmed the problem and translated it into the binary numbers the computer understood. He had not been out of the Hole more than a few minutes at a time for days. He would doze between sights, wake up and process one, then lie down again.

He had kept Kelly and Kovak on watch-and-watch as long as possible—although it was hard to get Kelly to rest. Lundy, Smythe, and Noguchi had continued to rotate, overlapping when the going got faster in order to help each other with plate changing and readings. For Max there could be no relief; he must process each sight, supplying from his card-file memory the information in the missing manuals.

All the Worry gang were there but Lundy. He came up as Max finished and ordered the correction. "Compliments of cookie," he announced, setting down a gallon of ice cream.

"What flavor?" asked Max.

"Chocolate chip, sir."

"My favorite. Just remember when you are dishing it that efficiency marks will be coming up one of these days."

"Now, Captain, that's not fair. The Chief has a lot more mass to feed than you have."

"And I have a very high metabolic rate," announced Noguchi. "I need more."

"Noggy, you have a built-in space warp in each leg. We'll let Kelly dish it and hope that pride will restrain him." Max turned to Kelly. "What schedule are we on?"

"Twenty minutes, Captain."

"Think we need that so soon?"

"Just to be safe, sir."

"Okay." They ran another sight and ate the ice cream, after which Max shifted them to transition stations. Kelly did not take the computer. A key punched by Kovak gave the same answer as one punched by Kelly, and Max wanted Kelly on the vernier stereograph where his long experience could make the best of poor data. Lundy assisted Kelly, with Smythe and Noguchi shooting and running.

At minus two hours Max called Compagnon, told him that they were narrowing down; the Chief Engineer assured him that he would nurse boost and vector himself from there on. "Good hunting, Captain."

On a ten minute schedule Max still found it easy, though he had to admit he wasn't as fresh as a still-warm egg. But he was kept comfortably busy and the corrections were pleasantly small—Compagnon must be doing a real job down there. When the preset on the computer said less than one hour to zero, he stood up and stretched. "Everybody all set. Somebody wake up Noggy. Everybody got a pepper pill in him? And who's got one for me?"

Kovak leaned back and handed him one, Max popped it into his mouth and downed it with a swig of coffee. "Grab a last sandwich if you're going to. All right, gang—let's hit it!"

The data flowed in a steady stream. After a while Max began to tire. He would no more than pick one correction off the lights on the computer and feed it to the power room than Kelly would have more data ready. A correction showed up that seemed off the curve, as if they were "hunting" excessively. He glanced back at the lights before applying it—then realized that a new set of data was being offered.

"Repeat!" he called out.

Kelly repeated. Max ran the figures over in his mind and found that they meant nothing to him. What had that last correction implied? Had he used a legitimate method in surveying this anomaly? Could you even call it surveying? Was this what a survey ship did to get out? How could they expect a man to. . . .

"Captain!" Kelly said sharply.

He shook his head and sat up. "Sorry. Hold the next one." With a feeling of panic he reviewed the data in his mind and tried to program. He knew at last how it felt to have the deadline bearing down fast as light—and to lose confidence.

He told himself that he must abort—slide past under the speed of light, spend weeks swinging back, and try again. But he knew that if he did, his nerve would never sustain him for a second try.

At that bad moment a feeling came over him that someone was standing behind his chair, resting hands on his shoulders—quieting him, soothing him. He began clearly and sharply to call off figures to Kovak.

He was still calling them out with the precision of an automaton twenty minutes later. He accepted one more sight, digested it, sent it on to Kovak with his eyes on the preset. He applied the correction, a tiny one, and called out, "Stand by!" He pressed the button that allowed the chronometer to kick it over on the microsecond. Only then did he look around, but there was no one behind him.

"There's the Jeep!" he heard Kelly say exultantly. "And there's the Ugly Duckling!" Max looked up. They were back in the familiar sky of Nu Pegasi and Halcyon.

Five minutes later Kelly and Max were drinking cold coffee and cleaning up the remains of a plate of sandwiches while Noguchi and Smythe completed the post-transition sights. Kovak and Lundy had gone below for a few minutes relief before taking the first watch. Max glanced again at the astrodome. "So we made it. I never thought we would."

"Really, Captain? There was never any doubt in my mind after you took command."

"Hmmm! I'm glad you didn't know how I felt."

Kelly ignored this. "You know, sir, when you are programming your voice sounds amazingly like the Doctor's."

Max looked at him sharply. "I had a bad time there once," he said slowly. "Shortly before zip."

"Yes, sir. I know."

"Then— Look, this was just a *feeling*, you see? I don't go for ghosts. But I had the notion that Doc was standing over me, the way he used to, checking what I did. Then everything was all right."

Kelly nodded. "Yes. He was here. I was sure he would be."

"Huh? What do you mean?" Kelly would not explain. He turned instead to inspect post-transition plates, comparing them happily with standard plates from the chart safe—the first such opportunity since the ship was lost.

"I suppose," said Max when Kelly was through, "that we had better rough out an orbit for Nu Pegasi before we sack in." He yawned. "Brother, am I dead!"

Kelly said, "For Nu Pegasi, sir?"

"Well, we can't shoot for Halcyon itself at this distance. What did you have in mind?"

"Nothing, sir."

"Spill it."

"Well, sir, I guess I had assumed that we would reposition for transit to Nova Terra. But if that is what the Captain wants—"

Max drummed on the chart safe. It had never occurred to him that anyone would expect him to do anything, after accomplishing the impossible, but to shape course for the easy, target-in-sight destination they had left from, there to wait for competent relief.

"You expected me to take her on through? With no tables and no help?"

"I did not intend to presume, Captain. It was an unconscious assumption."

Max straightened up. "Tell Kovak to hold her as she goes. Phone Mr. Walther to see me at once in my cabin."

"Aye aye, sir."

The First Officer met him outside his cabin. "Hello, Dutch. Come in." They entered and Max threw his cap on his desk. "Well, we made it."

"Yes, sir. I was watching from the lounge."

"You don't seem surprised."

"Should I be, Captain?"

Max sprawled in his easy chair, stretching his weary back muscles. "You should be. Yes, sir, you should be."

"All right. I'm surprised."

Max looked up and scowled. "Dutch, where is this ship going now?"

Walther answered, "The Captain has not yet told me."

"Confound it! You know what I mean. Our schedule calls for Nova Terra. But there is Halcyon sitting right over there—a blind man could find it with a cane. What destination did you have in mind when you boosted me into command? Tell me what you expected then? Before you tagged me."

"I had in mind," Walther answered, "getting a captain for the *Asgard*."

"That's no answer. See here, the passengers have a stake in this. Sure, I had to take this risk for them, no choice. But now there is a choice. Shouldn't we tell them and let them vote on it?"

Walther shook his head emphatically. "You don't ask passengers anything, sir. Not in a ship underway. It is not fair to them to ask them. You *tell* them."

Max jumped up and strode the length of the cabin. "'Fair,' you say. Fair! It's not fair to *me*." He swung and faced Walther. "Well? You're not a passenger.

You're my First Officer. What do *you* think we should do?"

Walther stared him in the eye. "I can't decide that for the Captain. That is why you are Captain."

Max stood still and closed his eyes. The figures stood out clearly, in neat columns. He went to his phone and savagely punched the call for the control room. "Captain speaking. Is Kelly still there? Oh—good, Chief. We reposition for Nova Terra. Start work —I'll be up in a minute."

# 22

# THE TOMAHAWK

Max liked this time of day, this time of year. He was lying in the grass on the little rise west of the barn, with his head propped up so that he could see to the northwest. If he kept his eyes there, on the exit ring of the C.S.&E. Ring Road, he would be able, any instant now, to see the *Tomahawk* plunge out and shoot across the gap in free trajectory. At the moment he was not reading, no work was pushing him, he was just being lazy and enjoying the summer evening.

A squirrel sat up near by, stared at him, decided he was harmless and went about its business. A bird swooped past.

There was a breathless hush, then suddenly a silver projectile burst out of the exit ring, plunged across the draw and entered the ring on the far side—just as the sound hit him.

"Boy, oh boy!" he said softly. "It never looks like they'd make it."

It was all that he had climbed the rise to see, but he did not get up at once. Instead he pulled a letter from his pocket and reread the ending: ". . . I guess Daddy was glad to get me back in one piece because he finally relented. Putzie and I were married a week ago—and oh Max, I'm so *happy!* You must visit us the next time you hit dirt at Hespera." She had added, "P.S. Mr. Chips sends her love—and so do I."

Quite a gal, Ellie. She usually got her own way, one way or another. He felt a bit sorry for Putzie. Now if they had all stayed on Charity . . .

Never mind—an astrogator ought not to get married. Fondly he fingered the sunburst on his chest. Too bad he had not been able to stay with the *Asgard*—but of course they were right; he could not ship as assistant in a ship where he had once been skipper. And assistant astrogator of the *Elizabeth Regina* was a

good billet, too; everybody said the *Lizzie* was a taut
ship.

Besides that, not every young A.A. had a new congruency to his credit, even now being surveyed. He
had nothing to kick about. He didn't even mind the
whopping big fine the Council of the Guilds had
slapped on him, nor the official admonition that had
been entered in his record. They had let him stay in
space, which was the important thing, and the admonition appeared right along with the official credit for
the "Hendrix" congruency.

And, while he didn't argue the justice of the punishment—he'd been in the wrong and he knew it—nevertheless the guilds were set up wrong; the rules ought
to give everybody a chance. Some day he'd be senior
enough to do a little politicking on that point.

In the meantime, if he didn't get moving, he'd have
to buy that taxi. Max got up and started down the
slope. The helicab was parked in front of the house
and the driver was standing near it, looking out over
the great raw gash of the Missouri-Arkansas Power
Project. The fields Max once had worked were gone,
the cut reached clear into the barn yard. The house
was still standing but the door hung by one hinge and
some kid had broken all the windows. Max looked at
the house and wondered where Maw and the man she
had married were now?—not that he really cared and
no one around Clyde's Corners seemed to know. They
had told him at the courthouse that Maw had collect-
ed her half of the government-condemnation money
and the pair of them had left town.

Probably their money was gone by now—Max's half
of the money was gone completely, it hadn't quite
paid his fine. If they were broke, maybe Montgomery
was having to do some honest work, for Maw wasn't
the woman to let a man loaf when she was needing.
The thought pleased Max; he felt he had a score to
settle with Montgomery, but Maw was probably settling it for him.

The driver turned toward him. "Be a big thing when

they get this finished. You ready to go, sir?"

Max took a last glance around. "Yes. I'm all through here."

They climbed into the cabin. "Where to? Back to the Corners?"

Max thought about it. He really ought to save money—but shucks, he would save plenty this next trip. "No, fly me over to Springfield and drop me at the southbound ring road station. I'd like to make it in time to catch the *Javelin*."

That would put him in Earthport before morning.

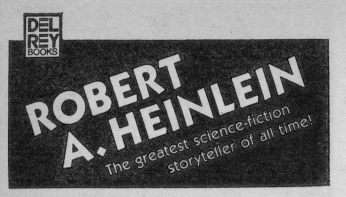

# From DEL REY, the brightest science-fiction stars in the galaxy...